Elexis Bell

Allmother Rising

Allmother Rising

Elexis Bell

This is a work of fiction. Any resemblance to person, living or not, is purely coincidental.

ISBN: 978-1-951335-14-4

Eager to stay up to date on the latest dark fiction from Elexis Bell?

Sign up for her newsletter at: www.elexisbell.com

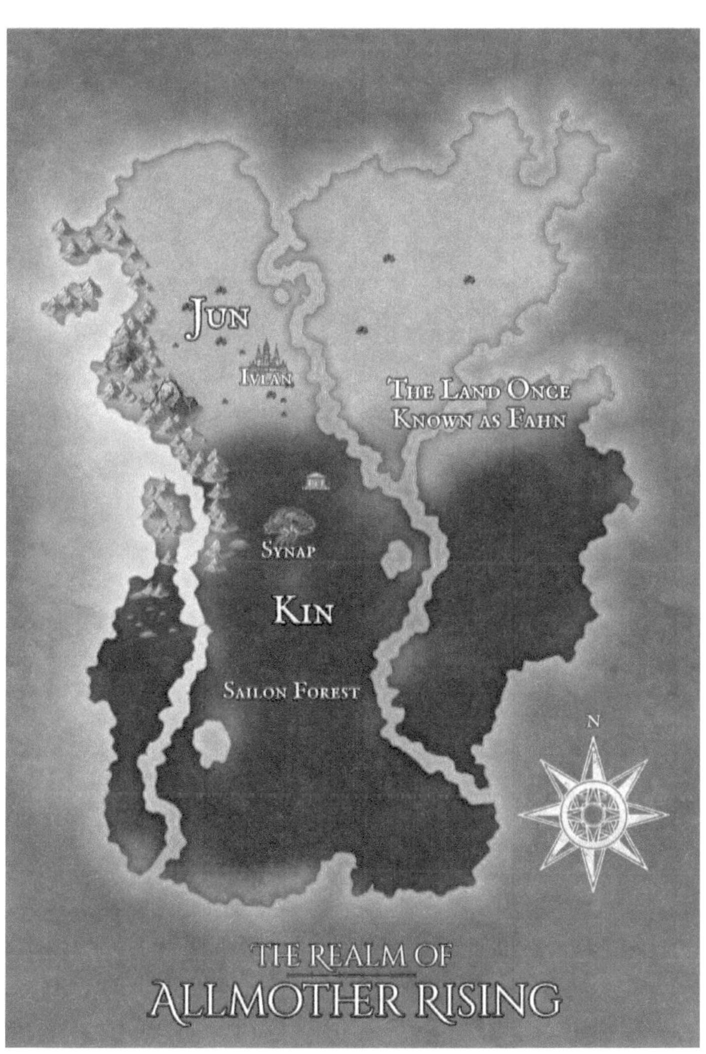
Jun
Ivlan
The Land Once
Known as Fahn
Synap
Kin
Sailon Forest
N
The Realm of
Allmother Rising

Chapter 1
Veliana

My blue robes flow behind me, trailing the wooden floor of my room. I part the heavy green curtain at my door and rush through, leaving it to flap shut behind me. Strands of golden hair flutter about my face as I run to see my parents. My feet pound the stairs which spiral around the tree at the center of our home.

They're back.

They're alive.

I breathe a sigh of relief. Yet, I need to see them for myself. I need to know they're safe.

"Priestess," an apprentice says, bowing her head as I rush past her. The overly large tips of her ears bob with the motion.

I mumble some benign acknowledgment but never slow my gait. Rushing down to the lowest floor of our treehouse, passing rooms with windows open to dismal grey skies, I beat a frantic pace to the main hall.

At the doors, two Rangers stand watch, freshly oiled leather armor gleaming despite the low light. They throw the doors wide at my approach.

And then, I see them.

My mother surveys my father with a dour expression. In place of the pristine white tips of their ears, flecks of dried blood decorate mangled edges. Flakes of it crust their necks and tattered robes.

My mouth drops open, and my pale hands rush to cover the gasp that falls from it. One faltering step is all I manage, shock stealing away the relief of their return.

They glance up in unison, braided energies lending them synchronization, but no smiles find their way onto their lips. If their broken, mangled ears weren't enough of an indication, this alone would tell me the news from Jun is dire.

Unable to bear it, I rush forward and wrap my arms around them. Our heads lean together and their dirty antlers knock against my clean white ones despite their backward slope. Dried bits of crimson sprinkle my shoulders. But I need to feel their energy, need to hear them breathe.

Nearly a full moon has passed since they left for Jun, so far from our land in so many ways. Every night of their absence, I worried. With rumors of regicide in Jun seeping over our border, I feared the worst. Every second, I waited for the Allmother to speak to me, to tell me something had happened to them.

A single tear rolls down my mother's cheek, sliding over her silver freckles to drip onto my own. Her white eyebrows furrow, and she leans her forehead against mine.

Reaching up to wipe away a tear, I ask, "What happened?"

Mother tries to speak, but a sob cuts off her words. She hugs me tighter and cries in earnest.

Father places a tender hand on my golden locks and kisses the top of my head. "Darling Daughter," he begins, shaking his head. His long silver beard quivers with the motion.

“There is so much we need to tell you, but first… know that I am sorry.”

“For what?” I ask, incredulous. “I’m sure nothing that happened there was your fault.”

A deep sigh lifts his chest, and he glances at my mother. Closing his eyes, he whispers, “Allmother, grant me strength.”

“High Priest, High Priestess,” a soft voice says behind me. I turn, and the same voice says, “Priestess Rising.” The apprentice I passed now waits with a tray of ointments and salves in her hands.

“Yes, please set that on the table,” Mother chokes out. “Thank you.”

The girl, surely no more than half my age, maybe 13 or 14 renewals, does as she is bid and leaves us.

The Rangers close the doors behind her. Only two rooms in our home have doors. This one and our petition room. We close the petition room doors any time we commune with the Allmother, but we only need *these* doors in times of great duress.

A maelstrom stirs within me as the doors click softly shut. Suddenly far more anxious, I ache for something to do. My eyes wander to the tray of ointments, but I know my parents will tend to each other’s wounds when I leave.

The sun of renewal hides, seeking shelter behind clouds and letting us fend for our own warmth. It sends only faint light in through the windows, so I light a few candles and gather furs from a chest. I drape them around my parents’ shoulders, careful not to nudge their ears as I pull the plaits of their hair from beneath the thick pelts.

They settle into carved wooden chairs near the window and motion for me to join them. Nervous glances pass between them, and the storm inside me intensifies. A million terrifying scenarios play out in my mind.

Are King Kelgon and Queen Halde really dead? Did Paikon really murder his own sister, his brother-in-seal, his nephew... All for the throne?

I can't imagine a land with so little of the Allmother's influence as to allow Aia, the god of greed and power, to poison someone so deeply.

Do they not know her? How will the new King lead without her hand to guide him?

My mouth goes dry, and I swallow hard.

Does the new King want some of the Allmother's land?

My questions go unanswered as my parents struggle for words. I glance out the window at Kin territory, eyes lingering over every branch of the magnificent Sailon Forest. Homes dot the trees at varying heights, connected by rope bridges. Moss hangs from them, and vines wrap around rope railings.

The High Seal has governed this forest, guiding the Kin according to the Allmother's will for so many generations.

If Paikon or his son, Tumai, want part of this land...

I shudder at the thought and turn my attention back to my parents. "Are the rumors true?" I ask, unwilling to wait any longer.

My mother nods, crisp blue eyes finally meeting mine. "Paikon has… taken the throne. The Furen family rules with no intention of peace."

The churning in my stomach intensifies and my palms begin to sweat. I rub them gently on my robes but it does little to help.

"He demands a third of the Sailon Forest," my mother says.

I gasp and my jaw falls slack. "He can't! They control so much land, already!"

"Aye," my father says. "But they have abused their land. Trees are scarce, and they tear great swaths of minerals from the earth for the sake of 'progress.' The Allmother's presence faded quickly as we moved into Jun."

"I wept for the loss of her, for the loss of so many feats of nature," he continues. "Crops and animals are butchered in great numbers. The surplus is gluttonous, yet so many go without."

He touches my cheek and the silver undertones of his skin glitter in the faint sunlight. "Darling Daughter," my father whispers apologetically.

My mother's hand finds mine upon the table, and she squeezes it tight.

"Paikon demands more than land."

A choked sob escapes my mother's lips, and I tense, preparing myself.

How bad is it?

"He wants a third of the forest, now. But he knows it is unusual for a Priestess Rising to go unsealed for so long…" my mother says, trailing off.

My stomach drops, filling me with dread. She struggles for words, mouth opening and closing silently.

Please… No…

A burst of loneliness spreads through me at the mention of my seal status, colored by images of Materva, the Light

Watcher I could have been sealed to years ago. Shadows flood my mind, tinged by his betrayal.

The smiles he seemed to save for that other girl, another Light Watcher. Laughter shared only with her. The sound of his voice telling me that he wanted her, wanted a life in the sun at the top of the trees with the freedom of the skies… without the burden of Rising.

Finally, Mother continues, "His son has recently… come unsealed. He wishes the two of you to be sealed so that, on his own death, Tumai will rule all of Jun and Kin territory. Kin will be no more."

"What?" Outrage burns hot within me, coursing through my veins, but it is not strictly my own. The Allmother's fury surges alongside mine, boiling my blood. "What makes him think we'd agree to that?"

"If we don't," my mother says, voice so small I barely hear her, "he promises to burn the entire forest to the ground."

The fury roiling within me hits a breaking point, and my veins run cold. "Have you already agreed?" I ask.

I survey their ears, maimed and bloody, and know that if they have, it was only under duress. Yet, that does little to shake the chill from my bones or free my heart of dread's icy grasp.

Silence greets my question and neither Mother nor Father meets my eyes. They exchange a look, and my mother whispers, "We told him we needed time, but… He expects us at the border on the next full moon. He expects *you*."

Pushing away from the table, I rise from my chair. "I must commune with the Allmother."

A third of the Sailon Forest now? All of it when Paikon dies?

Me, sealed to that vile welp, Tumai?

Fuming, I don't venture up the stairs to our Petition Room. I need more than that.

Tugging my furs tightly about my shoulders, I leave our home behind. My feet deftly lead me down the ladder to the ground. Running between trees, I put two fingers to my mouth and whistle. Golden curls fly behind me, fluttering with my robes.

Heavy footsteps sound ahead, signaling Tala's approach. The great white wolf breaks through the undergrowth, tongue lolling happily at the prospect of a long ride.

She skids to a halt in front of me, nuzzling my face with her own. She licks my face, wiping away the tears I didn't realize were falling. A soft whimper escapes her, and she steps closer to me, resting her massive head on my shoulder.

I sigh, hugging her neck, and whisper, "I need the Allmother, girl."

With one final lick of my cheek, she turns and kneels to let me climb up.

I settle onto her back with tears blurring my vision. Knotting my fingers in Tala's soft fur, I lean close to her and close my eyes.

She knows the way.

***

At the oldest Petition Temple in Kin, I dismount. The great stone building lies in wait with the filtered light of the moon shining through patchy storm clouds to reach it. On all sides, the Sailon Forest hums with the Allmother's presence, and she fills my mind with the chanting of my forebears.

Tension stirs within me, aching for release.

Can I truly be sealed to someone so vile? Could that be the Allmother's wish for me?

It would spare Kin from war…

But would it spare them the poisonous ravages of Aia's greed, spread through Tumai's influence?

Tala pads up the stairs ahead of me to the deserted building. Her massive frame dwarfs the delicate wooden handrails, and she turns to face me at the door. She sits patiently, amber eyes aglow.

My gaze roams over the Temple, raking over the wound in its back. A large tree lies across one side, caving in a section of the roof. It fell early in this year's renewal. Repairs will be slow as we never take more than the forest can afford. Gathering so many materials will take time.

Tonight, that means I have the Temple to myself.

Casting a glance at the forest around me, I sweep flaxen locks behind my ears and climb the stairs. My footsteps sound more substantial on the solid surface, lending weight to my presence in a way my petite figure never can.

The doorknob turns easily beneath my hands, and I step through into the sacred space. Scant light shines through the hole in the roof, but its desecration doesn't lessen the Allmother's presence. Her warmth sings in my veins, seeps through my muscles.

I'll know my course soon enough.

I breathe in the wonderful scent of an aged building, letting it tease the knots of worry from my back. Making my way to the altar with Tala padding along behind me, I lift my arms at my sides, raking them through the ancient air.

A silent petition to the Allmother lights the candles spread throughout the temple, filling it with a warm amber glow. The stone altar waits in the center, and Tala sniffs at the blood of old sacrifices. I run a hand over the edge, trailing it through stray leaves left over from former petitions.

Stepping around the altar, I approach the fallen tree and drape my furs over a limb that sticks into the temple. The warmth of the Allmother fends off the chill of the evening, so I shed my robes, leaving only the sheer white fabric of my underdress.

I pick my way across the flagstone to a chest. Candles perch on a shelf above it, sending flickering waves of light over the room. The old wooden chest creaks as I open it, and an herbaceous scent erupts into the room.

Jars and satchels galore await, but the ones I need rest on top. Communing is simple. I can do it easily enough without enhancements thanks to my place in the Rising line.

But tonight, my connection needs to be pure and strong. For my own peace of mind, I can't risk corruption.

Withdrawing the jar of powdered stag's hoof, a jar of blessed water, and a bundle of dried Allflower, I withdraw to the altar. Tala lays in the shadows of the fallen tree, leaving me to seek the Allmother.

A small wooden table beside the altar holds a stack of ceramic bowls. I take one, carefully mixing a pinch of powdered stag's hoof and a few drops of blessed water in it.

Slowly, I smudge the silver paste along my collarbones. Then, I reach up to color each tip of my antlers with it. The slender bones sweep back before curling upward, and five tines decorate each one. With the remainder of the stag's hoof mixture, I paint a single line down from my neck, under the light fabric of my underdress, between my breasts, all the way to the base of my ribcage.

Lifting the bundle of dried Allflower, I hold the tip, charred from prior petitions, over the flame of the nearest candle. Sweet smoke rises from it, drifting through the temple. I breathe it in, and nostalgia sweeps over me.

I've come here many times, seeking guidance.

The Allmother will provide.

She always does.

With a lighter heart, I walk the perimeter of the room, holding the burning Allflower aloft. A trail of purifying smoke follows in my wake, dancing in the candlelight.

Chapter 2

Tyrvahn

The Sailon Forest closes in around me, dark and foreboding in the night. A twig snaps behind me, and I know I haven't escaped them. With my parents dead and my kingdom stolen, a moon spent on the run has flown by.

Yet my cousin's men nip at my heels. I feel them getting closer each day.

I pick up my pace, refusing to give them an easy kill.

Sprinting through the undergrowth by the scant bits of moonlight that filter through the leaves, I remind myself who I am. Tyrvahn Mahrdur, Prince of the great nation, Jun. My last shot at an ally, at getting my kingdom back, vanished when the High Seal agreed to Paikon's terms, but I won't go down easy.

I try to think through how many of my assailants I've picked off, but it's no easy task. Their numbers change, and I can't be sure we haven't passed by another of their camps.

Sweat beads on my forehead and drips down my scalp. Droplets of it trickle around the base of my antlers, matting my thick black hair down. I force myself to focus despite the exertion.

Listen.

I strain my ears, desperate to pick any order from the crashing footsteps behind me. Yet, the cacophony is not as terrible as I expected.

Two of them?

Maybe three?

I try harder to siphon out the sounds of my footsteps and the violent beating of my heart. I pick out the sounds of the river and change direction, heading straight for the rushing water. My legs pump harder as I push myself toward the water and the promise of moonlight.

Behind me, a long, high whistle sounds, and realization hits me. These are scouts. The rest of the party follows behind, waiting for a signal before closing in. The whistle sounds once more, and my blood runs cold.

They're far too close.

I have to eliminate the scouts before the others catch up.

Maybe then I can slip away.

My heart stutters as I think of the other possible outcomes. Being overrun by a horde of assassins doesn't exactly sound appealing.

The trees begin to thin, and saplings claw at my clothes, already far from the glory they once were. My shirt rips as a small branch catches my side, but I keep going.

Another sapling reaches out, whipping a thin branch against the black tip of my ear. My breath comes in great gusts, but warmth builds in my chest. The warmth of the Allmother's approval.

I've only come to feel it recently. All it took was nearly dying, but I've seen her. And now, I feel her urging me along this path.

So, I run faster.

As I near the rushing river, fewer twigs crunch underfoot, and the sounds of my pursuers grow clearer.

Definitely no more than three.

I smile, liking my odds.

Allmother, grant me strength…

Here, in this wild place, her warmth seeps deeper into my body than ever before. As her powers channel into me, I feel her anger at my cousin and my uncle for taking the throne of Jun, just when I was beginning to see her will. Her ire burns red hot, galloping through my veins.

With the river before me, I turn to face the forest. I'm given no time to hide or think strategy. Two scouts burst through the foliage, but they come up short when they see the Allmother's power glowing at my fingertips.

No one in our land can feel her, let alone petition her for assistance.

So far from the wild, I couldn't do this either.

There, she is but a legend. But here, with the river rushing at my back and the trees looming behind my enemies, I feel her need for revenge, for closure.

I take a step toward the scouts.

They flinch, and I smile.

The moonlight shines on the tips of their black antlers and burns in their dark eyes. Fear stiffens their movements and scrunches up their faces. They didn't expect to catch me without the rest of their group.

Did they see the others I've left in my wake?

Raising one hand, I let the crisp white glow of the Allmother's power illuminate the riverside. Warmth flows through me, and I try to focus it into something I can use. I've had very little practice, but I think I manage alright.

The glow at my fingertips blossoms, engulfing my hand and spreading up to my wrist. Swirling around my fingers, I feel the weight of it.

One of the scouts, a woman with black hair braided back over her ears and around her antlers, charges me. Her sword shines in the light as she raises it over her head.

Rushing forward to meet her, I duck beneath her swing and land a solid punch to her stomach. The added force of the Allmother's power sends the scout flying. She smashes into a tree, and the leaves shake over her head. She lands in a crumpled heap at its base with blood seeping from her mouth.

I turn my attention to the remaining scout, a man who easily matches my size. He stands just beyond arms' reach, staring openmouthed.

I close the distance and grab his chest plate.

Please, Allmother. Lend me just a bit more strength.

And she does.

The warmth running through my veins spreads, oozing into each and every muscle.

Before the scout has a chance to unsheathe a weapon, I swing him around and throw him. His massive body soars through the air and into the river. The rushing water swallows him and carries him away.

I stare after him, matching the expression of disbelief he wore just moments ago. Glancing down at my hands, I watch the glow seep back into my flesh, fading from sight.

A whistle sounds in the forest behind me, seeking an answer from the scouts. When none comes, another whistle pierces the night, this one shaky but more intense.

They know.

Forcing myself into action, I sprint south, looking for a shallow place to cross the river. A bolt of lightning splits the sky, followed closely by crashing thunder, and I push harder.

Of course, it would storm, now…

My thoughts turn acidic as I run along the riverbank. A glance up ahead tells me that the river runs wildly for as far as the eye can see. Unable to cross, I dash into the forest. The assassins will break through the foliage soon, and I can't let them see me.

Trees pass by in a blur of shadows, and my feet beat an uneasy path. Rain rattles the leaves and drowns out the sounds of my footsteps. Another bolt of lightning flashes, showing me a fallen tree trunk just before I trip over it.

Vaulting over it, I thank the Allmother for the thunder that disguises my less than graceful landing. Desperately, I cast my gaze around, hoping some sort of shelter will appear.

But how much luck can I hope for?

And how much help can I reasonably expect?

Pushing further, I almost don't notice the new sound developing around me. A low hum shakes my bones. As I run, it grows louder, more insistent.

"Come to me…" a soft, feminine voice whispers through my mind, and a surge of warmth floods my body.

A brief moment of terror tries to tell me I've lost my mind, but the warmth eases my worries. So I run toward the hum. Pushing, legs pumping, I chase the Allmother for what feels like an eternity.

Then, I skid into a clearing.

A single building sits before me, an old stone affair with a tree collapsed over one side. Light burns within, and I almost turn away.

"Come," the Allmother whispers once more, and this time, I hear her clearly. High and delicate, yet impossibly low and sultry, her voice encompasses everything.

Slowly, I cross the clearing and make my way up the solid stairs. With every step, the hum around me grows louder.

Slipping through the door, I close it behind me, thankful to be out of the rain. I expect a chill to sweep over me as droplets run down my spine, but warmth fills this place.

Something growls behind me, and I freeze.

How many times can I call on the Allmother in one day?

Is there a limit?

The sweetest voice I've ever heard says, "Tala, be still."

Taking a deep breath, I turn around in time to see a petite Kin woman slip from a stone altar in the middle of the room. Her silvery-white skin glows iridescent in the candlelight, showing through the sheer fabric of her dress.

That's her underdress!

I blush and pointedly raise my eyes from the forms of her breasts, sweeping my gaze over silver lines painted on her collarbones. Antlers as white as snow sweep back from her head then rise, all points tipped with silver.

Against all odds, she approaches me with a smile. Silver freckles sparkle on her cheeks and nose, and flecks of silver dance in her grey eyes.

Is she… the Allmother?

But her voice is not the one that floated through my mind. Hers is not the voice that led me here.

"The Allmother smiles upon you." She pushes loose strands of gold back behind her white-tipped ear and says, "Come in."

No, she's not the Allmother.

Clearly.

I tell myself over and over, but it's hard to believe someone so beautiful could be mortal.

Then, the true voice of the Allmother whispers to me again. "Her…"

The voice goes on but becomes incoherent.

I stare out the window at Ivlan, the capital of Jun. An errant breeze reaches in, brushing my skirt against my legs. A light drizzle of rain coats the streets, shining in the moonlight. The castle looms in the darkness, towering over the city. Violent hatred flows through me with a shiver, only partly my own. Aia's dark presence slithers through my veins, twisting me, driving my anger deeper.

Clutching my necklace, I seek the Allmother. Freshly replaced, the tiny seed within my locket pulses with her energy. The old seed has found its home in my garden, bringing her closer.

But never close enough.

Closing my eyes, I try to remember how present she was in the Sailon Forest, back before Jun invaded Fahn. I see the trees, resplendent and plentiful. I hear the whisper of her voice drifting through my mind.

But I haven't heard her clearly in so long.

The little seed pulses anew, and a wave of comforting warmth seeps into my palm. Even here, even with so much oppression on all sides, she spares a thought to comfort me. She reaches for me, and I see a flash of her hand in my mind, trying so hard to help me.

But she can't reach me.

Aia is far too strong here, and the trees are almost gone. Paikon, filthy bastard that he is, has risen to the throne. The King and Queen are dead, as is Tyrvahn.

A pang of guilt tears through me, and Aia twists the knife. Floods of darkness surge through my veins.

Has he always been so terrible? So hard to bear?

Is it like this for everyone else in Jun?

But I know the answer.

To them, he's naught but a legend. A fanciful tale. His emotions and whims and manipulations are just part of their lives. They don't see him as separate. They don't see the way he darkens their hearts.

Nor do they know how the Allmother could help them.

But they will.

Turning from the window, I cross the room to my small dining room. Shelves line every wall, laden with plants and parchment. In the middle of the room, scrolls cover my table, spread wide. Stones, candles, and anything heavy enough to hold them open rest upon their corners. The fruits of my brief affair with Tyrvahn lay before me.

I just need them to tell me more.

A knock at the door draws my attention. I drop my locket, letting it fall into my shirt to rest between my breasts, then rush across my home. Staring out through a small window in the door, I see Flahren and breathe a sigh of relief. I haven't painted my antlers today, so I duck behind the door as he rushes in.

Untying the knots which fasten the hood of his cloak around his antlers, he wipes away the droplets of rain that somehow found his face. His hood falls, revealing dark, bushy hair. It tumbles out, spilling past his shoulders. So unfashionable here in Jun.

But I'm glad he hasn't cut it.

He holds true to Fahn, to our ways.

Shutting the door firmly, I welcome him. He hangs his cloak on a hook in the wall and follows me to the dining room.

His blue eyes sparkle in the candlelight as he surveys the scrolls. Rubbing his hands together, he says, "I hope we have what we need. We won't be getting back into the castle any time soon."

Aia laughs within my heart, chilling me to my core. I shiver, stroking my locket for comfort. Another wave of warmth seeps into my fingers, and I nod.

"I hope so, too," I whisper, voice breaking.

"Tala, be still," I say, easing the dire wolf's temper. Whoever this Jun is, the Allmother's power glitters on his fingertips.

Strange...

He turns to face me, dark hair dripping. Droplets shine in his scruffy beard. His clothes, clearly once quite extravagant, have seen better days. Yet, he stands tall with his shoulders back.

Slipping from the altar, I appraise the newcomer. The Allmother's light glows behind his eyes, so unusual for a Jun. Her warmth flows through my veins as my gaze rakes over his strong frame.

"He is the key," she whispers to my heart.

A smile lifts the corners of my lips.

"The Allmother smiles upon you," I say, pushing my hair back behind my ear. "Come in."

A blush spreads over the Jun's tan cheeks, and I remember myself. The sheer fabric of my underdress hides little. My cheeks warm at his reaction. The stranger lifts his dazzling green eyes from my figure, and a soft thrill shivers over my spine.

Turning from him, I cross the room and lift my robes from the branch I left them on. Rain falls behind them, splashing on the flagstones near the tree trunk, but they're dry enough. I wrap my robes around myself and fasten the buttons. Settling my furs back down upon the branch, I face the stranger again.

Tala stalks up to him, head bowed to keep her eyes level with his. She sniffs him, several times. With her appraisal complete, she wags her tail.

The Jun breathes a sigh of relief, eyes drifting to me. I nod, and he reaches out a hand to scratch behind Tala's ear.

"Your connection to the Allmother is strong," I say. "Much stronger than I expected for a Jun. Stronger than many Kin."

I tip my head to the side, considering him. "I wonder, could you feel her presence in Jun?"

"A little. Sometimes," he says, deep voice as smooth as silk. "But only recently."

Tala licks his hand and pads over to the tree trunk, resuming her position as sentinel. Her head falls to rest on massive white paws, dusty from the run here.

Wandering across the room, I open a chest butted up against the outer wall. One jar of dried venison rests in the bottom, left behind in case a traveler needed rations. I remove the jar and carry it to the altar, gesturing for the stranger to join me.

He approaches cautiously, feet stepping lightly across the floor. When he sees the contents of the jar, his hunger outweighs his hesitation. Stomach growling, he closes the remaining distance quickly.

I offer the jar to him, and his hand brushes mine as he takes it. Little sparks of lightning arc over my skin. My eyes snap up to his, and my cheeks flush.

I withdraw my hand and take a deep breath to steady myself. After all, I know nothing about this man. I shouldn't be reacting to him like this.

Taking another deep breath, I cross my arms before me. Leaning one hip against the altar, I ask, “What’s your name?”

We have to start somewhere. And clearly, neither of us is going anywhere in this rain.

I hide the excitement that sweeps through me at the prospect of being stuck here with him, chastising myself for being taken in so easily by an attractive man.

But my simple question seems to catch him unaware.

He hesitates.

"Tahrn," he finally answers, but the Allmother's light dims behind his eyes as he speaks it.

Tala lifts her head, tipping it to the side.

But why would he lie about his name? Whatever the reason, it can’t be good...

"Tahrn," I repeat, tasting the falsehood. "Do you know the power of a name?"

"Life or death?" The smile vanishes from his face, and he takes another bite of the deer jerky. He studies it closely, unwilling to meet my gaze.

My brows furrow, and I stare at him, wondering at his odd answer.

Is he a wanted man?

Yet again, a strange little shiver dances down my spine, defying all reason.

But... A wanted man beneath the rule of Paikon? That might not be... entirely *bad.*

"In some cases, I suppose it could be a matter of life or death." Taking a deep breath, I extoll the true purpose of our names. "Surnames tie the energy of one to those of others. The Allmother laces people together with names. When we Kin are sealed, we inherit each other's names and are tied to each other's families. Children inherit blended names. Only the High Seal is an exception."

A bolt of lightning flashes outside, a mimicry of that which tingled across my skin when our hands brushed.

Stop thinking about it.

Thunder rumbles outside. I wait it out before speaking, giving myself a moment to gather my thoughts.

Glancing at him, I continue, "The Vierna name is always handed down whole, maintaining a perfect connection throughout the Rising line, and a blended surname of all the Sealed forebears accompanies it."

Under his breath, the stranger says, "Veliana Vierna Alaken."

I nod, surprised that he knows all three of my names.

"Your kind weigh and measure bonds. The surname which affords them more power is kept, and the other is discarded. Names and power divide your land."

He finally meets my gaze, and his mouth falls open at my assessment of his country. But he nods, unable to deny it.

Self-conscious about my rambling, I bring myself around to the point, "Given names are different. When a child is named, the Allmother braids their given name into the core of their energy. Denying your given name denies your energy, dimming your connection to the Allmother."

I watch his chest rise with a sharp breath and tell myself that I'm only measuring his reaction. But even after he exhales, my eyes linger in the hollows of his collarbones, just barely visible, peeking out at the open collar of his shirt.

He nods slowly, and little drops of rainwater fall from his hair. Outside, the rain slows, and the winds die down.

"Now, knowing the power that your name holds, knowing how it hurts your energy to deny it, who are you?"

He swallows a bite of jerky, eyes searching my face all the while. My skin warms, and the Allmother's excitement sings in my veins.

If he's the key, I need to know who he is.

Tala rises to her feet and crosses the room with her head down, pulling our eyes along after her. At the door, she growls softly.

From the clearing, a deep voice shouts, "Well, well, well. I really thought you were smarter than this, Tyrvahn. Hard to hide when you light that many candles!"

The man continues shouting, but I hear no more.

Tyrvahn?

He's alive?

My heart expands, filling my chest near to bursting. My breathing accelerates, and the Allmother's warmth glows within me.

"Tyrvahn?" I ask, hopefully. "As in *Prince* Tyrvahn?"

Taking a deep breath, he nods. "I was on my way to approach the High Seal. At least, until I learned that they were going to take up with my uncle…" Dropping his gaze, he clenches his jaw and shakes his head. "I may go, still. Perhaps, if they knew I yet lived, that might change their minds."

This is perfect!

I couldn't have asked for better. Thank you, Allmother!

My excitement bubbles out, and I throw my arms around Tyrvahn's neck. Startled, he wraps his arms around my waist. My hand winds its way into his hair, pulling him in for a kiss.

I intend for it to be a soft peck, a small affair to show how happy I am that he's here…

But before I pull away, his lips part, and he kisses me back.

Heat builds in my stomach, coiling within me. His arms tighten around my waist, pulling me closer. Our mouths dance together, and he lifts one hand to the side of my neck. His thumb caresses my jaw, and fire skips along my skin. A shiver runs down my spine, moving me against him, and a soft moan eases past his lips.

Yet, the angry man outside has gone nowhere. He carries on shouting, and Tala lets out one sharp bark. A warning.

I jerk, pulling my lips from Tyrvahn's, and turn my head to look at her. A deep breath presses my breasts against him. I rush over to the tree trunk, grab my furs, and wrap them around my shoulders. My fingers fumble with the clasp.

Looking up at Tyrvahn, I smile and say, "Come on."

Grabbing his hand, I haul him to the door.

Tala steps aside, and I throw the door open. "Slow, Tala," I say.

She eases out into the night, white fur shining in the moonlight. Little drops of rain glitter on her coat.

At the edge of the clearing, three men freeze in their tracks. Their swords and armor gleam in the moonlight, but their eyes are dark. Slowly, they lumber across the grass, exchanging significant looks.

"If you were just running away to find a savage whore, you could have said as much," the man in front leers, adjusting his grip on his sword. "Maybe we wouldn't have had to follow you out here. But we've come all this way. May as well finish the job."

His fellows laugh, but Tala growls, chest rumbling beside my head.

They slow their advance, and she climbs down the stairs. All three men come to a halt in the middle of the clearing, looking warily at each other.

But I can't let Tala fight them. I can't risk her getting hurt.

Allmother, grant me the strength to shape these men to your will.

Grant me the strength to save my people.

The powdered stag's hoof still shines on my antlers and chest, amplifying my connection to her. The forest hums with her presence, and the Allflower's smoke drifts through the air, bringing her closer, still. Again, she fills my mind with the chanting of my forebears, letting their petitions strengthen my own.

I close my eyes, inhaling the sweet scent of her. Warmth runs through my veins and seeps into my muscles, flooding every fiber of my being.

Beside me, Tyrvahn gasps. In the clearing, the assassins follow suit.

I open my eyes. My skin glows with the Allmother's strength, and the world shines brightly with the power radiating from my eyes, turning night to day.

Swords tremble, but hands raise them high. The assassins step forward.

Another deep breath fills my lungs with the smoke of the Allflowers, and I lift my hands, palms open to the sky. All three assassins flinch, and I shape them to the Allmother's will.

My fingers move, running roots down from their feet into the ground. Slowly raising my hands, I let the roots transform them. Their legs become tree trunks, growing and fusing together. They scream out in pain, but it will only be temporary. They drop their swords and launch insults at me as they try to move.

My head tips back, and I breathe in more of the Allflower smoke. The glow of my skin intensifies, and I raise my hands higher still. I need to do this quickly, to end their suffering.

Bark spreads over torsos, splitting their metal cuirasses open. The husks of armor fall to the ground with a clatter. Organs become rings in wood, and I raise my hands higher. Arms become branches and fingers transform into twigs.

I raise my arms higher, pointing my fingers to the sky, and the transformation takes their necks, their mouths. The screaming stops, leaving only the hum of the forest and the chanting of my forebears to tickle my ears.

Leaves sprout from the ends of their branches, whispering in the light wind. Rain plays softly on the thick new growths.

Three trees breathe where three armed men once stood.

With my task done, the chanting quiets, and my mind is my own once more. Yet, the forest still hums with the Allmother's presence.

I smile and descend the stairs. The glow of the Allmother's power fades from my vision, and night falls around me once more. The grass is soft beneath my feet as I approach the new trees. Bending, I retrieve a sword and turn to face Tyrvahn.

He stares at me, openmouthed, sparing an occasional glance for the new trees as well as those at the edges of the clearing. He stumbles down the stairs and says, "How long…" He clears his throat and tries again. "How long will it take them to die in there?"

"What do you mean?"

"Surely, they can't breathe in there?" He meanders toward me, eyes repeatedly straying to the new trees.

"You misunderstand. They're not *in* the trees. They *are* the trees. They will live a long life in the Allmother's presence. We're good to the trees, here."

Tyrvahn casts one last awestricken glance at the forest around us.

"Arm yourself," I say, pulling his mind to the task at hand. "I'm taking you to my parents."

"Your parents? I need the High Seal. Why would you take me to your parents?" A strange look comes over him, scrunching up his face, and he asks, "How old are you?"

It catches me off guard, but I answer. “27 renewals. 27 times I’ve felt the cold leave us and watched the flowers bloom.” As he picks up a sword, I ask, “Why? How old are you?”

“28 snows.”

That’s right. Jun count differently.

Tala approaches and leans down. I climb onto her back, reaching out a hand to Tyrvahn.

“But if you’re 27, why do you need to take me to your parents? Surely, you’re old enough to take me to the High Seal yourself. Unless you’re sealed and need your parents to stay with your family while you’re away…”

His face falls, but he takes my outstretched hand, climbing up behind me. His hands land heavily upon his knees as he settles in. Tala is big, but Tyrvahn still has to sit close. My backside presses against him, and I suppress a shiver.

Turning to face him, careful of my antlers, I say, “I wouldn’t have kissed you if I was sealed, no matter how warmly the Allmother smiled upon you.”

Tyrvahn relaxes, and one hand brushes the outside of my thigh. His dark green eyes fall to my lips for an instant, then dart back up to hold my gaze.

I smile, and realization dawns on me. “I didn’t tell you my name, did I?”

He shakes his head.

“I’m Veliana, Priestess Rising,” I begin, chest swelling with pride, even as a bit of trepidation lingers in my mind. “I’m taking you to my parents because they *are* the High Priest and High Priestess of Kin.”

“Oh.” Tyrvahn’s lips quirk into a smile.

“Hold on,” I tell him.

His arms slide around my waist, and again, heat pools within me.

To Tala I whisper, “Home this time, girl.”

I knot my hands in her fur, and she carries us into the rain.

Chapter 5

Tyrvahn

The rain lets up as we meander through the forest. Veliana leans forward to spare me the sharp tips of her antlers. Her golden hair flutters before my face in the light breeze of the dire wolf's movement. The massive animal carries us far faster than I could walk but barely seems to exert itself.

Is it sharing in some blessing from the Allmother? Or are these creatures just this strong?

The animal, apparently named Tala, vaults over a small log, jolting Veliana and me. My arms tighten around her instinctively, pressing the soft flesh of her backside against me. I take a deep breath to steady myself, but waves of sweet smoke drift back from her hair, intoxicating me.

Swallowing, I try to stamp out the desire, the strange magnetism pulling me to her.

Focus. Beautiful as she is, there are more important matters at hand.

I force my mind back to practical matters. Thinking through the scene at the temple, I try to work through whatever I interrupted.

She must have been communing with the Allmother. Or was she performing a petition?

What was she doing there?

And how did she turn those damned men into trees?

The brief flood of confidence I felt after successfully managing to throw one scout and knock another back with the help of the Allmother's power vanishes. I thought, for a fraction of a sky, that I was wielding the power well. And maybe I was, given how little practice I've had.

But turning people into trees?

How often has she done that?

The great beast beneath us slows her gait, leading us down a small hill. Winding between trees, easily stepping over rocks half my height, Tala takes us closer to Synap, home of the High Seal.

Veliana turns to look at me, still glowing with the Allmother's light. Her eyes dance with it, and her skin shines a brilliant silver, illuminating her freckles. I gasp, and she smiles.

Could I have ever guessed the people of Kin were so powerful?

Veliana turns around, watching our path, and I fight the strange urge to lean forward and settle my chin atop her head, right between her antlers.

Would she lean back against me? Or pull away?

Or worse…?

Such an intimate gesture is far beyond our mere acquaintance, and I dare not try.

Why am I even thinking about that?

Chalking it up to a moon spent on the run, alone and cold, I shake my head to clear it. My mind drifts back many moons, and I see my parents sitting together, discussing Jun. Pompous as their early reign may have been, they were coming around.

Whispers of rebellion were forcing them to consider different tactics if only to placate the people and secure their throne.

"Perhaps we should look to the south? The Kin seem to manage fairly well," I suggested, gazing out the window of the solar at the distant forest shining like an emerald on the horizon.

My uncle gave me an approving nod, "Finally, a reasonable solution. The Kin are wasting the potential of their land. A bit of… negotiating…" He widened his eyes for significance. "Well, a new lumber mill would provide new jobs, new materials flowing into the economy. That ought to make the peasants happy. New land would spread their filth a little thinner."

Shaking my head, I said, "That isn't quite what I meant, Uncle."

My eyes drifted over his form, from his heavily oiled hair, slicked back, over the ridiculously intricate embroidery of his clothes, then down to his freshly shined shoes. He stood over my parents as if that might grant him power over them.

Quirking one eyebrow up, I said, "I meant we should look to them as a role model. Kin do not starve. They want for nothing. Their leaders rest easy, assured that their people will not rise against them."

My uncle sneered at me, pursing his lips. His hands tightened into fists at his side.

For the first time, I was curious. Some strange feeling in my stomach twisted, making me wonder. Perhaps, it hadn't been bad food. Perhaps, the cook my uncle swore tried to poison me really had been innocent. Perhaps, it was him.

But I dismissed the thought. I knew he wanted his son to inherit the throne, but I thought him above murder.

I looked at my mother and father, reclining in elegantly carved chairs, to see how they liked my idea. To my surprise, they were nodding. Slowly, thoughtfully. But they were nodding. The sun streamed through the windows to shine on their black antlers, far fuller than my own. My mother's dark red hair sparkled.

And the Allmother's warmth flowed through my veins. I remember taking a deep breath, trying to adjust. It still unsettled me. It showed me just how wrong things were in Jun, just how much needed to change.

Now, I crave her warmth.

Ever since the first time I felt her presence, the path Jun was on started making less and less sense. Glancing around me at the healthy forest, I marvel at how the Kin prosper.

Granted, some of these trees may well have been people at some point...

My gaze falls once more to the Priestess Rising, sitting right between my legs. The warmth of her body seeps into my inner thighs, and my arms tighten around her waist. She takes a deep breath, leaning back against me with her head bowed forward.

The Allmother's warmth surges through me. Or is that my desire? At this point, I can't tell.

Yet again, I have to force my mind onto a new path.

Desperate for a different topic, anything other than the images trying to flood my mind, I settle on the starkest contradiction possible.

My uncle.

My body screeches to a halt as the Allmother's anger sears my flesh. But I need to think of him, and not simply to keep myself under control. I need to figure out his next move.

So, I cast my mind over his previous moves.

He killed my parents. The poison worked quickly, thankfully. They wouldn't have suffered much.

My *accident* the bout of bad food that nearly killed me six moons ago…

Well, it's safe to say the cook was likely innocent.

Looking back, I remember the cold look in his eyes when I set my soup aside after only a taste. He tapped his fingers impatiently, eyeing me as the servants brought the other food around.

It was my favorite soup, too. Lamb, carrots, and potatoes. Fortified wine. I always finish that soup. When I set it aside, my mother asked if I was feeling well.

I wasn't.

Just a taste was enough to set my mind spinning. Waves of nausea and dizziness toppled me from my chair. Sweat dripped down my spine as I boiled alive.

One of the last things I remember was my uncle, standing at my bedside as smelling salts were passed beneath my nose, to no avail.

Then, the world went dark. My heart beat frantically in my chest, hammering away at my eardrums. My breathing grew shallow and quick.

But a bright light spread across my mind, enveloping every shattered thought and righting each one. A flash of a smile, a glimpse of vibrant green eyes.

My veins warmed, and she whispered to me. I strained to hear her, but all I could make out was, “The Kin are…”

The rest of her words faded.

I saw a flash of massive silver antlers reaching into the light around me, and then my eyes fluttered open. My bedchamber surrounded me rather than the light of the Allmother. I never thought I’d be so disappointed to wake up after being poisoned.

Not that I comprehended my narrow escape at the time.

Shaking my head, I wonder how much of a role the Allmother played in saving my life that day. She clearly has more power and influence than we ever gave her credit for. I loved hearing about her as a child, but we all thought the legends of the Allmother and her ill-fated son, Aia, to be just that. Legends. Stories.

Though we didn’t believe them, we knew the people of Kin took those stories seriously.

Now, I see why.

The soft glow hanging around Veliana’s petite figure, the strange connection she seems to have with Tala…

Trees growing where three assassins once stood…

I take a deep breath and glance at the forest around me with new eyes. Brief patches of moonlight illuminate a tree here, a mossy boulder there. An owl hoots in the distance. And somehow, it all feels connected. Suddenly, the magic of the Allmother seems far more real than ever before. Her warmth flows through me.

And these revelations couldn’t come at a better time.

The future of Jun rests within the hands of Kin and the Allmother.

***

Despite the late sky, voices greet my ears as we near Synap. Briefly, I consider the idea that, perhaps, the people of Kin stay up later than those of Jun.

But Veliana tenses in my arms, and Tala slows beneath us. The massive animal's ears twitch, then lay back against her skull.

Then, the tone of the voices dawns on me. Shouting, angry and fierce, fills the capital of Kin. Dread washes over me, draining the blood from my face in one sickening swoop.

And all my hopes vanish.

Chapter 6
Veliana

Raised voices grate against my ears, lifting the hairs on the back of my neck. Tala slows her approach, apprehensive of the anger filling our home. I hear my parents shouting back, pleading for order, but the mob doesn't care.

"Tala, we must go," I whisper to the great dire wolf. I pat her neck gently, and she picks up her pace.

As we draw nearer, words and phrases separate themselves from the angry buzz of too many voices.

"They'll only burn more…" one man shouts, but my ears fail to pick out the rest of his sentence.

"…side with Paikon?!" another voice cuts in angrily.

I blanch before their fury, but the Allmother warms my veins, pushing me forward with assurances of justice. "You can fix this," she whispers within me.

The people of Kin won't rally for this alliance, but maybe they'll rally behind the true Prince of Jun.

Even if it means going to war.

Riding into Synap, I stare up at the rope bridges leading from one home or shop to another, connecting all the beautiful trees. Small torches burn along bridges and beside doors, casting soft, warm light throughout the village. But the wonder this sight normally fills me with is buried beneath trepidation.

High in the trees, my parents try desperately to communicate the duress under which they agreed to such terms, but no one listens. A cacophony of fury roils above. My heart aches, imagining the pain they must have endured in Jun, yet I feel the anger, the fear of my people.

My hands shake, wrapped in Tala's fur, but I have to move, have to do something. So, I do the one thing that I know will catch their attention. Very softly, I howl, knowing Tala will join me. Her voice overtakes mine quickly, growing louder and louder by the second.

And slowly, the voices above grow quiet. All heads turn toward the white dire wolf, the Priestess Rising, and the Jun they don't yet know could be their salvation. Tala quiets, but the members of her pack howl in the distance, answering their alpha even as they lope toward us.

"Good people of Kin," I begin, raising my voice, trying to disguise the quiver that it holds. "We do not have to ally ourselves with Paikon. We don't have to become slaves to Aia, as he has. There is another way."

High above, my parents exchange a glance. If they speak, their words don't reach me.

"I went to the Allmother's temple, seeking communion. Yet again, she has provided for us." Sliding from Tala's back with the pack of dire wolves howling in the distance, I say, "Prince Tyrvahn yet lives! And the Allmother guided him to me!"

True to his status, Tyrvahn plays his role. He raises his arms, and the people of Kin applaud. Joy sweeps through them all, lifting their voices to the skies.

Smiling, I watch them, granting them a moment's reprieve. I can only make out the expressions of those whose homes are lowest, but their smiles and gleeful laughter warm my spirits.

But the difficult portion of my plan must come, at some point.

I gulp back a breath, thankful that enough distance rests between me and the people of Kin to hide my fear. A wave of warmth flows through me as the Allmother reaches out a tender hand, helping me along.

Another soft howl crosses my lips, and Tala follows suit. Her voice seems to shake the massive trees around us, and the crowd quiets, once more. Even the distant wolves fall silent, sensing Tala's plea.

"We must go to war, dear Kin. We must eliminate Paikon and Tumai." Pausing, I let my words sink in. "This is the only way. Their proposal to take a portion of the Sailon Forest now, to be used as they please, will last only so long. If I seal myself to Tumai, the Sailon will fall to them in its entirety. They will cut the trees. They'll burn the meadows. They'll chase the Allmother from these lands, just as they've done in Jun."

I stare at my people and add, "But they underestimate us."

My blood warms with the Allmother's approval, and I feel her power building within me. My skin glows with it, and she makes me brave. As it seeps further into me, her light allows me vision better than sunlight. Every face, no matter the distance, becomes clear.

And they hang on my words.

Holding the sword I took from one of Tyrvahn's would-be assassins, I say, "They think us defenseless because we don't ruin the earth for weapons like theirs." Passion and anger fill me, pushing me along. "Paikon doesn't understand that we don't need these paltry weapons."

Lifting my arms, with the Allmother's power sparking from my fingertips like tiny lightning bolts, I melt the blade of the sword. The molten metal drips to the ground, sizzling as it hardens into a lump at my feet. The hilt glows within my grasp.

"We live as we do because the Allmother wishes it so. She will protect us, so long as we honor her will and her land. We cannot let them drive her from these lands as they drove her from Jun."

Tyrvahn slides from Tala's back and stands beside me. I take his hand, raising it with my own, and shout, "FOR HER, WE GO TO WAR!"

Above me, Synap bursts into a chant of, "War! War! War!"

Tala tips her head back and lets out one long howl, beckoning her packmates to join her. And they do. Bursting from the undergrowth, they form a circle around Tyrvahn and me. Heads tipped back, they cry out for the Allmother and this wild place.

Tala's mate pads over to her. They nuzzle each other, and he sits beside her. Their voices join those of the others. And only one thing is left.

Raising my voice, I howl as loudly as I can, joining the wild rather than the continued chants of, "War!"

To my surprise, Tyrvahn throws his head back and howls with me, gripping my hand tighter.

And the people above us grow louder, screaming their assent.

***

Leading Tyrvahn up the ladder and through the circular halls of my home, I pass the doorway to my bedroom. I only blush slightly as thoughts of taking him in there flicker through my mind.

There's no cause for such thoughts. Control yourself.

Yet, they linger.

Memories of our kiss at the temple fill me with delicate tension, and I glance over my shoulder at the curtain leading to my bedroom. Briefly, I reconsider the wild fancy of leading him to my bed.

For half a heartbeat, I envision the wicked smile which would grace Kivala's face if she knew the path my thoughts travel, now. She'd certainly endorse it.

Though maybe slightly less on seeing him. He is Jun, after all.

Perhaps it could be a sign of uniting our lands?

And it isn't my fertile day. There'd be little consequence there.

I shake my head and keep walking. There would be other consequences, I know. I need a clear head, and so does he. Our people deserve that much.

I pull him along by the hand, leading him to the balcony my parents stood upon when last we saw them. We pass from one pool of flickering light to another, trekking past small candles along our way.

In the darkness, he clings tighter to my hand, sending shivers over my skin and making me wish for fewer candles to light our path. After all, I've long since grown accustomed to the staircases which spiral around the trunk of our home and the uneven boards of our floors. They don't trip me up as they do him.

I slow my pace, allowing for his unsteady footing, and he walks alongside me. A furtive glance finds his eyes shining in the low light and fixed on me. I blush and force my gaze ahead.

The lights of Synap glitter through the balcony doorway, and my parents turn to face us. Bandages hide the salves on their ears, and their freshly washed skin gleams. The glow of the Allmother dances beneath their skin. It does my heart good to see them looking healthier.

Sighing contentedly, I slip my hand from Tyrvahn's, placing it instead on his back. "Mother. Father. This is Tyrvahn Mahrdur, rightful Prince of Jun."

Turning to look at him, I find his head bowed slightly. "Tyrvahn, I present the High Seal, High Priestess Daerna Vierna Alasvena Lakenuta and High Priest Soolan Vierna Lakenuta Alasvena."

"I'm honored," Tyrvahn says, bowing at the waist.

"As are we, darling prince," my father says. "May the Allmother guide us in our alliance."

Tyrvahn glances up through his lashes, head still inclined.

"Please, dear Prince," my father begins, silver eyes shining. "We haven't time to stand on ceremony. Lift your gaze and follow us."

And at that, my parents lead us to the same room in which I conferred with them this morning. I light candles as my parents take their seats. Tyrvahn stands awkwardly at the doors until my mother waves him over to sit opposite them at the small table.

Rain still shimmers on Tyrvahn's shirt, so I drape my furs over his shoulders before taking the chair beside him. His gaze darts to my face, and I smile.

"Our guest mustn't be cold," I say. The Allmother's warmth flows through me, filling me with gentle peace.

The Allmother's words from the temple float through my mind.

He is the key.

He smiles, nodding slowly and sending my heart fluttering. His chest rises with a deep breath, but I keep my eyes carefully above the shadows beneath his shirt collar. My hand finds his beneath the table, lacing our fingers together. He squeezes my hand, and my eyes fall to his lips.

"We heard rumors of a rebellion forming in Jun," my mother begins, pulling our attention away. "Are they true?"

All traces of good humor vanish from Tyrvahn's face, but he nods. "Aye. The rumors are true."

"We need to reach the rebels," my father says. "They may be able to help us. Surely, they'll be glad to be rid of Paikon. Did your family have any idea as to who was orchestrating it?"

Again, Tyrvahn nods, shoulders stiff. I tip my head to the side, wondering at his odd reaction.

Shouldn't he want another ally?

"Garle Jahlon is leading them."

And then I understand. The reason he doesn't want this ally, the reason he isn't sealed.

Garle Jahlon left him. It sent rumors running wild throughout Jun and Kin alike. I always wondered why, given the value of power and name within Jun. Surely, a prince would be a suitable seal-mate. But it's clear enough, now. She wanted to take them down.

He was just a tool, a way for her to learn about them.

I sigh, squeezing his hand. The tightness around his eyes makes me wonder.

Does he still hold feelings for her?

A small spike of jealousy, some lingering remnant from Materva's betrayal, stabs my heart. Not that jealousy has any place here.

We've only shared a kiss.

My parents exchange a significant look. "Would she be amenable to an alliance?"

"Garle grew up near the Sailon. She knows of the Allmother. She's felt her warmth." A deep breath fills Tyrvahn. "She'll come."

"We'll call for her in the morning, then. In the meantime," my mother begins, "Tyrvahn, you have much to learn. If we are to stand a chance, even with Garle's forces alongside ours, you will need to channel the Allmother's power."

"Darling daughter," my father says, "won't you teach him?"

My face splits open with a smile, but I suppress it, tucking it away. Nodding sagely, I assure my parents that I'll do all I can to help him see the Allmother's light.

Veliana leads me through her home, scaling one staircase after another with my hand wrapped in hers. I trail my free hand along the bark of the tree they've built this place around, marveling at the elegant construction merging with nature.

Her sweet smoky scent drifts up from her furs, still wrapped tightly around my shoulders. I breathe it in, drawing comfort from it.

We drift from one pool of light to another, moving between sconces of carved wood and bone. Darkness closes in around us as we pass between them, stealing her from my view. I tighten my grip on her hand, hoping some change in her gait will tell me when we reach the landing.

Light reaches down toward us once more, and the sway of her hips takes shape beneath her robes. My mind flickers back to the temple and the brief glimpse of her gentle curves, barely visible beneath her underdress.

Rather pointedly, I lift my eyes from her hips to the next sconce, popping into view on the landing above. The delicately carved, swirling wood reaches out from the tree trunk, holding three interwoven bones. A single candle perches in their grasp with the wax of former candles hanging beneath it.

But my eyes meander back to her.

She crests the stairs and glances back over her shoulder. The candlelight sparkles on her silver freckles and the dusting of silver on the tips of her antlers. I step up even with her, staring down at the magnificent woman before me. Her grey eyes rake over me, and the corners of her lips lift into a smile.

A delicate heat builds within me. My hands ache to pull her closer. I draw in a deep breath to suppress the urge, but the scent of her floods my senses. I smile down at her.

"This way," she whispers, sparing me attempts at self-control.

She leads me forward amidst a light hum. We venture through a beautifully carved door and into a large open room. Candles burn all around, perched in sconces and sitting in stoneware on the floor. A single fur rug rests in the center of the floor, and three chests wait beneath a massive, open window.

Veliana releases my hand and meanders over to them. Her robes drift over the floorboards behind her. She pulls dark wooden shutters closed over the window and beckons me over to join her.

But this place feels too sacred for the likes of me.

I'm filthy from an entire moon spent on the run.

Can I really be here?

But the Allmother's warmth seeps into me, pulling me forward.

Veliana retrieves a robe from one of the chests and hands it to me. The soft green fabric shines in the low light.

"I'll wait outside while you change." She indicates a washstand waiting in a shadowed corner. "It isn't necessary for this, but if you'd like to clean yourself up, you may."

And she vanishes beyond the door. It closes softly behind her, and I shed my dirty clothes. Pulling a cloth from a small shelf, I wet it in the basin and wipe the dirt and sweat from my skin, cleaning whatever the rain left behind. I pull another cloth from the shelf and dry my hair. At long last, I slide my arms into the green robes, reveling in the feel of the smooth fabric gliding over my skin.

Quickly, I fasten the carved bone buttons at my waist. It leaves much of my torso exposed, but it doesn't feel out of place here. In Jun, our bodies are to be kept concealed. Showing too much is improper. Unless the act is strategic, that is.

But here, it feels natural.

I tell myself not to hope for some sort of reaction from her. These robes are normal attire here. Surely, she's seen plenty of bare torsos. As I fold my dirty clothes and the soiled cloths and settle them in the corner near the washstand, a thought strikes me.

Is showing this much normal for her?

She wasn't particularly embarrassed at the temple.

Suddenly, that feeling of it being natural to show more skin here deserts me. A flash of irrational jealousy sweeps through me, making me hope that no one else, or at least very few, have seen her as I saw her in the temple.

Chiding myself, both for the jealousy and the possessiveness, I take a deep breath and move to the door. Pulling it open, I invite Veliana back in, stepping aside to let her pass.

Her eyes linger on the opening of my robes, raking over me before coming back up to hold my gaze. A deep breath lifts her chest, and heat floods me.

She sweeps into the room and goes to the chests, once more, removing a small jar and two bundles of herbs. Closing the door behind me, I join her near the shuttered window.

Veliana settles the bundles of dried herbs atop the chest and says, "Kneel, please."

I do as she bids, taking a knee before her.

Opening the jar, she dips her fingers into the silver paste it contains and paints the tips of my antlers with it. To reach those furthest back, she steps closer, and the silken fabric of her robes flutters a hairsbreadth from my face.

Swallowing back the urge to run my hands up the sides of her legs to grip her buttocks, I close my eyes and tip my head forward to make it easier for her. But she doesn't step back. The gentle pressure of her touch tipping my head and the knowledge of how close she really is draws it out into an agonizingly sweet eternity.

"Please rise," Veliana whispers.

So, I do.

She reaches for me, and my heart stops. She draws silver lines along my collarbones, leaving trails of fire in the wake of her touch. A sharp inhale presses my chest against her skin, and I remind myself that this is probably normal for her.

This means nothing to her. It's just... normal.

But when her finger finds the base of my neck, dragging a thin silver line down my chest, I forget that little mantra. My heart gallops wildly in my chest as her finger slides down further still, and I cast my mind back to the temple, trying to recall how low the line on her chest went.

It vanished beneath her underdress... I couldn't see the end of it.

Gritting my teeth, I steel myself against the memory of her breasts, shrouded by that sheer fabric, and the silver line that… isn't there now. The rain washed it away, along with most of the silver which previously tipped her antlers.

At the base of my ribs, she lifts her finger from my skin, and I pull in a deep breath. Dipping her fingers back into the jar, she draws the same lines on her collarbones and asks me to tip her antlers.

I nod, expecting it to be a simple task. After all, her points are easily within reach as I'm a fair bit taller than her.

But she still stands close. And this simple thing turns out to be far more intimate than I expected.

In all my years, I've never actually touched anyone's antlers but my own. Not even Garle's. Even the one time I let my feelings for her show and rested my chin upon her head with my face right between her antlers… I never touched them.

Now, I paint the tips of Veliana's snow-white antlers silver, all the while fighting off the urge to trail my fingers down along the bone. Yet, it keeps my eyes from following her hand as she reaches into the neck of her robes and underdress to draw the line down her ribs.

With that finished, she looks up at me, tipping her antlers back. A smile graces her features. I smile back at her, utterly lost for words.

Turning from me, Veliana trades the jar for bundles of dried herbs and holds them over the nearest candle. The ends ignite quickly, but she blows out the flames, letting the embers lining the edges of each stalk and leaf and petal send up plumes of sweet smoke.

"Take this," she says, handing me one of the bundles, "and walk the perimeter of the room."

Our fingers brush on the dried bundle, and the contact sends my heart galloping.

Control yourself... This is important.

Yet, the Allmother's warmth buzzes in my veins.

But does she approve of my participation in this? Or my reaction to Veliana?

The answer seems clear enough.

Of course, her approval is of the alliance. Veliana likely has some potential seals that the Allmother would approve of a great deal more than some Jun who only recently learned she wasn't a legend.

Circling the room, holding the smoking bundle aloft, I rein in my thoughts. When we complete our circle, Veliana snuffs the bundles and places them atop the chest. Automatically, her hands find the buttons of her robe, and my heart jumps into my throat.

But her fingers pause on the buttons, then come away. They fall to her sides, idle.

"Habit," she muses under her breath. "Typically, I commune with the Allmother in only my underdress." She pulls in a deep breath and turns to face me. Tipping her head to the side, she adds, "But then, I usually commune alone. Tonight is another matter."

Veliana takes my hand in hers and leads me to the pelt sprawled across the center of the floor. She gestures for me to sit, and I do, crossing my legs beneath me. Her boots fall to the floor, and she steps forward, wiggling her toes in the soft fur.

The silver paste glitters on her chest and antlers as she stands over me. A smile warms her eyes, and anticipation builds within me.

Yet, I have no idea what to expect. I've never communed with the Allmother before.

Settling onto the fur, she crosses her legs beneath herself and smiles, resting her hands on her knees.

"Close your eyes," she says.

Pulling in a deep breath, I close my eyes. Veliana's hands wrap around mine, and my skin tingles at her touch. And I can't help it. I open my eyes to look at her with my face crinkling into a smile.

For a blissful moment, she smiles back, holding my gaze with eyes of liquid silver. "Aren't you supposed to have your eyes closed?" She teases lightly.

"Silly me." A soft chuckle escapes me, but I relent and close them.

Butterflies flutter within my stomach, setting my heart racing. Resting our hands upon my knees, I marvel at the intensity of the Allmother's warmth.

Does that mean this is the right thing to do?

A separate heat burns my skin where it touches Veliana's. A sweet, coy laugh whispers through my mind, but the Allmother offers no explanation.

"Now," Veliana begins, "much like this room, the Allmother dwells in a place of warm, amber light. Though no candles surround her, the air glows with the light of more candles than you or I could count. The sweet smell of Allflowers abounds, as it does here, tonight."

"Sounds wonderful," I whisper. The Allmother's presence builds, lending weight to the air. A low hum fills my mind, vibrating like a plucked bowstring.

“Did you learn of her, as a child, perhaps?” Veliana asks, soft voice somehow reverberating in my mind.

“No one thought her more than a legend, so we learned very little.” My voice shrinks with each word, vocal cords tightening with shame.

Yet, Veliana doesn't judge me, as I expect her to.

Rather, she tells me, “Our spirits reside within her. We are her heart. With every birth, her heart grows. She feels every death, every wrong we commit against each other.”

I pull in a deep breath and squeeze her hands. My heart beats faster in my chest, and the Allmother fills me with warmth.

“When we do well, we feel her joy. It warms us, filling our bodies with gentle heat. When we live poorly, we feel her anger. That used to be the way of it, so simple.”

The Allmother appears in my mind, full lips falling into a frown. As Veliana speaks, her image grows clearer. Brilliant green eyes glow in my mind like light shining through leaves.

“But she grew lonely. She created Aia. As he grew, she found that he inherited only her worst traits. Greed and a deep thirst for power ruled him. He grew jealous of her. He couldn’t create life as she did, but he soon found that he could corrupt it.”

The wind beyond the shutters fades, replaced by the hum of the Allmother's power. Her ire for Aia fills my veins with lava.

“He whispered to our ancestors, stealing some of them away to the North. He pushed them to tear out the trees, knowing the roots and branches connected the Allmother to this realm. As Jun rose, Aia corrupted hearts, stealing them and chasing the Allmother from the North.

“She was left alone, yet again.”

My mouth dries as the Allmother's loneliness shivers over my spine. My hands shake within Veliana's grasp.

"Do you feel her?" she asks.

"Yes," I whisper with a smile. Warm amber light seeps in through the cracks of my eyelids, prying them open. Blinding light surrounds me.

"Your connection must be strong," Veliana says, and I hear the smile in her voice. "As the moons passed, the Allmother looked inward. She found peace within the forests of Kin lands, within the pieces of her heart that Aia couldn't reach. The deepest parts of her heart, the safest places, she reserves for us. Her light is stronger here in the forests."

The sweet scent of the herbs we burned fills my nose, and I feel my spirit pulled forward. The Allmother's warmth spreads throughout me. It wraps around me like a warm embrace, filling the air with a glowing amber light.

All around, brilliant white energies hang in the air, tied together by glittering silver strings. At the center of each white light, iridescent blue symbols pulse. I've never seen their like and stand no chance of deciphering them. Yet, somehow, I know the energy immediately before me is my own, and its symbols spell out my name.

Veliana's explanation of names being braided into our cores floats through my mind.

I never would have guessed she meant it so... literally.

Gazing up in awe, I trace the silver lines reaching from my energy to the others around me. A few lines hang, broken and fluttering in some ethereal breeze. My heart clenches at the sight of them, and I realize they're the broken bonds Veliana spoke of, the ones my family deserted when they chose the Mahrdur name.

Yet, my eyes wander, drifting to a thick silver rope leading from my energy off into the distance. It hops from one to another until it disappears into the blinding white horizon.

But…

What is that one?

"Tyrvahn," Veliana's voice drifts out of the light, whisper-soft.

Pulling my eyes from the dazzling energy before me, I seek Veliana. She stands beside me, glowing in the light of the Allmother's realm. Her grey eyes shine as she gazes up at me.

"Are you ready to go?" she asks. "You need to rest."

And suddenly I realize how exhausted I am. My eyelids hang heavy over my eyes, blocking half the glory of this place.

Glancing up at my energy, I pull in a deep breath. I nod slowly and turn to gaze at Veliana once more. Trails of fire burn my skin as she wraps her hand around mine. Beside me, the light of my energy intensifies, and the Allmother's smile appears in my mind. Her warmth surges into my bones.

A smile lifts the corners of my lips, crinkling my sleepy eyes.

The silver lines on Veliana's chest and the tips of her antlers shine, dazzling in the light of this realm. She whispers, "Close your eyes."

Reluctantly, I do as she bids, robbing myself of the sight of this realm, the sight of her. She squeezes my hand, and the warmth surrounding us intensifies.

"Visualize the petition room in Synap," she says. "Imagine the fur beneath us and the Allflower smoke surrounding us, filling our lungs. Imagine the candlelight and our joined hands."

Slowly, I feel myself center on the physical world, tugged along by Veliana's grip on my hands. As she points out simple things, everyday sensations, the world becomes real again. I feel the hard, wooden floor beneath the rug, hear the wind beyond the shutters. I feel Veliana's hands in mine and hear her sweet voice whispering to me.

The blinding light of the Allmother's realm fades, but her warmth remains. It calms my restless spirit, loosening the knots that formed in my back over the past moon and filling me with the knowledge that I'm finally on the right path.

A smile splits my face open, and I remember that I have lips. The whole of my face bursts across my memory, telling me that, in this realm at least, I'm not a bright white light with strange symbols and silver strings.

Opening my eyes, I find Veliana gazing at me, glowing with the light from which we just came. The Allmother sings in my veins as Veliana's lips lift into a perfect smile.

Leaning forward, I pull one hand from hers. I tuck a loose strand of golden hair behind her ear, marveling at the fire burning over my skin as I brush the white tip of her ear.

And suddenly, it isn't enough. Our kiss in the temple floods my mind, and I ache for more.

Brushing my lips against hers, I savor the delicate sweetness of her. She parts her lips, ever so slightly, and I take the invitation. Pulling her to me, I crush my lips to hers.

Her hands tangle in my hair, and a sweet moan escapes her. Sparks dance across my spine, and heat pools within me, spurring me on.

But she pulls away.

Breathless, she leans her forehead against mine, and her thumb caresses my bottom lip. “We should rest,” she whispers, breath hot on my lips. “I’ll take you to your room.”

Disappointment burns me, churning in the pit of my stomach. Though my eyelids droop, I don’t want to rest. I want to learn about the Allmother and how I can save my kingdom.

I want to learn about the beguiling woman in front of me.

Chapter 8
Veliana

Wandering back to my bedroom after leaving Tyrvahn in his, my mind strays over the events of the evening. The beauty of the Allmother's plan, bringing him to me at just the right time. The heat between us which, I know, could just be the warmth of the Allmother, pleased that we're moving toward an alliance.

Is that all it is?

My boots hang heavy in my hand, swaying at my side as I drift up the stairs. The fingers of my free hand trail over the bark of the tree at the center of our home, and I use the texture of the bark to fend off the strange, irrational fear that Tyrvahn feels nothing more than the Allmother.

Wouldn't that be a good thing? It would, after all, mean he feels her presence, enough to be confused by it. If it were only a glimmer, a flickering of warmth...

We'd have a much longer road ahead of us.

My feet lead me across the landing, and I push past the heavy curtain hanging in my doorway. Dropping my boots, I strip off my stockings, happily letting the restrictive things fall to the floor.

My mind strays to the heat that built within me when Tyrvahn kissed me, the ache to pull him closer…

I haven't felt that way since...

I cut the thought off, unwilling to dwell on the past. Yet it tells me, beyond the shadow of a doubt, that I wasn't mistaking the Allmother's warmth for attraction.

Wouldn't it be more convenient if I were?

It would certainly make it easier to trust my judgment regarding this man. Not to mention the complications of getting involved with someone only for it to fall apart.

Again, my mind dredges up memories of Materva, my only real comparison for any sort of relationship. My thoughts fill with the sight of him walking away, deserting me for another, deserting me to avoid the responsibilities of the High Seal in favor of life as a Light Watcher, as his parents lived before him.

It's a noble calling, uniting all our lives with that of the stars.

But it left me alone.

Tyrvahn certainly isn't running from responsibility, but his duties will pull him away to Jun.

Not that it matters.

I remind myself, over and over, to control my thoughts.

Unfastening my robes, I drape them over the chair my grandfather carved for me years ago. Slipping out of my underdress, I suppress thoughts of Tyrvahn seeing me in the sheer fabric earlier in the day.

Redirecting my thoughts, though only slightly, I wonder at the oddity of his energy. Some of the silver strands were severed, fluttering uselessly. I expected as much. But there was one, thick and ropelike, that stretched further into the blinding white horizon than it should have. It wasn't as substantial as the Vierna line, nor did it glow as bright.

But the Vierna line is the only comparison I can draw.

Whatever family he descends from, it's an old lineage...

Turning down the covers, I slip into bed with a yawn. The soft fabric glides against my bare skin as I turn onto my side, antlers sticking out over the edge of the bed into open air. The Allmother glows in my veins. Her voice whispers through my mind, telling me to pursue this line of thinking.

But it's been such a long day, and my eyelids feel so heavy.

Again, I yawn, shifting in my bed. A deep breath fills my lungs, and thoughts of Tyrvahn fill my mind. I hear his howl echoing through my mind, helping me soothe my people as we push for the Allmother's will. I see his soft, full lips and thick hair, the ruggedness of his beard, the beautiful green of his eyes...

The feel of his hands on my skin.

A smile lifts my lips, and I drift into unconsciousness on waves of the Allmother's approval.

***

The wind rustles through the leaves around me, a gentle lullaby beneath the bird songs. A twig snaps beneath Tyrvahn's feet as he approaches, and my lips quirk up into a smile. A low, hollow sound reverberates through the forest as the local Light Watcher announces the sun's highest point.

Fifth sky...

If we leave now, we'll reach the temple by seventh sky, well before the sun dips into the horizon.

Putting two fingers to my lips, I let out a long whistle. Tala howls in the distance, answering my call, and I turn to face Tyrvahn.

His brows reach for each other, creasing his forehead. "How do you…" He shakes his head, struggling for words. Eventually, he simply repeats, "How?"

Gazing up at him, I pull in a deep breath to fend off the butterflies in my stomach. "The Allmother made the dire wolves when she first created Kin. The energies of all the pack members are tied to the High Seal and the Vierna line, as they've always been. Fahn was connected to massive black bears."

It seems like something he should know, but apparently, Jun paid little mind to their neighbors. Far less than we thought.

Perhaps we could use that in the coming days…

"So, the Mares and the Naivets?" he asks, eyes glittering with a sad curiosity.

I nod, lips turning downward. "The first Jun High Seal was bound to the Mares, and for a while, the connection with the Naivet line was maintained."

"What happened to them?"

Tala bursts through the undergrowth, rushing toward me. Sighing as she reaches me, I nuzzle my face into her neck. "The Mares were great creatures, far larger and far stronger than any other horses." My hands move slowly through Tala's fur, smoothing it appreciatively.

She licks the side of my face, pulling a sad smile from the depths.

"As Jun moved beyond the Allmother's reach, as Aia reached into their hearts, filling them with greed, they saw the

Mares differently. They weren't companions, but tools, commodities to be traded for all manner of wealth."

Turning to face Tyrvahn with my hand still smoothing Tala's fur, I say, "When the last Mare was traded from the Naivet line, the connection was severed completely."

He nods slowly, staring at the ground before him.

Climbing onto Tala's back, I relish the bond we have, thankful that Kin didn't squander the gifts we were given. I pull Tyrvahn up behind me, and his arms slowly wrap around my waist. My skin tingles, despite the tunic between his hands and my stomach.

"I need the Allmother," I whisper, and Tala carries us away.

***

A low hum fills the clearing, raising the hairs on the back of my neck. An intense wave of warmth sweeps through me, so suddenly that it sends a soft shiver rolling over my spine.

Tyrvahn's arms wrap tighter around me. "Are you cold?" he asks.

The warm air of the renewal season caresses my skin. "No," I say. "The Allmother is very present here."

Glancing at the temple, the old stone fills me with waves of her power. Her warmth surges through my veins, and I smile.

Tala kneels, and we slide down from her back. She meanders quietly to the three new trees in the middle of the clearing, settling beneath their swaying branches. The broken remnants of their armor lie beneath their boughs, undisturbed.

They live for the Allmother, now.

I walk toward the steps of the temple but hear no footsteps in my wake. Turning, I find Tyrvahn staring at the trees.

"Shall we?" My words shake him from his reverie, drawing his eyes away from the new leaves. He nods but doesn't speak, trailing along behind me.

Once inside, a silent petition to the Allmother lights the candles spread throughout the room, eliciting a gasp from Tyrvahn. Light streams through the hole in the ceiling, and the candles illuminate the corners. The bundle of Allflower still rests atop the chest from last night, and I light it quickly. The sweet smoke fills the temple, and I breathe it in.

After mixing a paste from powdered Stag's hoof, I hand it to Tyrvahn. Nothing we're to cover today will require my connection to be enhanced, but he's still learning.

"Same as yesterday?" he asks, cradling the bowl of shining silver paste in his hands.

Sunlight reaches through the ceiling and the windows, wrapping itself lovingly over his strong frame. Shadows play in the hollow at his collarbone, drawing my eyes.

Hoping he hasn't noticed my lapse, I pull my eyes up and over his rugged beard and force myself to hold his gaze. His eyes linger on the glittering paste within that little stone bowl.

"Yes," I say, swallowing my attraction to him. "The lines must be the same as yesterday."

Vaguely, I wonder if I should trace the silver lines on his chest or paint the tips of his antlers for him. He kneels, sparing me the decision. Dipping two fingers into the bowl, I gather a bit of silver and begin tipping his antlers.

He unfastens his tunic, and I keep my eyes studiously on my task. As he paints delicate lines on his chest, I focus on the way the silver sparkles against the black of his antlers. Yet, when his fingers stray to his collarbones, my eyes follow in their wake.

With the task done, he rises, immediately painting silver on the tips of my antlers. His chest rises and falls sharply before my eyes, and I almost tell him that I don't need the Stag's hoof for this. I even open my mouth to speak.

But he steps closer, robbing me of words. My skin flushes a deep red as heat surges through me, only to pool within my stomach again. Despite the wasted powder, the Allmother's warmth flows through my veins.

So, I unfasten the top buttons of my tunic, watching the muscles in Tyrvahn's neck bob as he swallows. His hand stills on my antlers for half a breath, and my heart skips a beat.

Dipping my fingers into the bowl, still cradled gently within Tyrvahn's hand, I draw the line from my neck all the way down between my breasts, then further to the base of my ribs. All the while, I ignore my sharp breathing and my pounding heart, rattling in its cage.

As I trace the silver along my collarbones, my eyes find their way to Tyrvahn's bare chest. The silver lines gleam in the light, and I trace them with my gaze. At the base of his neck, a small section of the vertical line grows thin.

Swallowing, I reach out, drawing a thicker layer. His chest expands, pushing his skin against mine, filling me with a sweet ache. His hand falls away from my antlers, landing gently upon my shoulder. He touches the side of my neck, thumb caressing my jaw.

Meeting his gaze, I wonder yet again if he truly feels this attraction… Or if he's just mistaking the Allmother's warmth for his own emotions.

Clearing my throat, I take the bowl from his hand and turn from him. Standing before those emerald green eyes with our chests open to each other is far too tempting. Meandering over to the trunks beneath the shuttered windows, I settle the bowl within them, using the moment away from him to calm my frantically beating heart.

After a few deep breaths, I rise and face him. A smile spreads over his face when our eyes meet, and my stomach flips.

"Today," I say, more huskily than I intend, "I'll be helping you learn how to petition the Allmother for the use of her power. We'll start with something simple."

I lift the nearest candle and blow it out. Approaching the altar in the center of the room, I gesture for him to follow. I lift myself onto the stone and sit cross-legged upon it, resting my hands on my knees. Suddenly, I find myself rather thankful I'm wearing pants rather than robes today.

"Come," I say, patting the stone before me. "Sit as we did last night."

He saunters toward me, holding my gaze, and I pull in another deep breath.

As he settles onto the altar and scoots forward to touch his knees to mine, I hold the candle up. "We'll start with lighting this."

He nods, and I say, "You must start by asking the Allmother for her help. Try, 'Allmother, grant me your light.'"

He takes the candle in his hands, and I ignore the burst of fire rushing over my skin as his fingers brush mine.

"Allmother, grant me your light," Tyrvahn whispers.

His fingers glow, dazzlingly bright. But the candlewick stays dark.

"Try again, but this time, visualize what you want. Really concentrate on the candle igniting."

Taking a deep breath, Tyrvahn nods again. Silence falls between us, and he stares intently at the candle within his grasp. "Allmother," he says, voice firm, "grant me your light."

The wick bursts into flame, far too bright. The candle explodes, spraying chunks of wax all around. I duck, covering my eyes and shrieking.

"Curses!" Tyrvahn shouts.

Peeking over my arm, I glance at him. The shock on his face mirrors my own, and I giggle. Slowly, my laughter infects him, lifting the corners of his lips.

"What just happened?" he asks, chuckling. "Is that normal?"

"Not quite." I try to stifle my laughter, covering my smile with my hand. I shouldn't be laughing, after all. It might discourage him.

Yet, I continue.

"Let's try again. I'll get another candle."

"You sure about that?" he asks, brushing little crumbs of wax from his lap.

"Well, I know to cover my eyes, now."

***

As the sun dips toward the horizon and the Light Watchers call out ninth sky, I call our efforts to a stop. Tyrvahn's eyelids droop, though not so much as I expected after such extensive petitions.

My eyes rake over him as I wonder at the strength of his connection to the Allmother. That strangely robust tether, reaching all the way into the light, must be the reason.

He has no trouble asking for her powers, or receiving them, for that matter.

He only lacks control.

My gaze dips to the shattered bits of wax lying beside us on the altar, and I suppress a laugh. But one candle burns beside me.

The glow on his face after he lit it flashes through my mind, and I smile.

I raise my eyes to his face. Reluctantly, I slide my hands from his and lift the bundle of dried Allflower from the bowl beside me. I smudge it against the inside of the bowl, snuffing the tiny embers at its edges.

My hands fall upon my crossed legs, fingers fidgeting, aching to reach out again. Our knees still touch, but I allow it, focusing instead on the matter at hand. "Have you petitioned the Allmother before now?"

Tyrvahn's lips lift into an alluring smile, and he chuckles. "Just before I met you, I tried. I asked for strength to fight a few of my uncle's soldiers. I thought I did pretty well, even. Let me tell you, I punched them really hard." He pauses, raising his eyebrows. "Then, I saw you turn people into trees and realized I wasn't as good as I thought."

He laughs harder, shaking his head.

Despite myself, I laugh with him. "To be fair, I've had more practice than you."

"Yeah, yeah, yeah," Tyrvahn teases. "You're just trying to make me feel better." He leans forward, and I have to fight not to lean toward him.

"I'm really not," I say. "It's just a matter of control and being specific within your mind as you use it. You can shape her powers, you just have to know what you want to do."

Tipping my head to the side, I smile and add, "Besides, you need to learn. Telling you you're further along than you are won't help you. I wouldn't just try to make you feel better. You clearly don't know me very well."

I chide myself for my teasing tone.

"Maybe I will in time," he answers, taking my hand in his once more.

A surge of heat rushes through me, begging me to lean in. His lips are right there, after all. My eyes drop, lingering over the lines of his collarbones, and my head tilts.

Clearing my throat, I forcefully clear my head.

Think of something else. Anything else.

Lifting my gaze to his, I open my mouth to speak but find no words.

Maybe say something that actually has to do with the alliance and saving our lands? You know, the entire point of this?

But when I finally speak, I surprise myself. "Will it be awkward for you, working with Garle?"

A knowing smile flickers across Tyrvahn's face, and he shakes his head. "No. My feelings for her died long ago."

A wave of relief floods me, and I try to hide it. But a little bit slips through the cracks, painting a smile across my lips.

"And you?" he asks.

"Well, I never courted her. Since I never had feelings for the girl, surely it won't be awkward for me," I tease.

Tyrvahn rolls his eyes but laughs despite himself. "That's not quite what I meant." Another laugh tickles my ears, but he quickly turns serious. "Are there any… prospects… that might be angry at me for this?"

Dropping his gaze to our hands, he caresses the back of my hand with his thumb. Turning my hand over, he trails his fingers up my wrist, leaving rivers of lava in their wake.

His eyes find mine, and I shake my head. "Not anymore. A fellow Light Watcher pulled his attention away a few renewals ago."

Again, I feel the urge to lean in, to brush my lips to his. But I need my head clear. There are more important matters at hand.

"I always wondered if Garle left you for the same reason, if she found someone else. Apparently not."

Tyrvahn shakes his head, and a small laugh escapes him. "It seems you know a great deal more about Jun than we know of Kin."

"Aye," I say. "We've kept a cautious eye to the north for many renewals. After the absorption of Fahn, we thought it might come to this. It just took longer than we expected. We dropped our guard."

Tala scratches at the door, pulling my attention away. Reluctantly, I pull my hands from Tyrvahn's grasp and slide from the altar. I feel his eyes on me as I walk away, and heat rushes up to color my cheeks.

Opening the door, I step aside to allow Tala in. She dips her head to pass through the door. But I stare up at the moon, once a thing of beauty, now a countdown.

It wanes, nearing a new moon. Soon, the night sky will mourn its absence.

And Paikon expects us on the full moon...

We have so little time.

I had thought to call an end to our lessons for the night, but now, I question my judgment.

Turning from the skies, I close the door and look Tyrvahn over. His eyelids hang heavy, and a dreamy smile plays across his face. His shoulders slump forward beneath the weight of exhaustion.

If it were anyone else, if circumstances were different, I would never consider pushing further tonight.

But can we afford to take it easy?

A great sigh lifts my chest, and I walk to the trunks. Kneeling, I lift the lid and retrieve a few herbs. "If you're up for it, I can give you something for more energy," I say. Deciding to leave this in his hands. After all, the fate of his land is at stake, too. "Or, if you'd like, we can go back and get some rest."

Rising, I turn to look at him, waiting for an answer.

He considers it for less than a heartbeat, green eyes sparkling in the candlelight. "I'll take whatever you have. I need to learn. My people won't do well under Paikon's reign. Neither will yours."

An ember of hope glows within me, and I smile, carrying the herbs to him.

Light glints off the river, sparkling brilliantly at fifth sky. Hanging at its highest point, the sun warms my skin and heats my dark clothes. Closing my eyes against it, I do as Veliana asked, focusing intently.

Before me, nestled within a tiny mound of dirt between Veliana and me, an Allflower seed awaits. Leaning forward, reaching over my folded legs, I place my hands on either side of the little dirt pile. The air around me hums with the Allmother's presence.

But I hesitate.

How many times can I fail?

I've only tried this a few times, I know. But I need to make this work. I need to do so much more than this. I have no weapons or armor, and clearly, Kin do not fight like Jun. I might be able to procure a bow and some arrows, maybe some leather armor.

But against Paikon and all his men... I'll need far more than that.

I need to figure this out.

Veliana reaches out, placing a tender hand on my arm. "Go ahead," she whispers.

Her soft words pull my eyes upward, and my gaze finds hers. Silver lines shine on her collarbones, and I swallow, remembering my fingers trailing over her skin as I painted them.

I nod, hating my uncertainty, my shortcomings. My people need me, but I can't even master what must be a simple petition.

Doubtless any Kin can do this. Even a child.

Staring into her beautiful grey eyes, I wonder at the confidence I used to have.

Losing a kingdom can really take it out of you.

Pulling in a deep breath, I nod, again. My eyes fall to the dirt between my palms, and I whisper, "Allmother, grant me the strength to shape this seed to your will."

My veins grow warm, and my skin glows. The tips of my fingers sparkle with her power. Nothing happens within the center of the dirt pile, but small sprouts of grass burst forth beneath my fingertips.

Sighing, I sit up and drag a hand through my hair.

"The new growth will please the Allmother regardless," Veliana says.

A frustrated chuckle pours over my lips. Groaning, I close my eyes. My hands clench on my knees as I say, "There isn't time for this, though. I need to be able to do this."

"You've come much further than you think, I promise." Her sweet voice reaches out, caressing my ears and tugging at the knots forming in my back. "Most people, when they're learning, struggle to successfully receive any of the Allmother's powers. You've already done that."

"That won't do us any good if I can't wield it by the time we meet with Paikon," I say, gritting my teeth.

"Tyrvahn, please," she whispers. "Open your eyes. Look at me."

Breathing deeply, I do as she asks. She gazes at me, eyes shining with compassion.

"You lack nothing but control. For how little practice you've had, that speaks volumes. No one else undergoes such rigorous training, pushing themselves to exhaustion day in and day out, to learn this. But you have. Since you came here, I've had to half drag you up the stairs to your room every night because you keep pushing." Her tone is light, soft, but I can tell she's serious.

"You need to go easy on yourself. You'll be fine. This just takes time."

She caresses my cheek. Her eyes roam over my face, dipping down to my chest, bare in the sunlight with lines of silver drawn upon my skin. My hands itch to reach for her, and my body tenses.

"Besides," she whispers, raising one eyebrow, "Paikon is mortal. If nothing else, you could always punch him, really hard."

Despite myself, I laugh.

"I jest, but only partially," Veliana continues. "The meeting with Paikon will really only be the official declaration of war. It won't be the actual war. There's more time than you think. But there's nothing wrong with a little… raw power."

I nod, thankful for the reminder that we have more time.

"When you tried last time, seeds grew, just not where you wanted. Did you pull your eyes away from it?"

I think back, trying to remember what I did. I remember my veins getting warm and the glow of my skin. And my fingertips sparkling…

"Yeah, I did. I looked at my fingers." I sigh, breathing out, "Damn it."

"Now, you know what not to do. Keep your focus. Ready to try again?"

"Okay."

Veliana pulls her hand away, and I place my hands beside the dirt pile, framing it with my thumbs and forefingers.

Just don't look away. Concentrate.

"Allmother, grant me the strength to shape this seed to your will."

My veins warm with her approval, and my skin glows with her power. But this time, I stare at the dark patch of soil. Slowly, the glow transfers from my skin to the dirt, shifting in my periphery, and sparks of light emanate from the seed buried within it. They surge outward, and I struggle to keep my eyes from following their glowing tracks through the soil.

A tiny sprig of green peeks out, sprouting from the earth. Giddy laughter bubbles up within me, but I focus quickly, stuffing it down.

The stem grows. Light radiates from it as a new leaf unfurls. It twists and spins, searching for something to wrap around as the vine gets taller. Another leaf, and another.

Then, a bud.

White petals sprawl, revealing the crimson at their center.

And my glee overpowers my concentration.

I laugh, lifting my gaze to meet Veliana's. A perfect smile shines on her face, and I rejoice over the little vine. It wouldn't reach my knee if I stood, but it doesn't matter.

"It worked!"

"Of course, it did!" she says.

Leaning forward, I pull her in for a kiss, letting my giddiness overflow. Our lips melt together, unleashing a mob of butterflies within my stomach.

I pull away, leaning my forehead against hers. "Thank you," I whisper.

"Come," she says. "Let's sit by the water and relax for a bit. You need some rest."

Chapter 10
Veliana

Our feet dangle in the water. Tyrvahn caresses the underside of my wrist, dragging fire along in the wake of his touch. I stare at the branches above us, luxuriating in the light shining through their leaves. It undulates as a gentle breeze tickles the canopy, shifting the light from one shade of green to another as it dapples the ground around us.

My chest lifts with an easy breath, and I close my eyes. Yet, the shifting shades of light through leaves do not desert my sight. My mind fills with them, and the Allmother's gentle voice whispers through my heart.

"She comes."

Who?

"She who is never as she seems. Remember that, my darling." Her words make little sense, but her voice fills me with a comforting warmth. It chases the worry from my bones, banishing the chilly fingers of uncertainty.

She who is never as she seems...

But why should that be something I need to remember?

Turning my head, I stare at Tyrvahn. He lays there, serene with eyes shut. Two tips of his antlers pierce the soft earth above his head, and he gently shifts to dig them deeper, reminding me how lucky I am that mine are nearly vertical.

I drag my gaze over him, taking in his tan skin and the dark lashes which fan out over his cheeks. Dark hair reaches out through the plush grass all around him, radiating from his head.

Our hands rest on the earth between us, and his fingers caress my wrist. Reluctantly, I raise myself up onto my elbow, pulling my wrist from beneath his questing fingers. To placate myself, I rest my other hand upon his chest.

Brilliant, dark green eyes open, and he smiles up at me. Reaching out, he places a tender hand on the side of my face.

I ache to lean in, to kiss him.

But more pressing matters demand attention.

"The Allmother spoke to me," I tell him.

"What did she say?" Tyrvahn's eyes flick back and forth between mine for just an instant.

"She said, 'She comes. She who is never as she seems…'" I trail off. Tyrvahn purses his lips, and I go on, "Could she mean Garle?"

"That certainly sounds like her."

"Then we should get back to Synap," I say. Despite myself, I slide my hand up Tyrvahn's chest and run my thumb gently over his neck, allowing myself just a moment more of peace. The scruff on his jaw tickles my skin, and I smile.

But my people need me.

Even if I'm not sure I'm ready to lead them, they need me to at least try.

I push myself to my feet and extend a hand to help Tyrvahn up.

***

Pacing the floor of our meeting room, I try to hash out a plan with Tyrvahn and my parents. If Garle joins us, all the information she gathered while recruiting others to the rebellion will be ours to use. Presumably.

Yet, the Allmother's words weigh heavy on my heart.

She who is not as she seems...

The Allmother isn't usually so cryptic. Why would she start now?

"Perhaps," my father begins, "we could lure them into the forest."

He winces as the Allmother burns his veins. Such a plan crossed my mind, too, but only for an instant. They'd burn the trees around them. Paikon made it abundantly clear that they hold no qualms about massacring the forest.

When Tyrvahn says as much, I nod and take my seat beside him.

"We can't let them into Kin, and we can't enter Jun." My mother stares out the window at the forest beyond. "We must maintain our border. That's our only chance."

My father nods and says, "We ride for the border in three suns, then. We'll meet Garle on the way. We'll be early for our meeting with Paikon, but we have little choice. A barrier of that magnitude will take time." His gaze darts to my mother, and he takes her hand. "Time and a lot of energy."

A deep, sick feeling swirls within my stomach, though I don't understand why. Some strange premonition tells me I won't like the path my parents tread toward.

***

As I meander between tree trunks with a basket of Allflowers and river moss, I listen to the woods around me. Tyrvahn speaks quietly with my parents up ahead, but I fall back. The birds chirp quietly overhead, and the wind rustles through the leaves.

The Allmother's beauty spreads out around me, and I breathe it in. My eyes trace the shifting patterns of dappled sunlight and chase the squirrels from branch to branch. One of the furry creatures skitters through the undergrowth, drawing my gaze down to land on Tyrvahn's strong figure. His loose-fitting tunic hangs from broad shoulders.

But I know the muscles that lie beneath...

My skin warms, and I drop my gaze. The feeling of his chest beneath my hand at the river earlier flashes through my mind, as does the sensation of painting the Stag's hoof paste on his skin.

Behind me, near-silent footsteps prowl, drawing my attention. I turn just in time to catch Kivala sneaking up on me. A smile splits my face wide open. I throw one arm around her, careful not to drop my basket.

She pulls me to her, chuckling near my ear. "I've missed you, so much!" Her light brown hair tickles my nose.

"I missed you, too!" I say. "How's your mom? Is her leg healed?"

"She's much better," Kivala answers. It'll take much more than a snake bite to keep her down for long."

She laughs easily, yet I remember the lines of worry on her tan face just last moon when I returned to Synap. "Sorry I couldn't stay with you longer."

"Please. I know who you are," she soothes. "You had to be here while your parents were gone. I get it."

Her blue eyes darken, and I know she's heard how their trip to Jun went. I even expect her to ask about it.

"How was it?" she asks, instead. "Taking over in their absence, I mean."

A deep sigh lifts my chest, and I begin walking again. She falls into step with me, easily matching my pace with her long legs. I pluck one flower from the basket, twirling it by its stem.

"Nerve-wracking, " I finally admit, letting it all out with her.

I'm not sure I'm ready to lead all of Kin...

All my life was too short a time to prepare. An entire moon was not enough time to adjust. With everything going on, people were restless, and I...

Was I good enough?

For a moment, I lose myself in the memory of waking with so many lives resting on my shoulders. The weight of it, something I've known all my days would fall upon me, felt so much heavier than I ever expected.

I always thought I'd face it with someone at my side, another pair of shoulders to carry the burden.

Someone to help with the decisions too small or too pressing to commune with the Allmother over, yet too large to be made by just one person.

Kivala places a gentle hand on my back, pulling me from my thoughts. Rubbing soft circles over my shoulder blades, she says, "I'm sure you'll get used to it, in time. From what I hear, you did rather well, even stopped a riot when they came back."

"I suppose the place didn't fall completely apart while they were gone," I whisper.

I lift my gaze, seeking Tyrvahn amongst the tree trunks and dappled light. I remember the sound of him howling alongside me as the riot drew to a close, remember the feel of his hand in mine. A chuckle escapes me as the scene flashes before my eyes.

Again, I blush and drop my gaze. Clearing my throat, I hope my slip has gone unnoticed.

But Kivala never misses much.

"So," she begins, tone carefully even, "tell me about this prince. Do we like him or is he a typical Jun?"

My eyes rake over him as he smiles at my mother. My father glances back at me with a knowing look in his eyes. I avert my gaze, staring up at my friend and willing myself not to blush.

She never blushes. Why do I do it so often?

"He's not what you think. He's…" I trail off, biting back a hundred praises. "We like him."

Kivala looks me over, tipping one dark eyebrow up toward her hair. The corners of her lips follow, quirking up into a mischievous grin. "Apparently, we like him a lot…"

I hurry my step, wishing to catch up to my parents and Tyrvahn.

Maybe then Kivala won't ask any more questions about this.

I'm hardly prepared to answer her. Thankfully, Tyrvahn stops, pointing at something in the distance. His mouth moves, full lips shaping some question or other.

My parents nod their heads gently, and my father places a hand on Tyrvahn's back before venturing into the undergrowth. He comes back with still more Allflowers in his hands. The white blooms glitter in the dappled sunlight, and their crimson interiors pulse with the Allmother's power.

A warm smile spreads my lips as I gaze at Tyrvahn.

Beside me, Kivala laughs. "Well, then," she says.

Her smug tone pulls my attention away from Tyrvahn's dark hair and muscled frame. She smirks down at me. A low chuckle escapes her dark lips, and she nudges me with her shoulder.

I step to the side, absorbing the minute force, and I can't help but giggle. Yet again, I blush, much to my embarrassment.

"Stop," I tease, gesturing to the basket hanging from my arm. "You'll make me drop my Allflowers."

"Mm-hm…" Again, she laughs, gifting me with a knowing smile. "Better walk a little faster. You might not catch up to your pretty prince otherwise."

I flash her an indignant look, but a smile stumbles onto my lips, regardless. Then, I pick up my pace.

I can almost feel the roll of her eyes as she follows in my wake.

***

I dump a handful of Allflower petals and stamens into the mortar and take the pestle in hand. After several full suns gathering them, each heartbeat bringing the meeting with Paikon closer, I'm glad to finally have enough to begin our preparations.

Grinding them up carefully, I watch the red nectar stain the white tips of the petals. Adding a few drops of blessed water, I work them into a paste.

Beside me, Kivala sits on the floor of the petition room. She pulls seeds from the flowers, dumping them into a satchel before letting the petals and stamens flutter into a stoneware basin. Her long brown locks dangle before her, hiding her face from my view.

Beyond the windows, the sun dips in the sky, casting long shadows through the forest. The little bit of light that reaches through sparkles on Kivala's small antlers. White at the base, they fade to black at the tips.

A few seeds fall beyond the satchel, clicking as they hit the wooden floor. Kivala reaches for them, hands shaking as she does. The trembling of her fingers draws my notice, pulling my attention from my work.

"Kivala?"

She makes a soft sound of acknowledgment but doesn't look at me. She picks up the dropped seeds and places them carefully in the satchel resting on her lap. She settles the stems into another satchel at her side and reaches over to drop the petals and stamens into my basin. A tremor rattles her nails against the side of the bowl.

Taking her hand within mine, I say, "Kivala? What's wrong?"

Was that a sniffle?

The wind sighs through the branches, disguising the sound.

I scoot my mortar and pestle away and turn to face her. "Kivala, please talk to me."

Finally, she looks at me. Tears stain her cheeks, and red rims her eyes. "It's so silly," she says.

Taking the satchel of seeds from her lap, I set it carefully on the floor, then pull her into my arms. "I doubt that," I whisper, throat constricting around a sympathetic lump.

How long has it been since I saw her cry? She didn't even cry when her mom hurt her leg.

She leans forward, resting her forehead on my shoulder. "Don't get me wrong, I'm glad you and your parents helped us," she mumbles. "This just… makes me wonder. We didn't know. We didn't have time to prepare… Maybe if we'd known before, Fahn wouldn't have fallen. Maybe—" A sob bubbles up, choking off the rest of her words.

I pull her into a tighter hug. Her arms slide around my waist. Her thoughts aren't hard for me to guess.

Maybe the massacre Jun called The Absorption wouldn't have happened. Maybe most of her friends wouldn't have been forced to abandon their customs to adapt to Jun society.

Maybe her two older brothers wouldn't have died, fighting to give her and their parents a chance to escape into Kin territory.

"We can't know what would've happened," I say, hating the guilt I know she still carries over her brothers' deaths. "But I'm sure Fahn would've given them something to think about."

She nods, moving her forehead against my shoulder.

"I'd tell you that you need to let this go, to live your life, but…" I pull back and look into her eyes before continuing.

"Maybe it's time for you to finally get your peace. Come with us. Fight at my side. You're burning good with a bow."

Wiping the tears from her eyes, she clenches her jaw. She pulls in a deep breath and nods. "I'll go with. Gladly."

I wipe away a stray tear hanging from her jawline, and she swallows back the lump in her throat.

"This won't be like Fahn. You won't lose another home," I say. "We'll make sure of it."

I just have to find a way to oust Paikon and Tumai without bringing them into Kin territory or venturing beyond the Allmother's reach.

Inwardly, I sigh at the difficulty ahead of me. Yet, I hold my tongue still. It won't do to fill her with doubts. I worry that my fears shine in my eyes, but if they do, she doesn't see them.

Nodding, she works through something in her mind. Kivala puts a hand to the side of my face and says, "Thank you."

I smile, and though it doesn't feel adequate, she picks up the satchel and another bundle of flowers. Quietly, she returns to her work.

Grabbing up my pestle, I drop a handful of petals into the mortar with a splash of blessed water. Steadily grinding away, I watch the shadows dance as the nearest candle hits some impurity or other in the wax, guttering and flickering away.

Kivala and I sit, working in silence for some time. The sun falls beneath the horizon, casting shadows across the land. A hollow call fills the air as the Light Watchers blow into their horns, calling out ninth sky.

The paste within my mortar grows thick, and I scoop it into the leather pouch. I take care to clean as much from my fingers as I can, wiping it into the folds of the leather before sprinkling more petals and stamens into the mortar.

I reach for my pestle, but footsteps on the landing draw my attention. Glancing up, I see Tyrvahn approaching, and my face lights up with a smile. He returns it, green eyes dancing with the light of the candles.

Striding into the room, he greets Kivala with a slight bow of his head. To me, he says, "You Kin are serious about your moss."

He settles down to sit beside me, and his hand finds its way to the small of my back. Leaning over, he drops a gentle, tantalizing kiss on my cheek.

My skin burns at the touch of his lips. I turn to gaze into his eyes, and the air between us swelters, blazing with the heat of a million candles. Remembering Kivala's presence, I clear my throat and return my eyes to the flower petals before me.

Of course, his casual touch and its not-so-casual effect on me do not go unnoticed. Kivala nudges me, smiling wickedly in my periphery.

"Well, that moss will come in handy," I say, keeping my voice low to hide any sultry notes that may creep in.

"What do we need it for, anyway?"

I glance up at him briefly, confused.

Surely Mother and Father explained how the barrier works.

Did they not?

"Not that I'm doubting you," Tyrvahn hurries to explain. "After all I've seen since coming here, I'm sure you'll use it for yet another miracle. I just don't know what it'll be."

I smile, humbled by the leaps his faith in us has taken since his arrival.

"I mean, I *made a plant grow*. I lit candles." Bumping his shoulder against mine, he teases, "Yeah, I know you turned people into trees, but… I'm pretty sure I'm catching up."

Giggling, I say, "Oh, you are, are you?"

Light dances behind his eyes, but not just that of the candles. Something else shines within him, some deeper happiness. It crinkles the skin around his eyes, and he tips his head back as he laughs.

"Well, I thought so," he says.

Recalling his insecurity earlier, I hurry to add, "You are actually doing quite well. Far better than I could've expected so quickly."

He holds my gaze until his eyes roam over my antlers, resting on the top of my head for just a moment. But they quickly fall to his hands, resting in his lap.

Was he thinking about…?

My eyes, or perhaps the flickering candles, trick me, sending a flash of color creeping over his cheeks.

Unless…

I tip my head to the side, trying to see better.

Is he blushing?

Kivala drops a few seeds into the satchel, and they clink softly onto the pile within it. The petals fall silently into the basin.

Finally, Tyrvahn clears his throat, and I return to my work. He looks over at me, asking, “Are we petitioning, tonight?”

“You haven’t taken much time to rest,” I say, “But if you’re up for it, we will.”

“I’m definitely up for it,” he whispers, deep voice rumbling through me.

And I can’t help it. My eyes desert my work, desperately searching his expression for a deeper meaning to his words.

Heat sings through me, pooling within the depths of my being. He gazes into my eyes, heavy-lidded, and his gaze dips to my lips.

“I’m going to clean up,” Tyrvahn says. “I’ll be back soon.”

I nod, trying not to picture the whole thing. Instead, I pour a few more flower petals into my bowl, steadily grinding away. He bids Kivala goodnight, and she returns his farewell. As he gets up and walks away, I keep my eyes carefully trained on the crimson nectar oozing from the stamens to stain the torn petals.

Tyrvahn’s footsteps meander down the stairs and disappear out of earshot. Immediately, Kivala chuckles.

“Well, then,” she says, voice heavy with mischievous implications.

Much to my chagrin, I blush. Yet again. Tipping my head down, I let my hair fall forward to block the color rising on my cheeks from her view. My hands move faster, gathering more bits and pieces of the Allflowers and mashing them up. All my frustrated desire pours into the motions.

"Wow," Kivala remarks. "You're going to grind that poor bowl to dust. There are much better ways to relieve that tension."

My head snaps up, mouth hanging open, and I stare at her. "Kivala?!"

Her hands fall into her lap and she throws her head back, laughing wildly.

Turning my attention back to the crimson paste, I scoop it from the mortar, quickly depositing it in the leather pouch. Yet my mind lingers on Tyrvahn. The flicker of his gaze to my lips, the way he looked at my antlers and the top of my head.

Heat floods through me at the thought.

"So," Kivala pries. "Have you two…?"

"What?" I hedge.

"You know."

I look up at her with shock coloring my cheeks. "Nestled?"

Again, I remember the way he looked at the top of my head, eyeing my antlers. I remember the strange, nearly insane desire I had just days ago to press myself to him, sliding my head beneath his chin.

"What? No. Of course not," Kivala says with a slight laugh. "I know you haven't done *that*."

I drop my gaze as she chuckles, hands still on the leather pouch. Waves of embarrassment wash over me, paralyzing me.

No. Move. You're being too obvious.

I wipe the red paste from my fingers, careful to move at a normal speed. "No," I confirm. "We haven't nestled."

"Well, no. He'll be going back to Jun if we can manage all this. Nestling is far too serious. I meant sex." Chuckling, she adds, "I thought that was pretty obvious."

"No, we haven't done that, either," I whisper. My hair tickles my forearm as I sprinkle more petals into the bowl.

But something in my tone must be off.

Kivala's hands fall to her lap with a partially dismantled Allflower hanging between her fingers. "Wait…"

My hands still, despite all my attempts to keep working.

Of course, she'd figure it out.

"You… You've thought about it, haven't you?" Her quiet words pierce my heart and still my lips. So, she goes on, "Allmother's warmth… But he's going back to Jun. You're just going to get hurt."

But I already know that.

I sigh, unable to meet her gaze, and force my hands to work.

Bright and early, the Light Watchers call out first sky with a single sound of their horns. The low sound resonates within my bones, but it isn't at all what I expected when I came here. I assumed the horns would produce a tinny sound, like the metal ones back home.

These sound richer, deeper.

I must say, these are much better to wake up to.

Stretching, I reach my arm out across the bed, surprised by the strength of my desire to have Veliana there with me. That isn't the only strange thought I've had since coming here, though. Not even close.

Briefly, I cast my mind over my conversation with her and the brazen desire to sit behind her, to rest my head atop hers.

There's certainly no way to justify that. I barely know her.

Compared to that, wanting her in my bed isn't strange in the slightest.

Rolling from my stomach to my side, I gaze out at the cozy room. Furs drape over the back of the lone chair, and a trunk with robes of a shockingly soft fabric tucked inside rests against the wall. A plush fur rug peeks out from beneath the bed, waiting to cradle my feet as I rise for the day.

Candles rest in sconces of wood and bone. For a moment, I consider lighting them for a bit of extra practice. But the day's first rays of sunlight reach in around the shutters, glinting on the hilt of the sword Veliana melted when we first came to Synap.

Better not light them.

The Allmother's warmth rushes through my veins, praising my decision to leave the wasteful ways of Jun behind.

I stretch once more, brushing the tips of my toes against the wall at the foot of the bed and tipping my head back. My antlers reach into the air at the head of the bed.

Rising, at last, I pull a robe on over my underpants and stride to the shutters. Throwing them open, I close my eyes, relishing the cool early morning.

Back in Jun, the butlers would have opened the drapes already. A lavish assortment of food would have sat on a side table in my chambers, waiting for me to wake. Most of it would have gone to waste, despite the poverty and food shortages in some areas of Jun.

Opening my eyes, I cross the room in a few steps. From a shelf near the door, I lift a stoneware jar of dried venison and another of dried fruits we don't even have in Jun. I retreat to my bed, crawling atop it with the jars in hand. Laying down, I prop myself up on one elbow and settle the jars down beside me. I snack on the preserved foods and watch the gray predawn light transform, bursting into a myriad of colors.

***

Walking along beside Veliana, I listen to the sled dragging in Tala's wake as we move for the border. The proud animal pulls the moss-laden thing easily, head aloft and tail wagging.

Kivala watches me carefully, analyzing my every move. I smile at her, hoping to alleviate some of the suspicions she so clearly holds. Yet, guilt toils within me every time I look at her.

How many loved ones did she lose in the absorption?

A strange, morbid curiosity makes me wonder if the Allmother could show me the nightmare my uncle and cousin inflicted upon Fahn, but the thought is cut off. The goddess gasps in my mind. Ethereal yet all too real, her pain and anger scorch my veins.

"They've begun," the Allmother hisses, and I see her clenched jaw, her gritted teeth.

She winces before my eyes, only to be replaced by the sight of a falling tree, clouding my mind with a million leaves fluttering as their host plummets to the earth. Birds take to the air, erupting into the sky in a cacophonous blur of wings. A nest falls, shattering eggs across the earth.

Immediately, nearby Kin howl. Their voices ring through the forest around the fallen tree, growing louder as they approach. The images fade in and out, but I know what's coming. My stomach sours.

No...

They'll slaughter them.

I beg the Allmother to stop them, to hold back their charge. Silently, I beg them to halt.

We're coming to solve this, please... Just wait...

But they can't hear me. And if the Allmother burns their veins, they take it as anger for the felled tree rather than a warning.

Through misty visions in my mind, I watch them filter into the sunny patch left in the tree's wake. Ruled by fury, they scream at Jun loggers. Axes fall and hands tremble as the loggers step away from the tree.

But the soldiers standing guard don't frighten so easily.

They draw their swords and step forward, almost eager. The early morning sunlight shines on steel, gleaming as it slices through one neck, then another. Bright red blood spills across the ground, and two Kin fall.

If only we were there so Veliana could melt their blades.

The thought reminds me of the hilt stowed within my pack, drawing me back to the here and now, stealing me away from the rest of the bloodshed. Veliana's hand grasps mine, tight enough to make my fingers ache. I loosen my grip, hoping I haven't hurt her.

Opening my eyes, I see the grass and dirt beneath me, far closer than they were just a moment ago. A small pebble digs into my knee.

But when did I fall?

The Allmother's pain and fury burn my veins, searing my muscles. I wince, hoping for it to pass. Yet, when it does, I know it is only because the soldiers have done their job. They've fended off any and all opposition on the forest's edge, leaving broken bodies on the ground.

My heart clenches in my chest, knowing that those brave people are gone.

Glancing to my right, I find Veliana on her knees beside me. I can't be sure if I dragged her down or if she fell of her own accord. Pulling myself up, I help her rise to her feet. Tears stain her cheeks, and she turns to face me.

"We're too late…" she whimpers. For half a heartbeat, she seems to consider stepping toward me, folding herself into my embrace for comfort.

Or maybe I'm just seeing what I want to see.

I don't get the chance to find out.

"What happened?" Kivala begs. "Why is the Allmother hurting so much?"

Did she not see?

For half a breath, I wonder if my connection to the Allmother is stronger than hers, if Veliana's curiosity about it may be warranted.

Veliana turns away, facing her friend. On seeing her expression, the Fahn woman pulls her into an embrace. Veliana wraps her arms around her friend, and a small surge of jealousy lances my heart.

"Paikon didn't wait for our decision… The loggers started working," Veliana whispers. "A few Kin were nearby. The soldiers…"

She chokes on a sob, and Kivala pulls her closer.

"Of course, he didn't wait," Kivala spits.

She keeps her eyes focused on the ground, but I can tell she wants to look at me, wants to accuse me. Guilt rages through me once more.

But what could I have done to stop this?

I was only fourteen at the time of the absorption. I had no role in deciding what would happen to Paikon and Tumai.

Sparing their lives was my parents' decision.

But glancing at this woman, seeing the tightness of her jaw, hearing her grit her teeth, the blame lands squarely on my shoulders.

Wouldn't this all have been easier if they would've been punished properly back then? Or even better, held in check to keep the absorption from becoming a massacre?

Pulling in a deep breath, I let her anger soak into me.

If I take the crown back, the responsibility of all that will be mine.

The weight of it all settles into my stomach, and I blow out a long breath. I've been preparing to lead Jun all my life, but with what I've learned since I saw the Allmother all those moons ago, with what I've learned since coming to Kin…

I can't lead the way my parents did.

The High Seal approaches, long robes dragging the dirt behind them. Soolan, Veliana's father, places a gentle hand on her cheek. "Dry your tears, Darling Daughter. Their deaths will not be in vain."

Pulling away from her friend, Veliana nods. I long to reach out and wipe her tears away, but I let her do it herself.

"Where will we place the barrier, now?" Kivala says, finally looking up from the ground. "They've already moved beyond the border."

"We place it at the border, in the flood grounds of the Krinai. Just as planned," Daerna says. Looking at her daughter's friend with a stern expression, she adds, "This is truly war, now. Blood has been shed. Any Jun within Kin territory when the barrier is in place is forfeit. The soldiers will pay with their blood. The men with the axes… They'll get their chance to see the Allmother's way."

"And if they don't?" I ask, surprising myself.

"They will receive the gift of her light, one way or another," Soolan says sagely, turning his silver gaze upon me. "This is war, and those people advanced into our territory, executing the commands of a greedy tyrant. Is this a problem of loyalty for you?"

My brows furrow, and I swallow, making decisions I'm ill-prepared for. I know peace can't be restored with Paikon or Tumai at the throne. There will be deaths, a great many of them.

"I understand about the soldiers," I allow. "But the loggers… Is there a way to do this without taking their lives, even if they can't feel the Allmother?" I find myself asking. I glance at Soolan and Daerna's ears, bandaged and healing without their tips. "We don't know the circumstances that led them to do his bidding."

They pause, and Veliana stares at me. Curiosity lights her eyes as she waits for me to explain.

But what can I say? That I want to spare the lives of my people, if at all possible? Of course, I do.

Perhaps they would come around, seeing the Allmother's way eventually. It just… might take some time.

And then, I remember the temple.

"If they do not see her light, if they refuse…" A smile lifts my lips, and I turn to the High Seal. "Well, I imagine the Allmother wouldn't mind the addition of a few more trees. They'd have all the time in the world to come to know her."

Maybe it isn't the best possible course of action.

But the compromise earns smiles from all around. Veliana wraps her hand around mine, and a deep breath puffs out my chest.

Soolan nods his approval. “Darling Prince. As always, the Allmother chose wisely. She was certainly right to place her faith in you.”

My heart swells at the compliment, and Veliana squeezes my hand, smiling up at me.

But still, I wonder.

Am I equal to this task?

***

Nine times, the Light Watchers call, and we stop in darkening shadows. Night falls quickly in the forest, far more so than in the open fields of Jun. Digging supplies from our packs by the light of a torch, we busy ourselves making camp.

My eyes dart to Veliana, watching the tendrils of hair that fall forward over her shoulders as she leans over her pack. Flickering shadows dance over her petite frame, and light glitters on her white antlers.

My heart swells with affection, and the Allmother warms my veins in approval. Dropping my gaze to my pack, I fish out the provisions the High Seal set aside for me with a smile on my face.

As I rise from my crouch, fully intending to sit near Veliana, Soolan approaches me. The wrinkles on his face converge as he smiles gently. His hand lands softly upon my arm, steering me gently away from his daughter. "Dear Prince. Won't you come gather sticks with me for our fire?"

I nod and hold my food up. "I'll just stow this away and grab a torch."

"No need for a torch. I'll show you a little trick."

I stash my food back in my pack and follow Soolan deeper into the forest, moving farther and farther from the light of the torches back at camp. With every stuttering beat of my heart, I wonder when he'll tell me to leave Veliana alone.

I can't exactly tell him how deeply I care for her. It doesn't make sense, given the short time I've known her.

Yet, the idea of actually giving up on her, just because her father might disapprove of me and my heritage...

My heart plummets.

Would he disapprove? If he knew how I feel?

Burn me alive... Should I disapprove? This is pretty rash...

I strain my eyes, peering into the darkness around us. An owl hoots loudly in the distance, stirring the nerves building in my stomach.

A stick snaps beneath my feet, and I nearly jump. Leaning, I pick it up, gathering both halves into my arms. Soolan wanders a few feet away and bends to pick up a few more sticks.

But how can he see?

"Are you faring well?" Soolan asks as I trip over a small vine.

"Um… I suppose."

"Petition the Allmother, Dear Prince."

I say nothing, wondering what I could possibly ask her for that would make this situation easier.

"Ask her for sight. We need to conserve the torches, burning as few as we can until we light the fire. There's no sense in burning them individually."

I suppose I should've thought of that.

"Allmother, please grant me sight."

Her warmth flows through my veins, and light gathers around me. My skin glows with it, illuminating the air around me. Slowly, the light sparkles in my eyes, allowing me to see my outstretched hands.

"Good," Soolan says. "Now, pull the rest of the light into your eyes."

In my mind, I can almost hear Veliana's voice telling me to relax and concentrate. I pull in a deep breath and focus, willing the Allmother's power to center in my eyes. At first, very little changes.

Exhaling, I close my eyes, blocking out all the things I can't see yet. The light gathers behind my eyelids, building to a blinding white and forcing me to open my eyes.

And the world appears, gleaming as if it were daytime. Trees shoot up into the sky, and though the lowest branches are well beyond my reach, somehow I can see each leaf clearly enough to count their veins. Moths flutter through the forest several fathoms away, yet I see the patterns on their wings.

A small chuckle bursts from me. I stare at the world around me in disbelief, taking in every detail. I spin slowly, seeing the forest as if for the first time, as if I haven't been surrounded by it since leaving Jun nearly a full moon ago.

Soolan chuckles softly. "It's remarkable, isn't it?"

I stare at him in disbelief as he smiles. All I can manage is a slow nod.

"Not everyone can do that. I'm impressed. Veliana did say your connection to the Allmother is unusually strong. She said you have a long lineage." He bends to pick up another stick, groaning as he does. "Though, Mahrdur is not a particularly old name."

He groans once more as he stands, and I rush forward to help him.

"No need, Dear Prince. I will manage. I always do." He takes a few steps forward, then groans as he retrieves another stick.

Deciding to spare him as much as I can, I set about gathering firewood in earnest, scouring the undergrowth. Yet, before I find even three more sticks, Soolan clears his throat.

"Do you know why I'm out here, gathering wood for our fire? There are more able-bodied people in our midst, I know that. In Jun, the King and Queen would never be expected to do such a task. But here I am."

I shake my head, genuinely curious, and resume my search. The pile in my arms grows steadily as he explains.

“The High Seal behaves differently. We are leaders, yes, but only because we're more connected to the Allmother. As such, we can communicate with her and decipher her will more clearly than others. We can learn from her and pass that knowledge on."

"Yet, we are still people," he says, hauling another stick into his weary arms. "Leaders are not inherently better than the people whose welfare they serve. We must pull our weight, whether that means divulging the Allmother’s will or petitioning for blessings on a hunt… Or gathering sticks to fend off the chills of a night spent beneath the leaves.”

I pause, staring openly. This man has access to more power than anyone I've ever met, yet he doesn't wield it to spare himself pain. He wields it carefully, respectfully. My jaw drops, and I have to urge myself to move again.

"You see, Dear Prince, when people must carry their leaders on their backs, not only do they become resentful, but they come to believe they can force other people to carry them. No place can go on for long like that."

Soolan pauses to gaze at me as if analyzing every move I've made since coming here. "Why are you trying to get your throne back, Dear Prince? Leading a nation is a great responsibility. You could be free of it. Yet, you aim to place that weight back upon your shoulders."

My hand stills on the stick I was about to retrieve, and I turn my head to look at him. Finally, I understand why he's brought me out here alone.

He's trying to see where the future will take Jun and Kin.

And consequently, Veliana.

I straighten to my full height, pulling my shoulders back. "Jun is broken. It can't continue the way it has, and I know my Uncle and Cousin will never stray from this path."

The Allmother's warmth glows within me. As it surges with her approval, I see even farther, picking out the grooves in the bark of trees many fathoms away.

Soolan nods. "And what sort of leader do you intend to be?"

The Allmother guides me to them, pulling me forward. She whispers through the leaves around me, shaking them with her breath.

"Come," she says. "They are here."

She fills my eyes with her sight, showing me just where to step, where to duck. Behind me, at a great distance, my followers sneak through the undergrowth by torchlight.

I take a deep breath, aching for the revenge I've been promised, and my breasts press against my leather chest piece. I swallow and pull the dagger from the sheath at my side.

They aren't the ones I want... But they'll do.

For now.

After all, they transgressed against the Allmother. They robbed her of her trees, her connection to this realm. Her connection to us.

And now, they'll pay.

Edging through the darkness that parts before my eyes, I approach the loggers' camp with the Allmother's warmth flowing through me. Yet, Aia twists my heart, corrupting my intentions.

"Only the soldiers, my Darling Rebel. Please," the Allmother whispers, yet again. "Fear is all that holds the loggers from my grasp. They may reach for me with the soldiers gone."

But Aia poisons me, stirring rage within me. He surges through the clothes I wear, products of Jun and their ways. He pulses in the weapons I use, born of metal ripped cruelly from the earth. But I have nothing else.

"Take them all," he urges. "After all, they work against your precious Allmother. They are your enemy. Spare no thoughts for them."

He slithers through me, freezing my heart and begging for blood.

A soldier stands idly by the fire. Her hands reach toward the flame, seeking warmth in the chill of the night.

If only they hadn't cut down the trees, they could have known the Allmother's warmth. She could have sheltered them from the cold.

But Aia holds their hearts captive, freezing them against her...

Pursing my lips, I cast my gaze over the camp and search for any others on watch. I find one more, but he paces far away from me. I smile at just how easy they've made this. My heart swells in my chest at the prospect of serving the Allmother.

Allmother, grant me stealth.

Within each boot, three cat hairs grow warm. Heat seeps into my heels, and I smile, once more.

Thank you, Allmother.

Now.

I shall do your work.

I duck behind a tent, then sneak to the next. Peeking around the corner, I make my way to the soldier at the fire. Her sword remains tucked away in its sheath. Her hands yet reach for the fire's warmth.

On the far side of camp, the other soldier peers into the night, willing his eyes to pierce the shadows which huddle beneath the trees. Beyond the ring of light provided by their fire and torches, the darkness must seem impenetrable.

Yet, my eyes cast it aside. One glance over my shoulder reveals the distant light of my followers' torches, still nothing more than a pinprick, a slightly brighter spot amidst the light of the Allmother's sight.

Turning my attention forward, I sneak across the remaining distance. One final push, one final step, and I reach the fire. Snaking my arm around her, I slit the soldier's neck in one quick move. She doesn't even make a sound.

As her blood gushes out, she settles into my waiting arms. I lower her to the ground, silent as a mouse. My hands come away slick with blood.

Grateful to have been able to give her a quick death, I turn my eyes to the man at the edge of camp. I have to get him before my followers get here so he doesn't wake the other soldiers. Ducking behind another tent, I sneak around it. Moving forward, I hop from one shadow to another, creeping up on my prey.

But every step brings Aia closer. Within their camp, no trees shelter me from him, and the vile products of Jun lie everywhere. He pulses through their camp and surges through me anew, twisting my heart to his will.

As I inch nearer, the soldier hears a twig snap, but not beneath my own feet. Beyond the limits of the campfire and torchlight, an animal saunters through the undergrowth.

Sneaking up behind him, I say nonchalantly, "It's only a raccoon."

He turns to face me, but too late. The blade of my dagger sinks into the side of his neck, and blood runs in rivers. It oozes over my hand, running down my wrist in rivulets. I pull it free and rush forward to catch him, easing his fall.

Recognition dawns on me. Lines have etched themselves into his face, deeper and deeper over the years. He doesn't know me, but he was there that night. I remember the sneer on his lips as he killed my friends, remember the laugh on his lips as he shouted orders to kill the *savages*.

To kill us.

He's one of Paikon's favorite soldiers.

Vrahnt...

I smile as the light fades from his eyes. Rising to my feet, I turn to face the camp and slink through it. I hear the Allmother's soft cry of anguish as Aia tightens my hand on my dagger. Her voice grows distant as he pulls me through the logging camp.

He laughs, voice booming through me and drowning her out.

Each tent I pass contains one or two sleeping loggers, dreaming their last dreams.

Guided by the Allmother's light, I venture back into camp with a few suhlroots and rehlberries for dinner. Kivala sits with a stoneware bowl full of water near our torches. I blink away the blessing of sight before letting my eyes wander from her features to the flickering flames.

I glance back at the trees, staring in the direction my father led Tyrvahn just before I went searching for fresh bits and baubles to accompany our dried venison. My heart stutters as I wonder what they could be talking about. Dropping my gaze to the grass at my feet, I watch the shadows shift over the soft, green blades as I approach our modest fire.

"I'm sorry," Kivala mumbles, drawing my attention from my thoughts.

I look at her with scrunched brows. "For what?"

"For being so… skeptical. About Tyrvahn and what you didn't *quite* say you wanted."

Somewhat embarrassingly, my cheeks grow warm.

Surely, she can't see it.

"It's fine, Kivala." I kneel beside her, pulling my legs up underneath myself. "It's so quick… I don't understand it myself."

Kivala falls silent for a few heartbeats, taking some of the roots from my hands. Settling them upon a slab of wood, she pulls a knife from her pack and begins chopping them. "I see why you like him, if that helps. He's nice, smart even." Teasingly, she adds, "For a Jun."

Dropping a berry into her bowl, I chuckle and cut my eyes at her.

Smiling, she adds, "He's handsome, too. Not my type, but handsome."

Laughter bubbles up, erupting from deep within me. "Yes," I say, "He's far too tall for you."

"Yeah, that's the problem," Kivala says, settling her knife on the wooden slab. A sharp bark of laughter bursts from her. "It definitely isn't his lack of breasts."

We devolve into riotous laughter. The knife lies forgotten on the cutting slab, and the berries rest in a pile in my basket. Shaking with mirth, I lean against her and toss another berry into the bowl. "I missed you."

"I missed you, too," she says. With another laugh, she adds, "Now, let's get this food made. I'm sure they're working up quite an appetite gathering sticks."

We set about finishing our preparations. Tyrvahn returns with my father, settling the freshly gathered pile of wood nearby. Despite the varied company to choose from, despite the presence of both my parents and many Rangers, Tyrvan settles in right next to me.

My cheeks warm, yet again, and I smile. A darting glance at Kivala rewards me with a quick raise of her eyebrows.

***

We make our way through the forest, approaching the river. The sound of it builds from a distant gurgle to a roar as we move nearer. I glance downriver, knowing how close we are to Kivala's parents. It's no more than a third of a sky from their home to the river.

Already, I can see the Light Watcher terrace, at the top of the highest tree around. Just one tree over from them.

My heart aches to see Shevari on her feet. When last I saw her, the snake bite on her leg still oozed, and fever held her in bed.

Kivala said she was better...

Yet, my mind holds only the image of her prone form, mumbling in pain. At my urging, our party moves faster. A steady pace brings us to the foot of the ladder leading to Shevari and Fluros' home before sunset.

With a warm smile, Kivala rushes up the ladder ahead of me. I follow quickly on her heels, and Tyrvahn follows. A blush spreads over my skin as I realize the view he must have, knowing how tightly these breeches fit. I shake my head to clear the idea away, but it doesn't work.

"Mother! Father!" Kivala calls out, already clearing the top of the ladder.

I always forget how much lower the people of Fahn build their homes. As I pull myself up onto their balcony, I look back out into the trees, marveling at the clear line of sight to the ground. Yet, my gaze doesn't linger on the natural beauty of the world for long.

"Kivala! Oh, Darling Daughter. I didn't think we'd see you again so soon," Shevari exclaims, closing the distance much faster than I would have expected. Her gait holds not even a trace of a limp. She embraces her daughter, dark hair cascading down to meet Kivala's.

Her eyes finally look up, landing on Tyrvahn and me. Rushing forward, she takes my hand. "You seem to have matured a great deal since I last saw you. I suppose leading a nation can do that to a person, though," she says, laughing. The sound wraps around me, seeps into my bones, warm and inviting and full.

I look down at myself, wondering if perhaps I've developed wrinkles or those funny little spots some people get on their hands as they age.

But no.

I look the same.

Of course, my reaction only deepens Shevari's laugh. I smile, blushing at having been taken in so easily, and she pulls me in for a hug.

"You look so much better," I say, sliding into a new topic. "I was so worried about you when I left…"

"No need to worry yourself over me, dear. It'll take the power of the Allmother herself to strike me down. Since I don't think she'll do that, I expect to live forever."

Behind me, Tyrvahn chuckles, drawing Shevari's attention. I make the introductions, and she regards him carefully. Her eyes sweep over him once, twice.

"What do you think of your uncle and cousin, young Prince?"

"They're vile," Tyrvahn says, simply.

The smile returns, pulling Shevari's lips wide and creasing her cheeks. "Then you're welcome here. Come. Let us prepare dinner. We'll eat at the banquet table down in the meadow. Fluros is out tending the garden. He'll be back soon, I'm sure, and he'll be glad to meet you."

***

The Light Watchers call out eighth sky as Kivala and I ladle soup into bowls. I hand two freshly filled bowls to Tyrvahn, relishing the little bolt of lightning that shoots up my arm as our fingers brush. Our eyes meet, and his lips lift into a sly smile.

Then, he turns, carrying the bowls off to the table. A young Ranger comes to take a couple of dishes from Kivala, clearly hoping to draw her attention as Tyrvahn has drawn mine. But the young man is destined to be disappointed in that matter.

Doubly so for, as he takes the bowls from her outstretched hands, a riotous noise erupts just out of sight within the forest. Kivala's eyes dart toward the sound of encroaching voices, letting the Ranger believe only that distraction stands in his way. His face falls, and he turns to carry the bowls away.

"She is here," the Allmother whispers through my mind. "She who is not as she seems."

She who is not as she seems? Why do you keep saying that?

"Because you *must* remember it."

And with that, her voice fades from my mind.

Kivala reaches for her stone dagger, sheathed at her side, but I put a hand on her wrist. "It's only Garle. We're safe."

She nods, and we resume our preparations, knowing that we'll need more food than previously expected. Tyrvahn comes back to carry more bowls, and I ask him to fetch more from the local Seal's house. Given directions, he hurries off.

And then, Garle's party breaches the clearing. My jaw drops at the sight of her.

Kivala blurts, "Burn me alive…"

Her exclamation temporarily diverts my attention. "What?"

"You see her, right?" She lifts a brow suggestively, cutting her eyes at me.

I chuckle, rolling my eyes. But I *do* see her.

Halfway between my height and Kivala's, Garle stands proud. Dark freckles decorate her skin, perching on high cheekbones. Full lips lift into a smile. Silky black hair hangs loose, draping in gorgeous curls.

Despite the shirt and leather vest, her cleavage spills out. Broad hips complete her figure, making me blush.

Because I know she's been with Tyrvahn.

Is hers the figure he desires? I don't exactly stack up.

My gaze drops to my chest, small, though not flat. My willowy frame seems lackluster by comparison.

Daring to glance back up, I finally notice what I likely should have seen first. Her antlers. Rather small for a Jun, they shine white at the base, only darkening to black as they near the tips.

She isn't Jun. She's Fahn.

And suddenly I understand her role in the rebellion.

***

"We can't go into Jun and expect any support from the Allmother," Garle says, sultry voice wafting around the banquet table. "She wants to help, but Aia pushed her out long ago. If we set foot in Jun, we're on our own. We keep seeds with us, in pockets or pouches, in necklaces or bracelets."

Her voice shrinks as she adds, "It helps, but it isn't enough."

My parents cast a glance at Garle, analyzing her words. Yet, their weighted expressions make little sense. She's spoken plainly enough.

Her words hang in the air, heavy like the smoke of our torches. I take a long drink of my wine, and frustration simmers in my stomach. "The Allmother is our protection. Without her…" I sigh, rolling the problem around in my mind. "We won't hold up to their steel weapons."

What have I led us to?

Was there a peaceful solution that I overlooked?

"We have a network of safe houses, with allies dotted across the landscape leading to the capital. There are gaps, though," Garle says.

Silence descends on us. My mother takes my father's hand in hers, and Kivala reclines in her chair, mimicking her own parents' posture. Tyrvahn sits forward with an elbow on the table, ramming one hand into his hair.

"So, the barrier is still our best option, then," my mother says. Shadows pool in the waves of her white hair and gather within her eyes. Sighing, she comes to terms with the current situation and says, "Perhaps we should take the evening to think this over. We can reconvene for further discussion tomorrow."

The Light Watchers call tenth sky, reminding us that even the sun has long since gone to bed. I nod and stand up, gathering the dishes before me. Across the table, Tryvahn rises, doing the same.

"Well, then," Kivala says, clearly surprised.

I glance at her, asking, "What?"

"Just never expected to see a Jun Prince clean up after himself…" she mumbles, her light tone keeping her words from biting.

I smile, thankful that he's proving himself to be better than Paikon and Tumai.

It doesn't take much to be better than them, but... He's far better.

A grin spreads itself over my face, and I blush at my own thoughts.

With my hands nearly full, I finally look up, just in time to watch Garle approach Tyrvahn. My stomach drops right into my boots, and I go still for half a breath. Only when I force myself to move do I come back to life. I reach for another bowl, moving at the speed of a tiny snail.

"So," Tryvahn begins, settling the bowls he was cradling in his hands back down upon the table. Now empty, his hands come to rest on his hips. "You're Fahn?"

"Is that a problem?" Garle asks, tipping her head to the side.

He didn't know? Did she paint her antlers?

I suppose that explains what the Allmother meant by 'not what she seems.'

"No." Tyrvahn chuckles. "No problem, at all. It does explain some things, though."

Butterflies erupt in my stomach as I watch the easy exchange. I reach for another bowl, adding it to my stack. Yet, my eyes watch Tyrvahn's gaze, hoping his eyes never dip to Garle's sumptuous lips or her ample bosom.

But the woman in question does so much worse.

She steps forward, reaching for Tyrvahn. Her fingers tangle in his hair as she says, "You look so handsome with your hair grown out. You always kept it so short, and I always wondered..."

Heat rises up my neck, coloring my skin, and my heart falters.

Stepping closer, she presses herself against him, nestling the top of her head beneath his chin.

And I can watch no more.

My stack of bowls clatters to the table, and I run, heart splintering even as my own stupidity dawns on me.

Of course, he would like her better.

Tears roll down my cheeks as my feet batter the ground.

Behind me, his voice calls out, "Wait! Veliana, please!"

But why should I wait?

To hear him apologize for leading me on?

To hear, from his lips rather than from my own mind, all the reasons why my wispy frame doesn't attract him?

To hear him sing her praises?

Holding my fingers to my lips, I let out one long whistle, calling Tala to my side. She howls in the distance, answering me from somewhere in the forest, and I run toward her. Torches hang from balconies, dotting the forest with light, but I crave the darkness beyond their reach.

Tears cascade over my cheeks, and I berate myself for thinking Tyrvahn would want anything to do with me, especially if he had a chance with someone like Garle.

And he clearly does.

It's Materva, all over again.

Again, I see him stroll away from me, arm in arm with that other Light Watcher. But now, I see Tyrvahn walking away, too.

Far away, I hear him shouting, "Nothing happened! Veliana, it was nothing!"

But it was certainly *something*.

The sight of her nestled up to him flashes through my mind, and embarrassment washes through me. A huge sob wrestles itself free of my lips, and my body shudders with it. My side begins to ache with the exertion of sprinting, and I slow to a stop. Gasping for air, my mind spins.

I'm just a little wisp.

How will the Vierna line ever go on if no one wants me?

Footsteps crash against the ground behind me, slowing to avoid barreling into me. "Veliana," Tyrvahn whispers, voice rasping through his throat.

I can't let him see me like this... I need to keep running.

My eyes, surely puffy and red, burn with the tears they've shed.

His arms slide around my waist, gentle and uncertain. I feel myself lean into him, hoping for half a second that maybe it means he's chosen me. Another sob tears its way up my throat.

Gingerly, Tyrvahn rests his chin atop my head. For a single beat of my heart, relief washes through me.

But then, I see Garle nestled up to him, and anger floods me, hot and fast.

I drop my head forward, controlling my anger just a bit, and step away from him before spinning to face him. But one tip of one antler catches the side of his cheek, tearing the skin. Blood drips from the cut, and shock spreads across his face.

"What are you doing?!" My hands ball into fists, and I shout, "That *means* something here, Tyrvahn! You can't do that with multiple people."

And then, I'm running, again. Another whistle, and Tala howls, so close. I sprint toward her, and this time, Tyrvahn doesn't chase after me.

Tala bursts through the undergrowth and ducks before me. Leaping onto her back, I bury my face in her fur.

"Take me away, girl," I mumble.

She pushes off, running toward the coast. The Allmother stings my veins, urging me to turn around.

But for the first time in my life, I ignore her.

My strengthened connection to her intensifies the heat of her disapproval, but I hold my lips still, letting Tala carry me away. So, the Allmother tries to comfort me, to ease my anger.

But I don't want comfort.

I want to be mad.

It's not like I'm doing any good here, anyway.

Chapter 14
Tyrvahn

Ten times, the hollow, wooden sound of the local Light Watcher's horn reverberates through my bones. Across the table, Veliana rises to gather bowls. Hoping to get some time alone with her after we take these dishes away, I stack the light stoneware bowls high, intending to follow after her.

Glancing up, I'm rewarded with the sight of a blush coloring her cheeks. With my heart swelling in my chest, I lift my teetering stack of bowls.

But Garle approaches, marching right up to me and impeding my plans.

"So," I say, setting the bowls back down on the table. Resting my hands on my hips, I continue, "You're Fahn?"

I suppose I shouldn't be surprised. She did always hold herself apart from everyone in Jun.

She tips her head to the side, the proper coquette, even now. "Is that a problem?"

Laughing, I say, "No. No problem, at all. It does explain some things, though."

Suddenly, I realize my mistake, hoping fervently that she doesn't ask me to elaborate. I'd rather not mention her insatiable appetites, certainly not in front of Veliana.

Somehow, I don't see that going over well.

She doesn't ask, presumably guessing my meaning. After all, she's Fahn. She knows perfectly well what their customs entail.

Instead, she steps closer to me, reaching for me, and I have to use every bit of my manners not to jump away from her touch. I'd rather have Veliana's hands reaching for me.

I go perfectly still, watching her face carefully. I remember all too well how casually she touches people, another Fahn custom that I never recognized within her.

Yet, it explains quite a lot. This could be nothing.

Twining her fingers in my hair, she says, "You look so handsome with your hair grown out. You always kept it so short, and I always wondered…"

My stomach drops. Before my eyes flash memories of her playing with my mother's hair, but this feels quite different. I tip my head back, trying to politely tug my hair from her grasp, but she takes it as an invitation.

Stepping closer, she presses up against me, nestling beneath my chin.

And I freeze, appalled at her assumption that I would still feel for her as I once did. The tips of her antlers shine in the low light, far too close to my eyes. Closing them, I step straight back as a stack of bowls falls upon the table.

Once free of the trap of Garle's antlers, I open my eyes just in time to see Veliana disappear between tree trunks, running at full speed.

Kivala stands at the table with lips pursed, glaring at me.

"Garle, what are you doing?" I ask. "We aren't together, anymore. You left, remember?" My feet carry me after Veliana, and my mind spins, wondering how I'll ever explain this to her.

"Well, if I knew Paikon's poison would lead you to the Allmother," Garle says, "if I knew you'd turn out like this, maybe I would've stuck around."

My heart freezes, and so do I. Staring after Veliana's rapidly disappearing figure, realization dawns on me, cold and brutal. I spin on my heel and take a few steps back toward Garle.

Fury boils my veins. "You knew?" I hiss.

She shrinks before me, realizing her mistake as my hands ball into fists at my side.

Shaking with rage, I spit, "Had you told me, my parents might still be alive."

Her gaze falls to the floor, but she says nothing.

Shaking my head, I turn away from her and sprint after Veliana. I can figure out the implications of Garle's betrayal later. Puzzling over it won't change the past. I can't let her chase away the one good aspect of my life.

"Wait! Veliana, please!"

Running in the direction she went, I beg the Allmother to let me catch her. My heart jumps into my throat as I weave between tree trunks and beneath balconies. Torches illuminate a small path, and I can do naught but hope Veliana followed it.

And then, I hear her.

Silently thanking the Allmother for my long legs, I push myself to run faster. Listening for Veliana's footsteps, barely audible over the crashing of my own, I follow. Each step brings me closer and closer, but not fast enough.

A single, long whistle rings out through the air, and Tala howls in the distance. I push myself harder, knowing I have to catch her before Tala gets here. I'll have no hope of catching the massive dire wolf.

My feet pound the dirt, and I call out, "Nothing happened! Veliana, it was nothing!"

But she doesn't answer.

A few more steps, and I hear her sobbing. My heart clenches painfully, dredging up what she told me about her old love, the man that was stupid enough to leave her for someone else.

What must she think right now?

But she isn't running anymore. The sound of her crying gets closer and closer, and I slow my pace.

Finally, I see her, standing in the middle of a path with her back to me. Her shoulders shake with the sobs that wrack her body. My brows furrow, and my arms ache to reach for her.

"Veliana," I whisper, my voice a hoarse mockery of its normal timbre.

I approach her, slowly, and my heart hammers away in my chest. My breath comes in gasps from the sudden exercise. I open my mouth to speak, but nothing comes out.

And still, she weeps.

Reaching out, I slide my arms around her waist, slow and gentle, testing the waters.

Please, don't run.

I pull her back against me, and for one breath, she leans into me. For one breath, I think maybe I can salvage this.

Her golden hair glows in the torchlight, begging me to rest my chin atop her head.

Or perhaps that's just my heart, aching to show her how I feel...

Taking a deep, shuddering breath, I do the only thing I can to make myself clear. I pull her tighter against me, gingerly nestling my chin on the top of her head, right between the sharp points of her antlers.

Still panting, I wait with my heart laid out before me. Veliana leans against me, and joy floods my body.

But she tenses in an instant. Tipping her head forward, Veliana steps away from me. She spins to face me, and one tip of her antler catches my cheek. But the pain of the cut is nothing to the pain of her rejection.

My heart convulses within my chest, and my jaw falls slack.

"What are you doing?!" Veliana shouts, face contorting in anger. "That *means* something here, Tyrvahn! You can't do that with multiple people."

And with that, she runs. Stunned, I stand in her wake, staring after her. She whistles once more, and Tala howls in answer, much closer than before.

I won't catch her, this time.

The world tips beneath me, and I fall to my knees. The corners of my eyes prick with the promise of tears, and I don't stop them.

***

Kivala leads me to a small temple built around the base of a large tree. Once inside, she fetches powdered Stag's hoof and blessed water from a trunk. I stare on, eyes unfocused. With the two mixed into a paste, she approaches me.

"How far have you made it into your training? Are you working on asking for the Allmother's power or have you moved on to receiving it?"

I shake my head. "Shaping it, controlling it," I mumble, half-heartedly.

She raises a brow, "Oh. Okay, then." Tipping her head to the side, evaluating me, she holds out the bowl of Stag's hoof paste.

I take it, dipping my fingers into the shining mixture. My eyes find the tips of Kivala's antlers, but somehow, it doesn't feel right to touch them. Shoving my awkwardness aside as some product of Jun society, I reach out to paint the tips of her antlers silver.

Kivala pulls back. "What're you doing?"

Confused, I hold the bowl up. "I was going to…"

"I don't need that. I'm not the one practicing," she says, walking toward the tree trunk at the center of the temple. Leaning against it, she adds, "Even if I was, it's been a long time since I've needed any enhancements for stuff like this."

"So… Veliana wouldn't need it, either?" My heart wars with itself, torn between the glee of realizing that maybe she just wanted me to touch her and the agony of knowing she thinks I prefer Garle.

"No. She doesn't need it. She only uses it if she wants to make sure she sees and hears the Allmother perfectly."

Leaning against the wall, I slide down. Slouching forward, I settle the bowl on the floor beside me and sigh. The world around me seems to shift, and I realize just how much Garle may have stolen from me.

My parents. My kingdom.

And now, Veliana.

Drawing my knees up, I rest my elbows upon them and stare at the floor beyond my feet. Images of her running, of her shouting at me, flood my mind, and I wince.

After a moment, Kivala comes to sit beside me. "Veliana let you tip her antlers, didn't she?"

Unable to form words, I simply nod.

Another silent moment passes, then, "You actually like her… Don't you?"

Again, I nod.

"Then, why would Garle…?"

"I don't know. She may as well be a stranger, now. She never really talked a lot about her life, and I apparently never learned as much about her as I thought I did. She was always lonely, though." I run a shaking hand through my hair. "Well, I suppose not always. Maybe not before…"

Shaking my head, voice small and weak, I continue, "The absorption… It wasn't supposed to be a slaughter. Paikon and Tumai… They got out of hand."

Beside me, Kivala clenches her jaw, just barely visible in my periphery. Her hands tremble in her lap.

And my mind spins.

"Garle said once that she felt out of place all the time. I think, I mean, *I wonder* if that was the only genuine thing she ever said to me. But I think she just wants somewhere to belong.

But she knew. She *knew* Paikon was going to try to kill me. And she just left. My parents…"

Taking a deep breath, I swallow back the lump in my throat. "And now, she's chased Veliana away."

I shake my head, and silence descends upon us once more. Kivala's fingers worry at each other, moving ceaselessly. When she eventually turns to face me, I don't look up.

"Your face," she begins, "When you… with Veliana… Does that mean the same thing in Jun as it does here?"

At her words, I remember the cut on my face, showing the world my rejection. Though it could have been much worse. The blasted thing starts to sting again, and I reach up to touch it. A few flakes of dried blood come away with my fingers.

"As far as I know, yes."

"So…" Kivala hesitates, something that seems unusual for her. "You love her?"

"Yeah." I pull in a deep breath and nod. "I thought she felt the same way…"

Suddenly, it's my turn to fidget. My fingers tug at a string in the seam of my pants, hanging loose on the side of my knee.

Kivala's tone softens, and she says, "Tyrvahn, she didn't run because she thought you broke a custom. She ran because she was hurt, because she has feelings for you."

My gaze darts to her, scratching my antlers against the stone wall. I search her blue eyes for any hint of a joke.

But I find only sincerity.

She stands up, reaching a hand down for me. "Come on. She's probably back, by now. If not, she will be soon. I don't think she'll stay away for long, not with everything that's going on."

***

Back at Shevari and Fluros' home, Kivala leads me in. My eyes scan the room, searching for Veliana. But I come up empty.

She isn't here.

My heart twists in my chest, but I get no time to process the feeling.

Gathered in a modest sitting room, lit up by candles resting in carved bone sconces, Garle stands with arms crossed. She faces the High Seal, dark brown eyes narrowed.

"You can have Paikon, but Tumai is mine. No argument. And I spare no one," she says, raising one eyebrow. "My followers are not prepared to leave survivors, not after what we went through in the absorption. We proved that at the logging camp. Agree to my terms, or we walk."

Soolan and Daerna exchange a significant look and sigh. The horror the Rebels must have inflicted upon the loggers flashes briefly before my eyes, but I blink it away. She wants us emotional and irrational, I'm sure. She wants to corner us in anger or frustration, only to bend it to her needs.

Gritting her teeth, Daerna says, "We consent that you may be the one to take care of Tumai. Readily, we consent to that."

Garle tips her chin up, daring them to oppose her. Her smug attitude joins with her reprehensible intentions to churn my stomach.

And to think my head was between her antlers earlier.

And back before she left, back before I knew what kind of monster she was…

All the things we did together…

I suppress a sick shudder, fighting off memories of sharing my bed with her.

“But if you insist on butchering innocent children,” Soolan says, picking up where his Sealmate left off, “simply because they’re Jun, we will find a way to move forward without you or your followers.”

“How exactly are you going to manage that?” Garle challenges. “We’ve learned how to fight without the Allmother’s power. You haven’t. If you set foot in Jun, you’re powerless. You need us, and you know it.”

“If you’re so capable,” I ask, tipping my head to one side and narrowing my eyes, “then why did you come here for an alliance to begin with? Clearly, you need help. But why?”

She clenches her jaw and steps toward me. “I don’t owe you an answer any more than I owe them one.”

Garle moves for the door, but Kivala sidesteps, blocking her path. A smile, sweeter than I’ve seen on her face yet, shines out, taunting Garle. Their eyes lock, and some strange shadow seems to shift across Garle’s features.

Kivala’s eyes rake over Garle’s face, and I stare on, confused.

At last, Kivala steps aside, letting Garle sweep out into the night. No sooner than the door shuts behind her, Soolan collapses into a chair. Daerna puts a tender hand on his shoulder, placing the other over her mouth. She stares into the guttering flame of a candle and shakes her head.

"She's right," Soolan says, voice a hollow shell of its former self. "We do need her. We're defenseless in Jun."

What happened when they were there?

My eyes drift to their ears, wrapped but obviously missing the tips.

Did Paikon or Tumai do that? Or did they have one of their soldiers do it?

Disgust wells within me. Sighing, I wish for Veliana's soothing presence.

She'd know what to do, I'm sure. She would've diffused that whole situation.

"Where's Garle staying?" Kivala asks.

I turn to look at her. My brows furrow, but Soolan doesn't miss a beat.

"She and her followers have taken up residence in the Ranger rooms. The Rangers have been spread across the village, sleeping in any home that could accommodate them."

Blue eyes glittering, Kivala says, "I'll talk to her."

Pacing back and forth across worn floorboards, I listen to them creak. The sound of the wood comforts me, easing the tension, albeit slowly.

Darkness moves within my heart, seeps throughout me. It creeps, slowed by the overwhelming presence of the Allmother in these lands.

But it doesn't vanish. It doesn't stop.

All I can do is close my eyes and push against it. Stilling beside my bed, I clench my fists and shut out the rest of the world for just a moment.

Allmother, please...

Loosening one hand, I reach for the locket at my neck, taking it in my grip. The seed within it pulses with her warmth.

Please... Help me fight him. Just a bit longer.

Her warmth flows through me, teasing the tension from my muscles. Yet, I hear his laughter, deep and horrid, simmering in the darkest recesses of my heart.

I recall my harsh words, my promises of slaughter, and I shudder. But I know I can't trust myself to resist him, can't trust myself not to hurt innocent people.

I proved that at the logging camp.

My eyes snap open, and I beg the Allmother for a distraction. For the first time in many renewals, I see her smile. In my mind, brilliant red lips part, showing perfect white teeth.

And a knock sounds at my door.

Turning, I swallow back the war within me. I open the door and find a smiling face, familiar in so many ways, though I only met her today. Kivala, best friend to the Priestess Rising and apparently, a skilled archer.

More importantly, a fellow Fahn.

An understanding heart.

"Hello," she says, leaning casually against the doorframe. Light brown hair falls softly around her shoulders, but her eyes hold shadows like mine. She saw it all. She lost people.

She knows.

Her beautiful blue eyes drop to my lips for half a breath, but she catches herself quickly, lifting them to meet mine. But not quick enough.

Rushing forward, I take her face in my hands and press my lips to hers, desperate not to think. After a moment of shock, she stands up straight, touching my waist as she moves toward me. I take a few steps backward, leading her into my room, and she closes the door behind her.

Her lips part in a beautiful invitation, and I take it. Our tongues dance, moving together gracefully, even as her hand moves to my breast. Teasing, gripping, she moves her hand skillfully, and I ache for her touch all over my body.

She kisses my neck, nipping gently at the tender flesh at its base. Gasping, I undo the buttons of her tunic, pushing the fabric back over her shoulders. It falls to the floor, landing in a heap. Her breasts fill my hands, perfect nipples taut and waiting.

My head swims with exhilaration, and my heart hammers in my chest. Her caramel skin shines in the light of the candles, and I move my hands over it, trailing my fingertips down her spine.

Kivala shudders in my arms, pulling her lips away from my neck. Meeting in a tantalizing kiss, our mouths melt together. Her hot breath fills me, and her hands unfasten my tunic. I shake the dreaded thing off, thankful for the freedom its absence allows her hands. They drift down my sides, sliding around my back, and she grasps my buttocks, pulling me tight against her.

A small moan of pleasure bursts from my mouth, and she pulls her lips from mine, smiling. Turning me, she maneuvers me to the bed. I sit on the edge, and she climbs atop my lap.

Our lips meet, once more, burning each other. And this time it's my turn. I leave a trail of kisses down her neck, whispering hot breath on her collarbones. Gripping her butt, I take one of her nipples in my mouth, letting my tongue play.

She groans, and my whole body tingles with desire.

Sliding my hands into the back of her breeches, I squeeze. Another groan, and heat builds within me, aching and sweet.

Pushing me back, Kivala kisses me, hard and deep. Her hand slides down my stomach, moving over my pants, teasing. Arching my back, I press my breasts against her, desperate for any contact I can get.

She quickly slips her hand inside my pants, letting her fingers play and tease before finally slipping one inside me. Moving slow, she bends her finger within me, stroking. I arch my back further, gasping and digging my antlers into the mattress.

Her hand slides free of my pants, and my insides beg for its return. Hot lips land on my breast, and I moan, begging her for more.

"Please," I whisper, desperate for her.

And she obliges, kissing all the way down my stomach. Pulling my pants down, she kisses lower and lower until her skillful tongue finds its mark. She works me to a fever pitch, then slips two fingers in, moving them inside me until I squirm on the mattress and the world shatters.

With a devilish grin, she rises, freeing herself of her breeches and boots. I take her hand, pulling her down on the mattress beside me, and our lips meet once more. She grasps my breast, and my skin burns beneath her touch.

Shallow breaths rattle my body as my hand dips down between her legs. Deserting my breast, she grabs my buttock, gripping tight. My fingers play and tease, slowly sliding into her warmth. I move faster and faster, then pull free, working my fingers at the tip of her mound until she falls to pieces beneath me with her nails digging into my skin.

Violent, shuddering breaths rock our bodies, and we curl into each other. Her lips find mine, suddenly sweeter, gentler. My eyes roam over her face and dart between her clear blue eyes. A smile graces her lips, and I match it.

Pulling me close, she slides one arm beneath my head. We lay there, staring into each other's eyes until sleep claims us.

Chapter 16
Veliana

The wind whips through my hair, and the trees thin out around us. Tala slows to a walk once more, and I lift my head. A few trees stand before us, stubbornly rooted in rocky soil. Beyond them, the rocks grow more plentiful, and the Krinai River opens into a dark bay. Further out, the bay turns to a vast ocean, and everywhere, the water reflects the night sky.

Tala clears the trees quickly, carrying me into the open. Finally able to stop after several skies spent walking or running, she kneels. I slide down from her back and stare up. More stars than I've ever seen before glitter above me and sparkle on the waves before me. My jaw falls slack as I gaze at their infinite beauty.

No wonder Materva couldn't abandon the stars for me.

That makes sense, I suppose. But Tyrvahn...

Breathing deeply, I push away the sight of Garle nestling up to him. Then, I shove away the shock and hurt on his face when I pulled away from him.

And the drops of blood on his cheek.

I thought I stepped forward far enough. I thought I leaned my head down far enough.

Sighing, I look to the horizon. The gentle ululations of the water moving against the shore pull me forward. Tala stays behind, sprawling out near the tree line. But I leave the shelter of the forest behind.

With every step, the Allmother's voice grows quieter. Her warmth deserts me, but so does the sting of her disapproval.

A gentle wind teases my hair, lifting it from my shoulders along with the burden of leading. I breathe it in, pulling the salty air deep into my lungs.

It feels strange, this crisp freedom.

But not unpleasant.

The Light Watchers call twelfth sky, and though quiet, the twelve sounds of the horn slowly draw me from the warmth of sleep, dredging up memories of a day long past. Half-awake, the sound of the horns echo in my mind just as they echoed through the trees when Paikon and Tumai came to my village in the absorption.

The fire came first, burning our homes to the ground. Screams burst from within them, piercing my ears. Shrill agony and hoarse shouts filled the air, riding the smoke into my lungs until I made the same sounds. Pulling the shutters open on my window, I froze for just an instant, watching Jun soldiers set homes alight.

I turned, running headlong down the hall until I skidded to a stop at my parents' doorway. Pounding my fists on the side of the door frame, I shouted for them to rise. My mother came to the door first, pulling the curtain aside. The light of the fire reached in, flickering angrily over her naked body.

"We have to move," I whisper, voice a raspy little mockery of its former self. "Jun has come for us."

Horror filled her eyes, and she coughed on the smoke seeping in through the windows. Behind her, my father slipped free of their bed.

But outside, the Jun soldiers were moving quickly. Fire already lapped at the sides of our home, crackling madly. Sparing little time for clothes, we grabbed only the furs which hung near the door to the forest.

Stepping out onto our balcony, we watched a torch soar through the air, only to land within arms' reach. Its flames lapped at our home, and my parents pushed me toward the rope bridge that would lead us to another tree.

In the distance, across the river, I could see the rest of Fahn territory, safe from the blaze. I thought they might be safe from Jun, but we were merely an example. The capital of Fahn fell that night, and my parents fell with it.

The rest surrendered, thinking they might be spared.

So foolish. Only those who ran survived the wrath of Paikon and Tumai.

Now, I sit up. Glancing around, I reacquaint myself with my surroundings. Desperately, I try to blink away the image of my parents' bodies on the ground, the feeling of running away from them, scared and alone.

Beside me, Kivala sits up, planting a tender kiss on the back of my shoulder. "What's wrong?" she asks.

And because she knows, because she felt the pain of the absorption, I tell her. "Just… remembering."

Her hand moves in reassuring circles on my back.

The darkness within me slithers, and Aia's cruel laugh rumbles through my head.

"You're not actually going to kill the kids, are you?" Kivala asks, but her certainty makes it seem more like a statement.

"Jun *must* pay." I grit my teeth, wishing I could be as strong as my followers need me to be.

"And they will. But none of the kids alive now were even born when the absorption happened." Kivala pulls my hair back over my shoulder, gentle fingers brushing my skin as she does. "Making them pay for what their parents and grandparents did… doesn't make sense."

My parents flicker in my mind, their battered bodies revealing themselves to me as the light chases the shadows away. The fire behind them gutters, hiding them from me once more.

I sit still, uncertain. Her words make sense, I know they do. And I know I'll kill Tumai.

But will I kill the children?

Again, I hear Aia's cruel laughter, and I know better than to trust myself to overcome him.

"Look, I get it," Kivala says, voice breaking. "I know it hurts. I still weep for my brothers. Sometimes, it feels like I'll just fall apart if I let the pain out. And I don't think you're all that different from me. I lock the pain away with smiles and jokes. You use anger and bravado. You pretend you don't feel anything, at all."

Her sincerity, the way her voice cracks as she says it, cuts my heart open. Agony washes through me. But she's right.

So, I say, "Don't act like you know me. You laid with me once."

"I'm Fahn," she says simply. "You know we read people. And we're good at it."

"So that's why you came up here? To read me?" I accuse, scooting to the side of the bed as I push her out of my heart.

“I came up here to talk. I certainly enjoyed what just happened, don’t think otherwise. But I came here to talk.”

Standing up, I snatch my tunic from the floor. I wrap it about myself, shoving my arms through the sleeves, but I don’t button it.

Sighing, Kivala says, "Come back…"

"I can't. My people need their leader." But my voice breaks, betraying the strength I need to portray. In my periphery, her brows furrow.

“They need a leader who can think clearly. They need a leader who won't turn them into their enemies.”

Don’t I already know that?

I spin on my heel, desperate to flee, but Kivala takes my hand. “Come back. Please.”

Finally looking at her, I whisper, "Why? So you can learn more about me?” A single tear tracks down over my cheek.

“No,” she whispers. “So you can grieve. It doesn't seem like you have.”

“I can't.” Tears fall from my eyes, far more plentiful than I can afford. Balling my free hand into a fist, I say, more to myself than to her, “I can't fall apart right now.”

I can’t give Aia the chance to break me.

“I'll keep track of the pieces.” Reaching up, Kivala wipes the tears from my cheek.

I take a single step toward the bed, and she tugs at my hand gently. Climbing in beside her, I curl up in her arms. Our antlers tangle in the air beyond the bed.

Kivala slides one arm under my head and wraps it around me, tracing patterns on my shoulder. Her other arm slips beneath my tunic, caressing my waist as she pulls me closer.

Leaning my forehead against hers, I cry harder than I have in all the renewals since the absorption.

Chapter 18
Veliana

Staring out at the water, I wonder if this is how everyone else feels. The Allmother makes passing whispers, reaching for me, but I barely hear her. I get flashes of her eyes, pleading for me to come back. Little bursts of warmth trickle through my veins, aching with sympathy.

I've never been so distant from her. All my life, she's been present, filling me with the deep peace of knowing she was there, even as I labored beneath the weight of Rising. Each step I took, each day my parents aged, I knew I walked toward leading all of Kin.

But here… I barely feel her, barely feel the duty which has rested upon my shoulders my entire life.

I can't even hear the Light Watchers. The night drifts idly by, unmarked, as the stars move about. A chill wind blows in off the sea. I shiver, but I settle upon the rocky ground, pulling my knees up to my chest. My arms rest upon them, and my chin falls onto my wrists.

With eyes closed, I listen to the waves. They crash gently, like whispers in the night. Far behind me, Tala sniffs at the ground, whining softly.

She must not like being so far from her pack...

But I can't be there, right now... I can't see Tyrvahn with Garle, again.

And I don't have much to offer my people. All I can do is lead them to a war we can't even fight, a war we wouldn't be fighting if I'd just accepted the deal Paikon offered.

If I hadn't been so selfish...

A tear rolls down my cheek as the remnants of my anger fizzle out. Another shiver rolls through me, but this one has nothing to do with the cool coastal air. My heart clenches as a pit of loneliness opens within me, swallowing me up.

I consider calling Tala to me so I might curl up against her. I spare a glance for her, only to find her staring longingly back at the forest. My heart twists, knowing how far I've pushed her, how far I've pulled her away from her mate.

With a sigh, I tug my furs tighter around myself, seeking comfort from the little warmth they contain.

But a strange chill tinges every beat of my heart, every breath. The light I've grown so accustomed to feeling thanks to the Allmother disappears, replaced by smoky darkness.

***

After what must have been a full sky, I wander over to Tala, swallowing my pride. I don't want to sit alone anymore. I don't want the unsettling cold that pulses through every heartbeat spent away from the trees. And every step I take brings a little trickle of warmth from the Allmother.

Tala watches me with her head on her paws. As I draw near, she lifts her head to greet me. I scratch behind her ear and lean my forehead against hers.

She never strayed far from the trees, thin as they may be here on the coast, and it's harder to ignore the Allmother here.

But her presence warms my veins, easing the loneliness which swelled within me in her absence.

I settle on the ground beside Tala, leaning into her warm fur. She flicks her tail forward, draping it over me. The Allmother whispers through my mind, soft and distant. Indecipherable.

But she's there.

And her sweet voice makes me smile.

I curl my hands up in Tala's fur, only to find a small seed stuck near her shoulder. The Allmother's warmth pulses within it, leaking into my skin as I pluck it from Tala's coat. Wrapping my fingers around it, I hold it to my chest and let it chase the cold, coastal evening from my bones.

Drawing in a deep breath, I sit up, staring over Tala's back at the forest. The rich, earthy scent of my home wafts toward me, calling for my return.

But I'll have to stand by as Tyrvahn chooses Garle, over and over. My mind fills with the sight of him smiling at me, but it shifts, bending like smoke in the wind. Lurking behind it, I see Tyrvahn and Garle pressed together.

As the smoke of our short time together dissipates, all that's left… is them. I close my eyes, exhaling, trying to forget the sight.

I try to replace them with thoughts of my people, of the things we need to do to oust Paikon and Tumai. But no answers present themselves. Still, I have no means to win the war I started.

I'm as helpless, as worthless as I was before I came here.

Shaking my head, I blink away the pain in my heart and focus on the little seed held safely within my grasp. With one finger, I dig a small pit and drop the seed down in it. After pushing the dirt and all its tiny pebbles over the seed, I place one hand upon the small mound of earth.

The Allmother's power moves through me at a simple request, and I push it down into the seed, willing it to grow. It quickly takes root, and a little stem reaches up through the ground. A leaf unfurls, tickling my palm. I pull my hand away, but let the Allmother's power continue to flow through me.

As the little plant grows, Tala relaxes behind me, letting out a long breath. More energy flows, and the seed becomes a sapling, easily reaching my full height. Placing a hand upon its spindly trunk, I whisper to the tree, "I don't know how long you'll last here, but you'll have a chance."

Reveling in the familiar comfort of the Allmother's warmth, I let the growth continue until the lowest branches of the tree are out of reach. I gaze up at it, and the Allmother grows clearer in my heart.

She speaks within me, voice clearer in the presence of this new tree than I've heard it since Tala carried me away from Tyrvahn. "Thank you, Darling," she says, smiling beautifully in my mind.

And suddenly, I know what we must do.

It means facing Tyrvahn and Garle, but Rising requires sacrifice.

And Kin cannot fall because of my broken heart.

Chapter 19

Tyrvahn

After the High Seal introduces Garle to our small party of Rangers as well as those stationed here in Forn, Garle introduces all of us to her Rebels. Nearly all of her followers are Fahn, perhaps all that remains of the once-prosperous people. They stand rigid beneath the boughs of the trees. Each rebel eyes me warily, questioning the alliance their leader advocates.

Surprising me yet again, Kivala takes Garle's hand. To the assembled rebels, Kivala says, "He's one of the good ones. We can trust him."

Of course, she doesn't need to assure them that The High Seal can be trusted. Kin never turned from the Allmother, never slaughtered an entire territory only to cut down their homes.

My stomach flutters, and I do everything in my power to appear trustworthy. I search my mind for some sort of feat, some gesture that might reassure them I'm not like my uncle or my cousin or any of my ancestors.

That I'll do better.

But so many parts of me wonder if I *can* do better, if I'm equal to the task before me. After all, I have to restructure an entire nation.

If I can even regain leadership of it.

Yet, I smile warmly, projecting a calm air to the people before me.

"Thank you, Kivala," I whisper, and she smiles at me.

With the introductions out of the way, all leaders retreat to the privacy of Shevari and Fluros' home. We gather around their table, desperate for answers, yet we come up with little.

"Veliana should be here," Garle says, glaring at the table before her. "No wonder she's unsealed… Running off when her people need her. She'll be a terrible leader."

"Garle!" I shout, rising to my feet. The Allmother stings me, burning my veins. Taking a few deep breaths to calm myself, I add, "She's just upset."

"Are you defending her? Or just trying to make yourself feel like less of a fool?" She sneers at me, tapping her cheek to remind me of the cut upon mine.

As if I need reminding…

The sight of Veliana running away from me has seldom left my mind. I grit my teeth, holding back any ugly retorts that might otherwise spring from my mouth.

To my surprise, Kivala places a hand on Garle's arm. The two share a look, and Garle's features soften as she nods.

At the head of the table, Soolan says, "He's right. Veliana doesn't shirk her duties. She'll be back soon."

***

The morning creeps onward, and the tension between Garle and the High Seal builds. Whispered exchanges pass between Soolan and Daerna at every turn. Garle huddles with her fellow rebels, sharing words and plans. Kivala inserts herself into both groups, playing the mediator in a way I didn't expect.

Shouldn't I be doing that?

Yet, my hands are busy in another way.

Shevari stands beside me, hands outstretched above the river moss upon Tala's abandoned sled. She whispers petitions to the Allmother, nudging me to repeat them.

So, I do.

The old woman smiles and reminds me to focus, to let the Allmother's power transform the air above the moss. She pulls her hands back, turning to face me. "Visualize it in your mind, remember the way the hairs stand on the back of your neck as the air shifts. Feel it on your skin."

And I try.

The air around my hands grows heavy and cold, but little else happens. Frustration bubbles within me, clouding my mind. It breaks my concentration, and the small progress I made dissipates in an instant. Pulling in a deep breath, I clench my fists.

Shevari pushes her long silver braid back over her shoulder and breathes, "Relax." Stepping forward, she places one gentle hand on my shoulder.I stiffen, glancing at her with furrowed brows.

"Let me show you," she whispers, closing her eyes.

And then, I feel the Allmother's warmth gathering beneath her calloused palm and seeping into my shoulder. It oozes up my neck and over to my other shoulder, then spreads down my arms. The hair on the back of my neck rises, and the scent of the air shifts.

Hurriedly, I unclench my fists and hold them out over the river moss. I whisper another petition to the Allmother. Her warmth builds within my chest and spreads to the tips of my fingers.

The air around my hands grows cold and crisp, yet somehow, it weighs upon my skin. As the Allmother's power flows through me, Shevari helps me shape it, condensing the air at my fingertips. Gradually, it grows darker, thicker.

Electricity jumps between my fingers. Tiny bolts of lightning send jolts of energy into my body like static from dragging stocking-clad feet over a rug. The smallest thunderclap I've ever heard follows, somehow cuter than anything I could have imagined. The little clouds around my hands grow larger, obscuring my fingers as they darken.

And the first drops of rain fall upon the river moss. My jaw falls open when a tiny downpour erupts from the clouds gathered around my hands.

"Be sure to hydrate the moss evenly," Shevari says with a chuckle in her voice. "It'll do no good to drown a small portion and starve the rest."

Awestruck, I glance at her. Shock spreads through me when I see her hands hanging at her sides.

When did she pull her hand away? How much of this was me?

Jubilant, I move around the sled, taking my wondrous storm clouds with me. The smile never leaves my face.

Shevari stands by, gazing on with pride. She nods her head, approvingly, and my heart swells within my chest.

If only my mother and father had known this was possible! No wonder the people of Kin never suffer drought or famine. The Allmother truly provides everything they need.

Jun could have done so much better had we only held fast to her.

Turning my attention to the moss, I watch the little drops of water fall on brilliant green. Another bolt of lightning hops from one of my fingers to another, and thunder rumbles softly in my ears.

My smile widens, splitting my face wide open.

As I move around the sled, positioning my little rain clouds above the remaining dry patch, another sound draws my notice. Feet, heavy yet padded, crash through the undergrowth.

I've heard them before. I've felt them rattle my bones.

Tala.

Veliana's back!

I jerk my gaze away from the storm and the river moss, suddenly even happier.

Tala slows as she enters the village. Veliana sits atop her back, powerful and mesmerizing. The tips of her ears shine silver, marking her fertile day and making her even more beautiful. Her glowing blonde hair falls about her face, wild from the ride here, and her eyes find me.

And for a second, as she rakes her gaze over me and takes in the storm clouds around my hands, she smiles. My heart leaps into my throat, gazing upon her radiant joy.

But then, she remembers.

I watch it all flicker across her features as Tala carries her closer. The smile falls from her face as her soft grey eyes find the cut on my cheek, the cut from her antlers.

Veliana drops her gaze, shaking her head as Tala carries her past me.

And my heart shatters in my chest. The storm clouds disappear as my arms fall to my sides. The last little bit of moss still needs more water, but none flows from me.

With a soft hand on my back, Shevari says, “Go. There is much planning to be done. I’ll see to it that someone else hydrates the other sleds, and then I’ll be along.”

***

Fluros opens the shutters all around the first floor of his cozy, circular home as I enter. The sunlight glitters on his grey hair and beard, getting lost in the wrinkles on his face. The man smiles at me as he walks from one window to another.

Off to my left, Veliana calls up the stairs which spiral up the trunk at the home’s center. “Mother! Father! Come quickly!”

Kivala bursts in through the door behind me, rushing to greet her friend.

Yet, I’m rooted to the spot, staring at Veliana. She avoids my gaze as her feet pound back down the stairs. She throws her arms around Kivala, closing her eyes as she does.

“Where have you been?” Kivala demands.

“I went to the coast,” she whispers, dropping her gaze.

“The coast?”

Veliana nods. “I needed some time to myself.” For just a moment, she looks up at me, clenching her jaw.

Then, Soolan and Daerna wind their way down the stairs, stealing her gaze from me. Reaching out, Daerna takes her daughter’s hand, welcoming her return.

Kivala glances at me, offering up a soft, comforting smile.

But it reads like pity.

"We must go into Jun," Veliana says. "Paikon will meet us at the border, but Tumai will never leave the safety of the castle. If we truly want this done, we have to go into Jun."

Soolan's face falls, and he shakes his head. "We cannot, Darling Daughter. The Allmother can't reach us there."

"Then, we must take her with us."

Take her with us? How are we supposed to do that?

I gape at her, but her eyes spare no glances for me. My mind whirls, trying to piece together what her meaning could be.

But amongst people who conjure storms at their fingertips at the whisper of a few words, I can't even fathom what might be possible.

Trailing into the room, Garle sidles up next to Kivala. Bored and condescending as ever, she says, "Wasn't that *my* plan? We all keep seeds on us to keep her with us as we sneak from one safe house to another. We're just going to have to paint your antlers and freckles and hope your dainty frames pass for weak or undernourished Jun."

Veliana doesn't flinch before her criticism. Staring her dead in the eye, she answers, "We're using seeds, certainly, but far more of them. And we're not using stealth."

She pauses, lifting one eyebrow. "They will *know* we're coming."

Chills trickle down my spine, even as the Allmother celebrates Veliana's decision, flooding my veins with warmth.

Another afternoon passes on my knees, laying swaths of moss along the border. Only a thin strip will be needed for the barrier, but it must stretch quite a distance. Amiable conversation fills the air around me as Fahn Rebels work alongside Kin Rangers.

Even Tyrvahn joins us, crawling along in the dirt as he lays strips of river moss. But he works much further along the border. I can't hear his words, can't understand the twinkle in his eyes as he laughs with the High Seal.

Memories of him flicker through my mind.

One instant, I see him impatiently tapping his feet at the window as the butler set up his breakfast, a little late because of a minor fire in the kitchen.

He'd had to draw his own curtains, and that simply couldn't be.

I remember rolling my eyes at him and muttering curses against Jun in my mind.

The next instant, I watch him throw out an entire outfit because of a tear in his jacket sleeve. It could have been repaired, but then it would have had an unsightly seam.

Now, he crawls on hands and knees in the mud, *working*, in roughly hewn garments. A completely different man. A welcome surprise.

Back then, he was only a tool in my plans, a means to an end. He gave me access to the royal family and their library of scrolls.

And I learned so much, made so much progress toward my goals.

But apparently, I didn't learn everything I needed.

I didn't learn the exact means to accomplish my goal, though I got close. And I didn't learn the potential for growth within our hearts.

What a change the Allmother has worked in him in such a short time. Has it been just six moons? Seven?

Did I ever think him capable of this?

My answer is quick and certain.

No.

Not once did I believe him capable of change, capable of being better. Perhaps, if I'd looked beyond my hatred for Jun, I could have intervened and spared his parents, could have kept the loggers from going to Kin.

I could have spared the lives of everyone who died at the logging camp, Kin and Jun alike.

But I didn't. Aia blinded me.

Now, still more blood stains my hands.

I remember his cruel laughter shaping my thoughts, his darkness slithering through me, encouraging me, as I moved through the logging camp. I flinch before my own memories and lay another cool, damp strip of river moss down upon the earth.

Footsteps move toward me, and the familiar, hollow slosh of water in a gourd draws my attention. My eyes drift upward as I recall just how long it's been since I've had a drink.

"Thirsty?" Kivala asks, smiling down at me.

I return her smile and nod. Taking the gourd, I unstopper it and pull in a long drink.

Kivala kneels beside me. "Take a break. You've been working nonstop." She lifts a strip of moss from my pile and drapes it over her shoulder. Then, she picks up another, laying it out carefully at the end of my last piece. Crawling to its end, she pulls the other strip from her shoulder and places it, as well.

I lift another and hand it to her before taking another drink. Placing the stopper in the gourd, I push myself to my feet. Pulling half of the pile of moss strips into my arms, I follow Kivala down the line as she places them.

My gaze drifts to Veliana, carefully apart from Tyrvahn. She's been distancing herself from him since my arrival. A small twinge of guilt rises within me.

Have I ruined my own plans?

Have I ruined her heart?

But darkness simmers in my heart as I remember the look on her face when she saw me press myself against Tyrvahn. Aia urges me to twist the knife.

"If you give her a chance," Kivala says, following my gaze, "you'll probably like her. She's nice. And sweet. And smart. And she does what she needs to do for the Allmother and her people."

Kivala takes another strip of moss from my outstretched hand and goes on. “Strange, that you two have all of that in common…” She quirks one brow up, sparing a glance for me.

“Nice? We have *that* in common?”

“Well, when you aren’t determined to pretend otherwise.”

Pretending isn’t quite what I’d call it.

Failing to overcome Aia... That seems more fitting.

I feign a laugh and purse my lips at her.

Leaning closer, she kisses the outside of my thigh. Heat trills through me, and I suppress a shudder, remembering our times together in my bed and hers. A devious look crosses her face as she stares up at me, and I know her thoughts travel a similar path.

She clears her throat, silently placing another strip of moss. We’ve nearly reached the portion of the border that Tyrvahn started with.

I hand her the last strip of moss and turn, going back for the remainder of my pile. It’ll be just enough to reach the next section. Each one has been carefully measured, with stacks of moss distributed perfectly.

As I heft it into my arms, Kivala speaks, once more. “You really should give Veliana a chance. I think you’ll like her.”

But I can’t.

I can’t befriend someone I may have to kill.

Again, Aia’s cruel laughter slithers through my heart, chilling me to my core. And I know Veliana’s blood may be the only way I can be rid of him.

My hands busy themselves, pulling seeds from pods. It doesn't even matter what kind of seeds. We just need them. Hundreds of them. Thousands.

As many as we can get our hands on.

A few Rangers work quickly beside me, deft fingers freeing seeds from stems far more quickly than should be possible. They put me to shame, and I have to remind myself frequently that they've likely done similar things before.

I certainly haven't.

Whether I'm here for busy work or to learn patience, I can't be sure. But I know Veliana isn't beside me. She stands at the border, just beyond our little camp, chanting with the High Seal to raise the barrier. The light of our torches and that of the moon drift toward her, outlining her delicate figure with fragile highlights.

Their voices blend, growing deeper, softer. The hum of the Allmother fills the air, resonating in my bones.

Before my eyes, the moss lining the border shimmers. It spreads out, growing wider, twining together. It reaches outward, all the while digging its roots deeper.

A single, glittering wave ripples over the moss, spreading outward from the center. Each leaf, each little stem shines as the Allmother's power passes over it, and the entirety of the moss border plants itself firmly in the ground.

Standing between her parents, Veliana joins hands with them. Their chanting grows more intense, and they glow with the power the Allmother grants them. Slowly, they funnel it into the moss before them. The entire length of the border pulses with it, yet still they channel more.

Then, with an audible rumble, the air above the moss border glistens, transparent yet somehow solid. Colors play upon its surface, cascading through rainbows.

The wall reaches higher, and their chants fill the night. Their voices wrap around my heart. Only when the wall reaches higher than anyone could ever hope to climb do they stop. The rumbling stops. A deafening silence settles over us.

And the wall stops shining, stops glittering in the moonlight. The torchlight no longer casts a million rainbows upon thin air. I see only Jun land beyond.

"Did it work?" I ask, hands motionless. A single seed pod rests between my fingers.

"Of course," the Ranger next to me says, matter-of-factly.

As if invisible walls were built every day. As if moss had always been the only thing necessary to keep hostile forces from burning homes to the ground and slaughtering the masses.

Amazement lifts my lips into a smile and pushes a soft laugh through my lips. My hands resume their work, pulling seeds loose and dropping them into a satchel. But I stare at Veliana.

Are her hands trembling? Or is that the flickering shadows of torchlight?

My brows furrow as I strain my eyes, trying to see. Briefly, I consider asking the Allmother to grant me her sight.

But Veliana turns, catching me staring at her. I smile weakly, and my heart begs her to smile back.

But she hasn't smiled at me in several suns…

Pain lances my heart as I sit beneath her gaze. My stomach churns, begging her to speak to me.

She looks away.

And my heart shrivels.

Chapter 22
Veliana

The sun peeks out over the horizon, but we've already risen. I stand with my mother and father, with Tyrvahn and Kivala and Garle on our side of the border. The moss before me glitters with the Allmother's power, reassuring me that our barrier still stands.

Yet, my heart beats far too quickly in my chest.

My gaze drifts over the entirety of Jun, so vast next to my small frame. The journey before us humbles me.

How will we ever make it there before they kill us all?

I don't expect an answer, but the Allmother whispers to me, "Wolves and Bears, Darling Priestess. How else?"

Her voice fades from my mind without further explanation, and my eyes fall upon the camp beyond the border. My hands tremble, and my knees threaten to buckle beneath the weight of the coming confrontation.

So much depends on this moment.

So much depends on me saying the right things, doing the right things...

The Allmother sends a comforting wave of warmth through me, and it chases the weariness from my bones. But only for a moment. It returns quickly, settling heavily on my shoulders.

Beside me, Tyrvahn glances at me. He's been doing that a lot, trying to talk to me. But I can't handle his explanations, can't handle his halfhearted apologies. I can't handle knowing that Garle was in his arms, pressed up against him…

Nestled up against him.

So, I keep my gaze steady, staring straight ahead at the camp of Jun soldiers in the distance. They set up far from the border two suns ago, cutting it rather closer than I expected them to.

In my periphery, I watch Kivala and Garle link hands. My parents do the same. But my hands hang limply at my side.

If I reach out, would Tyrvahn lace his fingers with mine?

Can I reach out?

It seems like Garle has moved on to Kivala, but I'm clearly only Tyrvahn's second choice. Could I stand that?

My heart sinks because I know the answer.

No.

I know myself well enough to know that I want to be someone's first choice. I want to be the one they look forward to seeing every morning.

Not the one they settle for.

Sighing, I refocus my attention.

My people deserve better than a distracted Priestess Rising.

Birds chirp carelessly overhead, flitting from branch to branch, completely oblivious to the struggles below them. Yet, even they must play their part in this.

In the distance, a small group splits from the Jun camp, making their way toward us. Their metal armor gleams red and orange in the early morning sun, and the occasional flash of bright white reaches off of it, blinding me.

As they move toward us, another larger group leaves the camp, following behind as they all make their way to the border. Their feet batter the poor broken earth beneath them as they tromp across the field.

I keep my gaze straight, waiting.

But Tyrvahn wraps his hand around mine. My heart flutters as warmth flows between us. Our fingers lace together, and for half a heartbeat, I draw strength from his comforting touch.

But Paikon shouts ahead, desperate to be heard long before I can see the whites of his eyes. “I didn’t think you had it in you, nephew.”

Marching closer, he stops just outside the reach of the Sailon. At a run, I could reach him in three breaths if not for the barrier. Tala could reach him in one.

“It does complicate things for me, though,” Paikon continues. “I was under the impression I was here to collect my son’s bride-to-be. Yet, it looks like I’m not the only one after Kin territory.” A sneer twists his features.

My lungs falter, and my palms grow sweaty. Tugging my hand from Tyrvahn’s grasp, I turn to face him, appalled.

Was this all a ploy?

Some game played only to trick my stupid, lonely heart into giving our land away willingly?

"What? NO!" Tyrvahn shouts back. He turns toward me, eyes earnest.

But is that only a trick? An act?

Voice softening, he says, "Veliana, I swear, that isn't what this is. I didn't come here to trick you. I actually feel something for you."

But all I can see is Garle nestled up to him.

All I can hear is Paikon's accusation.

The Allmother rages in my veins, burning me alive. But I can't tell if it's rage at the situation I've fallen into or my reaction to it.

But there are more important matters to tend to at the moment.

I hold up a hand to still Tyrvahn's lips. "Tyrvahn," I begin, voice breaking over the sounds of his name, sounds I held so dear just a few suns ago. Starting over, I will my voice to be steady. "Your affection for me, or lack thereof, real or contrived, is not why this alliance exists. The Sailon cannot fall. The Allmother *cannot* fall."

But all my attempts at strength fall short. Tears well in my eyes, betraying me as they show him just how deeply I hurt.

The birds overhead chirp restlessly, filling the silence between us as Tyrvahn struggles for words. His mouth opens, working soundlessly.

He takes a deep breath, gazing at me with those marvelous green eyes. "My affections for you exist. They're not contrived." He shakes his head gently. "They're not."

And my entire world ruptures beneath me. The impossibility of the situation, of him choosing me over her, of him wanting me to begin with, of him wanting me for any reason other than gaining control over Kin…

None of it fits together with the things I've seen, the things I've heard.

Flashes of Garle pressing her ample breasts against his chest flicker through my mind to the tune of Paikon's words.

Memories of Materva walking away, choosing another and a life with the stars over me.

The weight of my life, my position in the Rising line is too great a burden to ask another to bear.

And my frame is not weighted enough, falling far too near to flat to tempt anyone.

Paikon's words make sense when I consider myself. But do they make sense in light of Tyrvahn's actions?

I try to puzzle it out, staring into his eyes. They soften, and he even takes my hands in his once more.

But the birds overhead… Oh, how restless they are.

They want to play their part. They want this to be over.

"I can't do this, Tyrvahn, not now," I croak. The lump in my throat strangles my words, making them small and quiet. "I can't handle any distractions."

Another moment of strained silence falls over us, and I drop my gaze, failing before his.

"Is…" Tyrvahn clears his throat. "Is that all I am to you? A distraction?"

I can't look at him, can't breathe. Swallowing, I give the only answer I can come up with, "You are, now." But I can't own these words, can't watch their impact shape his face. My eyes never leave the moss beneath our feet.

Beyond the barrier, Paikon groans, finally pulling my eyes from the ground. "Ugh. Archers, spare me."

From the back of their ranks, the archers raise their bows. They nock their arrows and pull the strings back.

Letting Tyrvahn's hands fall, I turn to face them. I pull my shoulders back and lift my chin.

Paikon stares on, astonished that we do not flinch before his assault. He stares on, dark eyes hard and cruel. The sunlight shines in the grease which holds his dark hair back around his antlers and black-tipped ears.

"Fire!" he shouts.

And they do.

The arrows fly toward us, but neither I nor any assembled wince. The Allmother warms our veins, reminding us of her presence. The moss shimmers beautifully.

And one hundred arrows smash into the barrier. They fall to the ground, utterly useless, in a rain of mulch and splinters.

My heart swells as I watch Paikon's jaw drop. The foot soldiers and archers behind him grow still, even as the cacophony of wings and chirping grows louder above us.

Stepping forward, I place one hand upon the barrier, feeling the buzz of the Allmother's power within it. "You must think us truly stupid if you thought we'd come here unprotected."

I pull my hand away from the barrier, wriggling my fingers, and Allflower vines reach up from the ground beneath Paikon's feet. I raise my hand, and the vines climb, twining around his legs. They crawl over him, and he tries desperately to move.

But this is war.

And he is the enemy of my people, the enemy of the Allmother.

"What in Aia's name is happening?" Paikon shouts. Empty words from an empty man.

Lifting my other hand, I raise more vines from the ground, sending them up and around his torso. Every soldier behind him stands motionless, mouths hanging open. A few drop their weapons as I raise my hands higher and wrap the vines over Paikon's shoulders.

A few delicate tendrils tickle his neck. They twist and wrap, but not too tight.

"Even if you kill me, my son will inherit the land," he reasons, practically spitting the words in his exertion. "Why do you think I left him in Ivlan?"

"Yes, that's true," I allow, nodding.

I consider his words and the massive undertaking before us. His face shines with sweat, but his eyes sparkle with the hope that maybe I'll reconsider. Maybe I'll let him go.

Then, I let out a breath. This decision was made before he ever came here.

The Allmother cannot fall.

"Your death will pass Jun into Tumai's hands." I narrow my eyes and drop my voice as I add, "But it's half the job done."

Clenching my fists, I wrap the Allflower vines tighter around his neck. His hands claw at them, anywhere they can, trying desperately to reach the slender plants cutting off his air. But they wrap tighter, twining together into thick ropes. His face grows red, then purple as the last bits of air escape him.

The soldiers gasp. Most run, desperate to escape.

But they'll find no such refuge today.

My parents raise their hands, and the feet of Jun soldiers and archers transform. Their legs become tree trunks, and their toes extend into the earth, rooting them to the ground. They scream and bat at their legs, then their torsos as the change progresses up their bodies.

But as the transformation approaches completion, their faces grow placid, finally feeling the Allmother's warmth.

She sings her approval in my veins as I gaze out through the barrier.

Where once stood an army poised against us, there now stands a small forest.

Tucked in the gap between the greater Sailon and this new branch stands a dead man wrapped in Allflowers.

Ready to burn.

I stare at the new trees and the grotesquely mottled face of Paikon, wrapped in Allflower vines. Even his blotchy face, made pallid in death, cannot quell their beauty. They sparkle in the waning sunlight, crimson centers glittering spectacularly.

Behind me, Rangers and Rebels busy themselves, checking their weapons. The High Seal prepares dinner for us all with the aid of Kivala and Veliana. Tyrvahn strips seeds from still more branches.

Yet, I struggle to tear my eyes from the sight of the dead man before me.

I can almost see Aia lifting Paikon's lips in a smirk, taunting me, reminding me that he moves in my heart, too.

For a moment, I'm gripped by the irrational need to scale the barrier, to vault over the top of it, chancing great injury in the landing, only to check for a pulse. Suddenly, seeing isn't good enough. I need to feel it, to *know* that Paikon's heart has stopped, that one more of Aia's dwellings has been ripped from him.

He's gone…

I repeat it, over and over, desperate to convince myself.

Paikon is gone. And with him, part of Aia's hold on this realm.

But it isn't enough.

A gentle breeze drifts over the fields of Jun, whispering through the new obstacles which reach for the greater Sailon. Their branches bow and sway, and I wonder if the soldiers feel peace, now.

Has the Allmother chased him from their hearts? From their bones?

Do they feel only her warmth?

I tug my boots off and discard my stockings. Stepping forward, I wriggle my toes in the moss which edges the barrier. The Allmother's power tingles on my skin, seeping into me in soft waves.

Pulling in a deep breath, I lay a hand upon the barrier. The gentle buzz of pure power shivers over my spine, warming my entire body.

Watching the new trees swaying with the breeze, I wonder, yet again…

Do they feel only her warmth?

How much easier that must be.

***

The sun lingers here at the edge of the forest, taking longer to say goodnight than it did in Synap. Here, it seems to know we cannot rest so easily, so peacefully. We have so much yet to do.

My hands busy themselves with the preparation of nets, but my mind whirls with all I know must come and all I may have to do. I spare a glance for Veliana every so often, and my heart twists each time.

She raises a patch of Allflower vines, only to harvest the seed pods. She summons a storm to water the moss. She petitions for the Allmother's power, seamlessly transforming it into a fire to keep her people warm. She twists ropes and braids nets beside me.

She smiles at everyone, despite the strain of Rising.

She even smiles at me, though that gesture is sheepish and only in Kivala's presence.

Could I spill her blood?

Aia simmers in my heart, and I know… if it comes down to it…

I drop my gaze, unable to hold hers. Yet, she sees nothing amiss. Or perhaps she merely has the grace not to question me.

Likely the latter.

Tyrvahn approaches, settling to the ground beside her. He struggles for words, a sight painful even for me.

But Veliana rises. "I'm needed elsewhere," she whispers. "I'm sure the two of you have this well in hand."

A deep sigh grates through Tyrvahn's lips, and again I wonder why I did it.

Why did I have to be so damned lonely? Why did I think he'd take me back, even for a night?

Why did I think I could twist him into doing my bidding?

As if in answer, Aia rises to a boil. I feel his disdain, his hatred of such compassionate regret. He begs only for one thing.

"Take what you want," he whispers coldly.

A shiver rolls down my spine, but I resist him.

Forcing my lips to move, I whisper, "I'm sorry."

How long has it been since I said those words? How long since I admitted fault outside the confines of my mind?

Tyrvahn twists a few vines idly, not quite braiding them. For a moment, the old him seeps out. "A lot of good 'sorry' will do me, now."

Inwardly, I flinch. And I know, had I left him alone, I may not have needed Veliana's blood. But my actions and Aia's influence have, yet again, converged to demand death.

Clenching his fists, Tyrvahn pulls in a controlled breath. The torchlight casts a wavering shadow off of him, and it shivers over the vines laid out before us.

"Sorry," he croaks. "I'm just… overwhelmed. I don't know what to do, anymore. Everything here in Kin, everything the Allmother lays a hand upon… It's so much better than we ever knew. And now, I have to fix Jun. I have to because no one else will. Tumai will destroy it, and he'll take Kin down with it." He drops the vines he'd been toying with, staring out into the darkness. "But how? How can I do this? I couldn't save my parents. I was too blind. I'm supposed to fix an entire kingdom, but I can't even convince Veliana just how much she means to me…"

I stare at him, openmouthed as he admits to fears and worries. My hands still on the vines.

Another feat I never thought him capable of...

How often did he attribute his failings to the shortcomings of servants and teachers, refusing to admit his faults because he didn't have to? Too many times to count.

But now?

How often did I attribute his shortcomings to his own feeble, selfish personality? How often did I overlook the effect Aia may have had on him, even knowing how Aia shapes my own heart?

Too many times to count.

I struggle for a solution, mind spinning uselessly. My eyes search his face, but he refuses to meet my gaze.

Before I can say another word, he says, "I'll just have to keep trying, I guess." And with that, he rises to his feet, leaving me behind.

My heart shrivels in my chest. A single tear slides down my cheek as I realize the full extent of the damage I've wrought. The chasm of destruction laid out before me yawns, opening up to swallow me.

Because I know I'm not done.

***

My hands ache from the braiding, but I keep on. Every so often, I stop to stretch my fingers, bending them, popping the joints. But I always resume my work, even after the Light Watchers in the distance call eleventh sky.

I have to do something *good here.*

Only when two forms move into view do my hands still. Their pale robes drift over the ground, torn and dirty at the bottom. I lift my eyes to look upon the High Seal.

They gaze at me with far more comprehension than I can afford. But their features are soft, not the masks of disapproval or anger I expect.

"May we have a word, Darling Rebel?" Soolan says, voice a gentle dream.

And I know I can’t refuse him.

They link their hands as I haul my sorry self up from the ground. They lead me just beyond the edge of camp. The light of the fire in the center of camp flickers, playing gleefully with the shadows it casts upon us.

Swallowing back my fear, I wonder at how much they've guessed. Or how much the Allmother told them. She sees my heart, after all. She knows that Aia lurks within me. She knows the path I've contemplated to be rid of him and the joy he takes in such violence.

When Soolan and Daerna stop, turning to face me, I expect a torrent of condemnations. Yet, their faces remain gentle. Kind, even.

My mouth dries out, and I swallow uselessly. My hands clench and unclench at my sides, palms sweating profusely. But I lift my chin, determined to make my side of these matters known.

The darkness of the night drapes the forest in a blanket of silence, making me wish for the incessant chatter of a thousand impatient birds. Anything to cover the sound of my fraying nerves, my hammering heart.

Perhaps a raucous cry in the canopy could even hide the words I know must spill from my lips too soon.

But the birds sleep quietly, leaving me to the chaos within me.

"Darling Rebel," Soolan begins, soft voice filled with pity and all too clear in the quiet night. "You have so much to fight against, do you not?"

Unwilling to incriminate myself unnecessarily, I remain silent.

"You were an anomaly, my dear. For so long," Daerna says. Firelight dances on her silver freckles and glows in her tender blue eyes. "When Tyrvahn posed the question of your need for the alliance, we puzzled over it, watching you."

My skin grows cold and clammy. A single bead of sweat rolls down my spine.

"As we watched, though," Daerna continues, tipping her head to the side, "we saw two sides of you where there should only have been one. One side soft, the other hard and hiding desperation with coldness. Kivala says it's how you've learned to cope with the Absorption, with living in Jun."

She pauses as if waiting for me to answer. Her perceptive eyes pierce the depths of my soul, watching me squirm.

But how much could I tell them?

And how much do they already know?

Soolan nods sagely, as though some great revelation had just been bestowed upon him. Not waiting for confirmation, not needing it, he says, "But there is more to you than someone recovering from tragedy. There is darkness in you."

My veins run cold, and my heart falters.

They know...

"That is what you need us for," Daerna says.

I can only nod. My jaw will not unclench. Every word I might have said in my own defense remains locked behind my lips.

Because what defense do I deserve?

"Do you know what it takes to purge a God from this realm?" Soolan asks.

Still, my lips remain motionless. I stand, transfixed, before them. My heart thuds behind my ears.

"It requires an undivided High Seal, Darling Rebel."

My stomach drops into my boots.

I was right. But that means...

Veliana...

"Did you know that?" Soolan whispers.

"I…" My voice comes out a croak. I clear my dry, raspy throat and try again. "I suspected…"

Sighing, I force myself to own up to this. "The scrolls in the royal library in Jun… They mentioned an attempt, made by Kin, to purge Aia. It was so long ago, hundreds of renewals ago, and the scroll didn't say much about *how* it went wrong, just… that it did. It said that the High Seal of Kin and the Rising Seal joined together to channel…"

I trail off. Voices nearby drag at my attention, but never fully wrest my focus away from the matters at hand. Soolan picks up the thread of my thoughts.

"They nearly died, all four of them. Seeing their error at the last moment, the High Seal broke the connection with the Rising Seal." His voice softens as he adds, "The High Seal perished. Their connection with the Allmother's realm was open, and they were exhausted. Aia took advantage. He pushed their energies from their bodies, turned them to stone. But the Rising Seal lived on."

"Exhausted as they were, they couldn't finish the job, even after they Rose. It took them months to heal." Soolan's silver eyes shine in the firelight, nearly reflecting it upon me as he weighs and measures my worth. "Aia laid dormant for many renewals after that. They may not have completely purged him, but they chased enough of him from this realm that he had to find a new foothold."

"And he found it, as Jun moved further and further beyond the Allmother's reach."

My shoulders lift with a deep breath as I process all I've just learned.

It can be done. Aia can be purged.

But at what cost?

There's always a cost…

I wipe my sweaty palms on my legs and lift my eyes to meet theirs.

Daerna meets my gaze, unwavering. "It will take an undivided High Seal to fully purge him, something Kin hasn't seen in many generations." She squeezes Soolan's hand, nodding. "But it is time. Our efforts in the invasion, given our age, will be our end. The Vierna lineage will center solely on Veliana as soon as our energies join the Allmother's realm."

"You'll shed no more unnecessary blood, Darling Rebel," Soolan whispers.

Relief washes through me. Mouth agape, I fall to my knees with tears streaming over my face. Yet, it wars with the anguish of knowing that such gentle people will soon give up their lives.

Slow, halting footsteps carry someone closer. In a small, strangled voice, I hear Veliana squeak, "What?"

My fingers dance, quickly braiding vines into rope. For a moment, I consider a petition to the Allmother to speed the process. I consider the time we have left and the number of people working on this. We have time. And besides, the tedium, the repetition, is soothing.

My eyes dart to the edge of my periphery, tracing Garle's form. The shadows of the evening deepen the set of her cleavage, and my cheeks grow warm.

Yet, Tyrvahn insisted earlier...

My heart spasms, trying desperately to decide what to believe.

Could he truly have feelings for me?

Another glance at Garle, at her strong legs and wide hips, and I chasten myself.

Next to her... I'm nothing.

Kivala carries another stack of vines over, dropping them before us. She mouths something to Garle that looks a lot like, "Told you."

I glance between them, uncertain, but offer up a tentative smile for the both of them. Then, Kivala disappears into the shadows of our camp once more, leaving us in awkward silence. Garle looks at me occasionally but remains silent.

Yet, I know this can't be the way of things. We'll be working side by side for many suns, and our people are depending on us.

I can't let them down.

So, I open my mouth to speak, fully intending to shove my feelings down in favor of the alliance, in favor of doing what's best for my people.

But footsteps draw my notice, and no words form.

Sheepish despite his large frame, Tyrvahn settles on the ground beside me. He takes a few vines in hand, manipulating them into ropes, then into nets. His skillful hands work quickly, but he glances at me.

Studiously, I avoid his gaze. My own hands work furiously, and I concentrate on the knots they tie rather than the knots bound up in my stomach.

Sitting between Tyrvahn and Garle, my cheeks burn hotter than any fire. My palms sweat, and I'm sure I'll drop the Allflower vines at any moment.

His shadow shifts as he turns his head, looking at me, again.

Or maybe he's looking over my bowed head...

Maybe he's looking at Garle.

And suddenly, I can't take it anymore.

I push myself to my feet and croak, "I'm needed elsewhere." Beneath my breath, petty as it may be, I add, "I'm sure the two of you have this well in hand."

I walk away toward the edge of camp with tears streaming down my face, craving the darkness beyond the fire's reach.

***

I rest my head on my arms, braced on drawn-up knees. I close my eyes against the darkness, blocking out the world.

The soft flutter of wings caresses my ears as the cluster of birds above me shifts, rearranging themselves peacefully on the branches. As they settle in, a new sound drifts in to fill the void they leave behind.

Footsteps.

Turning in the darkness, I wish I'd thought to petition for sight rather than sitting in the darkness, pouting like a child. Briefly, I consider getting up, moving away. There aren't many who would seek me out.

Even fewer who I want to see.

"Veliana," Tyrvahn says. His voice is quiet, uncertain. He takes small, shuffling steps, getting closer and closer.

Maybe, if he walks far enough away, I can sneak back to camp.

I hold still, hoping he hasn't petitioned for the Allmother's sight. His footfalls lead him slightly beyond me, just skirting past, and I know he hasn't.

I feel like a coward, but a sigh of relief eases past my lips. He slows to a halt, and I wonder if he heard me.

"Veliana, please," he whispers hoarsely. "I know you're out here. Please, just talk to me."

And the pain in his voice roots me to the spot. All notions of avoiding him desert me.

His voice, that little quiver of pain, makes me wonder. A shadow of doubt floats through my mind, and my stupid heart dares to hope.

Does he actually want me?

Have I blown all of this out of proportion?

But then I remember Garle's recent fascination with Kivala.

Am I his second choice?

I pull in a deep breath, but anguish chokes it, turning it into a hitching, ragged thing. And Tyrvahn hears me.

"Veliana, I'm so sorry," he pleads, inching closer.

But I'm on my feet and moving away. Of course, he hears me.

And of course, he follows.

But I can't just sit here and listen to him tell me he still loves Garle. My heart stutters at the thought, bringing my hand up to my chest.

I hear voices nearby and cling to them. My feet turn, rushing to be near other people.

If we're not alone, maybe he won't feel compelled to explain why I'm not good enough to be his first choice.

Again, my heart clenches, and I propel myself faster toward the voices.

"Veliana, please. Nothing happened with Garle," Tyrvahn says, following behind. But he's getting closer. His long legs can easily outpace mine.

"Nothing?" I hear myself say, despite my better judgment, despite everything in me crying out to leave it alone. "So nestling is nothing to you?"

I throw the words behind me, unaware as they cross my lips of just how deeply they'll hurt me. The feel of Tyrvahn's arms around me, the comfort of his chin resting atop my head, the warmth and intimacy of it floats through me for a single heartbeat before my own words rip it away.

Because if that act means nothing to him, it means that nestling with Garle was meaningless.

But it also means that it was meaningless with me.

My poor abused heart shrivels in my chest, and I stumble to a stop. The voices, now clearly my parents and Garle, are so close I can make out their words. Something about Jun moving further and further beyond the Allmother's reach.

But the wound I've just inflicted upon myself knocks me to my knees. Tyrvahn bumps into me in the dark, nearly tripping over me.

"Veliana?" he asks. "Are you alright?"

His hands reach down, finding my shoulders and sliding under my arms to pull me up from the ground. My feet, still unsteady, find their place beneath me. I move to step away from Tyrvahn, but he grips my waist loosely, just enough to hold me in place.

For a moment, neither my parents nor Garle speaks, and only Tyrvahn's breath, so close, pricks at my ears.

Then, I hear my mother say, "It will take an undivided High Seal to fully purge him, something Kin hasn't seen in many generations. But it is time."

Her voice tugs at my attention, pulling my face in her direction. The darkness shields her from view, but I hear her. And her words fill my veins with ice.

An undivided High Seal? A purge?

I shudder.

But my mother continues. "Our efforts in the invasion, given our age, will be our end. The Vierna lineage will center solely on Veliana as soon as our energies join the Allmother's realm."

My stomach drops, and my hands shake.

"I swear, *nothing* happened with Garle," Tyrvahn says. "I didn't *want* anything to happen with her."

But my brain doesn't process a bit of it, not a single word from him. Each one drifts over my ears, known but lost on me. My leaden feet drag me from him, and his arms fall slack, slipping from my waist.

They can't...

They can't die. They can't leave me alone.

My heart falters in my chest.

"You'll shed no more unnecessary blood, Darling Rebel," my father whispers, and a weight falls softly to the ground.

Tyrvahn walks behind me, pleading, "Veliana, what is it?"

Yet, I walk on. I stumble, nearly tripping over my dread. My hands tremble at my sides, palms sweating profusely despite the cold hands wrapped around my heart.

They can't leave me.

The fire back at camp flickers in the distance, filling the world with a warmth I'll never know again. It casts half shadows over the faces of my parents, over Garle's slumped form. She sits, weeping before them.

But then, I look at my parents, really look at them.

And my lungs collapse, chasing the air from my body.

My voice comes out, small and weak, "What?"

They glance up at me in unison. Frowns carve wrinkles into their faces, far deeper than I've ever seen.

But they are aging. I know that. I've *known* that for quite some time. Everyone knows their parents are aging, but no one thinks about it. Their bodies change so gradually, it goes unnoticed.

And now, forced to think of it, forced to see them as old…

Every wrinkle seems deeper. Their silver hair seems duller now, more grey. Their complexions, pale as ever, seem pallid. Their wispy frames, a hallmark of our kind, seem somehow hollow and fragile.

They seem like two completely different people.

Gone are the powerful, wise, *vital* people I know and love, replaced by people who could be broken by a gentle breeze.

And their time has come?

Tears drip down my cheeks. They splash at my feet, lost to the darkness. Tyrvahn places a comforting hand on my back, but the world falls out from under me, regardless.

Guilt twists within me, growing and growing until no room remains for my lungs or my heart. My parents close the distance between us, and I look back and forth between them, from my mother's crisp blue eyes to my father's glittering silver irises.

And my stomach flips within me.

"I didn't know…" I creak. "I didn't know it would kill you. I wouldn't have suggested it. I would've come up with something else, something better. I didn't know the invasion would…"

A strangled sob cuts me off, and I clench my hands into fists. All my willpower, every bit of strength left in me focuses on finding something to save them.

I can't lose them…

"I'll do it," I say, forcing myself to blubber out the words between sobs. "If you're not strong enough, I'll do it."

My father places a hand on my arm, thin fingers gripping softly. "Darling Daughter. Attempting it alone would kill you," his warm voice quivers with the tears in his eyes. "I have many reasons to oppose that course of action, but I know you'll listen when I say… You can't leave Kin without an heir."

A sob wrenches its way free of me, spluttering as I choke out, "But I can't lose you." I throw my arms around them, pulling them toward me. Our antlers clank together as I twine my hands into their long braids.

"You will have to purge Aia," my mother whispers. Her tears drip onto my shoulder, soaking into the fabric of my tunic. Yet, her voice is no steadier than my father's.

Pulling back, I look at them, incredulous. "But… I *can't* purge him alone. I need you here."

My father looks at Tyrvahn rather pointedly before telling me, "You're not alone."

I shake my head, vehemently. My entire world seems to have fallen in on itself, and all of it comes down to one simple thing.

I'm not enough.

I'm not strong enough to purge Aia alone. I'm not wise enough to lead Kin.

I'm not attractive enough for Tyrvahn.

My heart twists in my chest, shrinking from the pain my admissions inflict upon it. I shake my head again, softer this time, slower.

Truly defeated, I force myself to say, "Though he fights by my side, he can't help me channel. Not that much energy. Only a Seal can do that."

Behind me, Tyrvahn says, "That's easy enough to fix."

All the air rushes out of my lungs, and my chest collapses in its wake. Turning to face him, I struggle for words. The shifting light of the distant fire casts more shadow over his face than light, making his expression impossible to read.

Finally, I manage, "I can't ask you to do that."

Stepping closer, he says, "You don't have to."

And a wave of fresh tears spills over.

Garle climbs to her feet but has the good grace to remain silent.

Only my mother speaks. "We'll see to it tomorrow, then. We have little time to spare."

So little time...

Another sob rattles my body, leaving me shivering. Tyrvahn wraps his arms around me, whispering about keeping me warm.

But a deep despair sweeps over me, scooping everything out and leaving me hollow. My arms hang limply at my sides, though Tyrvahn tightens his hold on me.

Tears yet fall, and my body still shivers.

But I feel nothing.

Chapter 25
Tyrvahn

For a moment, Veliana lets me hold her close. Her tears drench the thin fabric of my tunic, and the evening air cools them quickly.

Eyeing the tips of her antlers, I contemplate resting my chin atop her head. Thanks to the backward sweep of her antlers, those sharp points aren't quite so close.

Perhaps the result would be better this time.

Perhaps now is the right time.

But she pulls back, wiping the tears from her cheeks.

"After all this," she mumbles, more to herself than to anyone else, "I'll still be sealed to a man who doesn't love me. I'll lose my parents and take my people to war to unite two lands that never wanted to be one."

Finally, she looks me in the eye. But all traces of the woman I love hide, cowering in the darkest depths of her. Only uncertainty shows in her eyes. "Is this any better than my parents' plan to deal me to your cousin? At least then I wouldn't have brought war upon my people or led my parents to their death."

My mouth falls open, and I struggle for words. Eventually, I say, "But the Sailon and *the Allmother* will still stand. That's the point of this, isn't it?"

"Will they, though? There will still be a Jun ruling over Kin, just like Paikon said. Was that your intention in coming here?" she asks. Her brows furrow, carving deep, angry lines in her face. But her lip quivers, and she flinches as if stung by the Allmother.

"No!" I say, more forcefully than intended. Calming my temper, easing the sting of the Allmother's disapproval, I take a deep breath.

Somewhat more gently, I say, "When I came here, when I met you, I was stunned. The Allmother isn't the only one who showed me I can be better. It was you, too. Your capable nature, your confidence—"

"Confidence…" she scoffs. "Perhaps you don't know me as well as I thought you did. I am *not* confident."

"I thought you were." My voice adopts a wistful tone as I add, "You certainly should be."

Still, she won't meet my gaze.

"My only intention in coming to Kin was to form an alliance and wrest Jun from Paikon and Tumai. I was already terrified of ruling Jun. You *know* that. You can't seriously believe I sought to rule Kin, too. The idea of leading Jun *and* Kin shakes me to my core."

She backs down, unable to hold my gaze. Her grey eyes drop to the ground. She knows, at least this much is true.

"Veliana, I only offered to be Sealed to you because…" I trail off, searching desperately for the words that will convince her that I love her. Clearly, nestling up to her wasn't convincing enough.

But what can I say?

She doesn't give me a chance.

"Because we have to purge Aia. I know," she says in a voice so small I barely hear it. She turns and walks into camp. The light of the campfire reaches for her, pulling her away from me.

"What? No," I say, reaching for her.

But she's gone.

I move to follow her, but Daerna puts a gentle hand on my arm. "Don't fret, my son. She'll see your heart in the Sealing. The best thing you can do right now is to give her space. She has all the pieces. She merely needs time to put them together."

When I glance at Daerna's calm face, none of the anguish of a few moments ago lingers there. The placidity of wisdom and acceptance has reasserted itself over her features.

And despite the bone-deep need to comfort Veliana, to let her know that I *do* love her, the calm of the High Seal is contagious. It doesn't assuage my fears or chase the ache from my heart. It doesn't lessen the burden of knowing that Veliana is hurting.

But it convinces me that I'm doing what's best for the long term. It tells me that I'm on the right path.

I breathe deeply and nod. The Allmother's approval warms my veins, gentle and soothing, and somehow stronger than usual. Yet, my eyes find their way back to Veliana, now just a silhouette near the campfire. She sits with hands reaching toward the flame for warmth.

My legs itch to carry me toward her. My heart burns to reach out.

But I don't.

I've shown her how I feel. She just has to open her eyes to see it.

My heart clenches and stutters, hoping she'll see before we're Sealed, hoping she'll nestle up to me. But still, excitement buzzes through me.

We're to be Sealed...

Circumstances could be better, obviously. But it's going to happen.

And Kivala said Veliana thought about nestling up to me...

Fortified by my musings, I take another deep breath. The Allmother smiles within my mind, and I nod.

She'll see my heart in the Sealing.

I settle onto the ground, crossing my legs beneath me. The moss we laid at the border provides a gentle cushion, and the soft rustle of feathers and leaves overhead caresses my ears. The light of the fire in our camp burns so far away that only the faintest flickers of its light reach me, leaving the moon to illuminate my view of the Sailon.

Everything looks so soft, so gentle. It contrasts sharply with the maelstrom of violent emotions whirling in my gut, making me nauseous.

So, I close my eyes against it all.

Leaning back against the barrier, I face away from Paikon's rotting corpse, laced throughout with Allflower vines. The Allmother's power buzzes against my back, rippling through the barrier. Her warmth seeps through my veins as I seek communion with her.

I long for the Stag's hoof paste, not because I need it to commune with her, but because I want to be certain I don't misunderstand her.

Yet, we will need it for the coming invasion far more dearly than I need its comfort.

Laying my hands on my knees, palms turned up to the sky and the branches above me, I envision her. My mind fills with her kind yet piercing gaze, a more vibrant shade of green than I've seen anywhere in the mortal realm. I picture her sweeping red hair.

I imagine myself in her realm, surrounded by a warm, amber light. I imagine the clear, pulsing light of all our energies, imagine the blue symbols at their centers and the silver strings and ropes connecting them all.

And her warmth intensifies. The night air around me disappears, replaced by her gentle heat. The moonlight vanishes, and her soft radiance envelopes me.

The Allmother saunters toward me, silver antlers gleaming. She smiles down at me and reaches a hand out.

She's never touched me before...

I hesitate, but only for a second. Reaching up, I take her hand. Silky smooth skin slides against my palm, rough and dirty from my work today. Yet, I don't feel shame or insecurity. All the work I did was for her.

Her warmth penetrates my body, tugging all the tension loose within me. A deep sense of calm overtakes me, replacing the storm that churned in my gut just moments ago.

I gain my feet, and she releases my hand. But much of the calm remains.

As she smiles at me, I look back over the past days and see my life as she must see it. A small detail in the grand scheme of things, yet important in the same way that every link in a chain is important.

And my choices seem clearer.

I must be Sealed to Tyrvahn, whether he loves me back or not.

The full admission that I love him startles me, but only for a heartbeat. I already knew it, it seems. I just hadn't faced it, afraid of the pain it might cause me, was *already* causing me.

I'll be Sealed to him...

Because it's what my people need from me.

I pull in a deep breath and turn to face the Allmother. She smiles, filling me with her warmth, and I know she knows my decision.

But questions yet linger in my heart.

"Will this plan work?" I ask, voice breaking despite myself, despite the relative calm of this place.

Her gentle voice whispers through my mind, "Too many paths still shift, Darling Child. Nothing is yet set in stone."

My heart falls.

What was I hoping for? A steadfast assurance that I can't fail?

Of course, I can fail.

Internally, I chide myself for expecting a clear cut answer to something so complicated.

"Is this the best way I can serve you?" I ask.

"Yes," the Allmother says aloud, nodding once.

I breathe a sigh of relief, grateful, at least, to know I'm doing all I can for her.

"Is this the best way I can serve my people?"

Again, she nods and says, "Yes."

Another burden falls from my shoulders and crumbles at my feet. Two crystal clear answers, two assurances that I'm on the best path.

For the Allmother. For my people.

And that's what matters.

Yet, for all the peace I've found with these two answers, my heart is still broken. Because I have one more question.

Will I be happy?

I don't speak it. I don’t dare to.

But the Allmother nods, surprising me with yet another straightforward answer. No shifting paths. No qualified answer.

And even better, it's yet another answer in the affirmative.

I pull in a deep breath.

I'll be happy.

I don’t dare ask when or how. I don’t ask how much I’ll have to sacrifice to get there. I don’t know if Kin will fall to Jun, don’t know if I’ll eke out some sort of happiness in whatever new society comes out of that. I don’t know if I’ll perish, finding happiness in the Allmother’s realm.

But I smile at the Allmother and whisper, "Thank you." My voice comes out small, but stronger than before.

I stand straighter, lifting my chin so that I look the part of Priestess Rising rather than a defeated child. Shame spreads through me for half a heartbeat as I realize how close I've come to messing things up. But I push the shame down.

I know my path.

And somehow, eventually, I will be happy.

A deep breath lifts my chest, then wafts out of me. I nod, accepting my fate. “Thank you,” I whisper.

“Stay the path, Darling Child,” the Allmother says, silver antlers gleaming in the amber light.

A weak smile lifts the corners of my lips, and I close my eyes.

Focusing on the mortal realm, I remember the soft, spongy texture of the moss beneath me and the gentle light of the moon. The soft rustle of a million feathers and leaves brushes my senses. The faint scent of smoke floats toward me, and the breeze which carries it plays with my hair.

I pull in another deep breath, exhaling quickly this time. My eyes spring open to find the forest just as I left it.

The peace of the Allmother’s assurances, though still present, is faint here. My stomach ties itself in knots at the prospect of being Sealed, finally, but to someone who doesn’t love me. My heart burns at the thought of losing my parents.

My lungs freeze when I think of leading Kin, collapsing under the weight of my burdens. The idea of failing with everything I’ve ever known hanging in the balance terrifies me.

So, I remind myself.

This is the best path, for the Allmother and my people.

And I’ll be happy.

Somehow.

Pulling myself to my feet, I force myself back to camp.

Eventually.

Lying in Garle's bedroll, I wait far longer than expected. When I saw her leave camp with Daerna and Soolan, I thought she'd return quickly. The High Seal isn't particularly fond of dragging conversations out for the sake of pleasantries.

But I've been here, nearly naked in Garle's tent, for an entire sky. At first, the anticipation was phenomenal. Now, it's soured in my stomach, slowly turning to annoyance with each passing breath.

Sitting up, I snatch up my tunic and thrust my arms into the sleeves. Buttoning it up hastily, I wonder if I should go looking for her, wait here, or give up and return to the tent I'm technically sharing with Veliana.

I reach for my trousers, but my hands still as footsteps approach the tent. It opens, and Garle's voluptuous form greets me, a sexy silhouette thanks to the campfire beyond her.

My breath quickens, and my hand deserts my trousers.

"Well," I whisper huskily, "It certainly took you long enough."

I expect her to giggle, or perhaps to rush forward and straddle me. I lick my lips, waiting, and swallow hard.

But her hand rushes to her mouth, stifling a sob as she ducks inside the tent.

My desire shatters, replaced by concern. I slip out of the bedroll and beckon her forward.

"Garle, what's wrong?"

Shuffling forward, she falls to her knees before me. Curling into my arms, she weeps openly. My mind spins, trying to come up with an explanation. My heart pounds, furious at whoever made her cry and shocked by how much I care.

A flutter in the pit of my stomach tells me this isn't quite so simple as I thought. I'm not just attracted to her, and I'm certainly not just getting to know her.

Burn me alive...

I actually have feelings for her.

The realization hits me hard, and I tighten my hold on her. And for a moment, we sit just like that. Her tears stain my tunic. At a loss for someone to defend her against, not knowing why she's upset, I marvel at how quickly she's put down roots within my heart.

When she pulls back, staring at me in the darkness, I say, "What is it? What's wrong?"

But she shakes her head. "Not yet. I can't say it, yet."

She leans forward, pressing her lips to mine for an instant. She pulls back, and her eyes, just barely visible in the faint light that seeps through the fabric of the tent, dart between mine. Shining like warm molasses, they peer into the depths of my soul.

Fear shifts within them, the reason she peers into my soul. Hope brings her closer, brushing her lips against mine, once more.

Desperation tinges the kiss, and she nips at my bottom lip.

Her hair sticks to her face, clinging to the tracks of her tears. I smooth the strands away, pushing them behind her ear. The tip, usually grey, glows a soft silver, telling me her fertile day has arrived.

Though it holds no bearing over us, it makes me want her more.

Her hands find the buttons of my tunic, undoing them quickly. She kisses my neck, hot breath making me shiver. She pushes the fabric back over my shoulders, and then her hands find my breasts. Her thumbs play, circling my nipples.

Moaning softly, I pull her onto my lap, grasping her buttocks. Our kiss deepens. I feel her hunger, and it frightens me. Gone is the gentle woman I've shared this bedroll with for several nights, now.

And I can't help but wonder why.

She pulls my hands forward, placing them on her breasts. Despite my trepidation, it sends a shiver of delight cascading through me. Squeezing lightly, I try to put my reservations aside.

We need to talk about whatever upset her…

But her hands move quickly, unfastening each and every button of her shirt. My heart beats ferociously in my chest, begging me to wait, to talk later.

She tugs her shirt off, throwing it to the ground, and my hands find those perfect breasts. She pulls me in, arching her back to allow me better access, and I kiss her neck, then her collarbone, then her breasts. My tongue teases her nipples, working them into taut little points.

Garle's breath comes faster, but she sits up. Pushing me back, she slides her hand down over my stomach, easing lower and lower. Her fingers move in circles, teasing me until I gasp. She dips them into me, moving slowly, kissing my neck.

I push her trousers down past her wide hips, sliding my hands over her buttocks. She moves faster, and I squeeze, digging my nails in as I gasp.

Releasing her flesh from my grasp, I slide my hand forward, trailing my nails over the sensitive skin of her stomach. Moving slowly downward, I feel the warmth of her.

But she uses her free hand to pull mine away. Pinning it by my head, she whispers against my neck, "This is just for you."

I swallow hard, afraid of what she's apologizing for.

But her thumb makes tantalizing patterns as her fingers dance within me, and I tip my head back, arching until my breasts push up against hers. My entire body buzzes with the promise of release, and she pushes me toward it, faster and faster.

Nipping at the soft muscle where my neck meets my shoulder, she shatters me. I gasp as waves of pleasure rock me, and she bites just a little harder.

"Garle," I breathe, despite myself, despite my worries.

My nails dig into her back as she pushes me toward another freefall. Her lips roam over my neck, my chest. Her fingers move skillfully, taking me higher and higher.

I grasp her breast as she nibbles at my ear. And then, her lips are on mine, panting as we kiss. I ache to slide my hand down over her body or push her back and let my tongue work her into the same fevered state I'm in.

But she keeps my hand pinned by my head, a firm reminder that this is meant to soften some sort of blow.

And her thumb moves faster, pushing harder. Her fingers dance inside me, and her tongue teases mine.

Suddenly, I'm falling again, and the only name I call is hers.

Chapter 28
Veliana

Pulling my knees up, I lay my arms atop them. I shake my head, then drop it onto my wrists. A deep sigh leaves me.

Tomorrow…

With the knowledge that I lead my people toward the best path, the upcoming Seal skitters back into my mind. I've awaited my Sealing Ceremony for so long. I've looked forward to it eagerly, longing for the day when my energy would be braided with that of the man I love.

I just never thought it would be… like this. I always thought, when the day came, whoever I was Sealed to would love me back.

I thought that would be the reason I'd be Sealed… Not for duty.

I'm so naïve.

Another sigh.

I lift my head, rubbing my hands over my face. Thoughts of my parents and their coming sacrifice slither into my mind, pulling tears from my eyes as an even greater agony crushes me. I bury my face in my palms. The weight of my tears digs my elbows into my knees.

Kivala pushes aside the flap of my tent, and I jump, hastily wiping away tears. She sits on her bedroll across from me but doesn't lie down. I assume she'll sleep in Garle's tent, again. But she's here for now, gazing at me in the near-darkness.

I clasp my hands, fingers laced and pressed against my lips.

Reaching out a hand, she strokes the side of my face. Her thumb wipes an errant tear from my cheek, but her gentle touch tugs a flood of them loose.

"Well, that's not what I wanted to happen," she says with a sympathetic smile.

I laugh, soft and full of self-deprecation. "I know," I sob. "Sorry."

"Don't apologize," she says. "It's been quite a day."

A huge breath puffs my chest out, then whooshes from me. I nod, unleashing a torrent of tears as the full weight of the past few days drops onto me. My hands shake, and sobs wrack my body. I curl forward into my lap, wrapping my arms around my head.

Kivala abandons her bedroll, coming to sit beside me. In less than a heartbeat, she tries to pull me into her arms. But I fall sideways, unable to lift myself beneath my burdens. My face lands on her lap, and my tears soak into her trousers. She slowly rubs my back, making large, comforting circles.

Between sobs, I mumble, "My parents…"

But I can't say another word. The thought of them dying slams into me, stealing the air from my lungs.

"I know. Garle told me," Kivala whispers, sparing me the agony of saying the words aloud.

"If I knew… If I had any idea…" I choke, gripping the loose fabric of her pants. "I would've found something else, some other way."

"But the Allmother—" I try to continue, but a sob cuts me off. My heart shrivels then spasms, battering my lungs. "She said this is the best way, and I just…"

"I know," Kivala says. Her hand never stills on my back, moving slowly and trying desperately to infuse my body with some semblance of calm. Her other hand smoothes my hair as she does her best to pull loose strands from my face.

But the tendrils lie beneath my face, and the full weight of my future rests upon them.

"What am I going to do without them?"

They'll be happy and at peace, warm in the Allmother's realm.

But I'll be here…

Alone.

My parents have been such a big part of my life. They've been there through everything. They taught me everything, from communing with the Allmother to the importance of humility.

They lead Kin.

Without them, that falls to me.

And I'm not ready…

"You'll do exactly what you're meant to do," Kivala says. Her voice is gentle but unwavering. "You'll lead Kin, as you were born to do. You and Tyrvahn will purge this realm of Aia and his influence, according to the Allmother's will."

“But I’m not ready to lead…” I whisper. “And Tyrvahn doesn’t love me.”

Tugging gently at my shoulder, Kivala pulls me up to face her. She places her hands on my cheeks, wiping my tears away with her thumbs, and a soft smile lifts her full lips.

“I wouldn’t be so sure of that,” she says.

“Of which part?”

Not that it matters. I’m right.

I’m not ready.

And he doesn’t love me.

Certainty washes through me, and despair follows in its wake, chilling me to the bone.

“Either.” She presses her lips to my forehead, then gestures for me to lay down.

Then, she surprises me, laying down beside me and pulling me into her arms. The warmth of her body seeps into me, joining forces with the Allmother’s gentle, comforting heat.

Though my agony doesn’t dissipate, and though my tears continue to fall, I slip into unconsciousness in the arms of my best friend.

Veliana lies within my arms, sleeping peacefully. Every so often, her breathing hitches in the aftermath of the tears which have only just dried upon her cheeks.

And to think I could've lost her.

I breathe deeply, willing myself to be calm lest I wake her.

Blinded by a pair of breasts... I've been clinging to Garle. I didn't see what she really is, what she's truly capable of.

Yet, even as I think the words, I know it's deeper than mere physical attraction. My stupid, silly little heart is involved.

And it almost cost me Veliana.

My stomach churns angrily, and my heart shrivels before the thought of losing her. I tighten my hold on her, and her arm slides over my waist.

"Why couldn't you be attracted to women?" I whisper. "This would've been so much simpler."

It's been so long since I entertained ideas of anything more than friendship with Veliana, since the first days of her relationship with Materva. But here, in my agony, with her in my arms, I can't help but wonder what could've been.

"We could've been Sealed, so long ago. We could've adopted a kid. The Allmother would've passed both our legacies onto them," I whisper.

Garle wouldn't have hurt me. You wouldn't be hurting over Tyrvahn.

"But the Vierna lineage would've been continually divided, as it has been for generations. And purging Aia would still be impossible without blood."

Veliana's chest rises and falls softly, and she presses her forehead to mine. Our noses brush, but the only heat that flows through me is that of anger.

Would Garle have really gone through with it?

I think back to the tears streaking her face as she defended herself. She insisted that she didn't want to, that it was merely Aia twisting her desperation, steering her toward bloodshed. But I've never thought Aia powerful enough to do that.

He isn't as strong as the Allmother, I know that much.

But is he strong enough to twist mortals, even in the midst of the Sailon Forest? With the Allmother breathing life into everything here, could he still push Garle to such terrible extremes?

Or is she just weak and venomous?

I shudder, unsure which alternative I like better. Betrayal seethes within me, dark and foreboding. It churns in my stomach, and for a moment, I feel sick.

Breathing deeply, I try to calm my nerves. Staring at Veliana, I focus on the little flecks of silver sprinkled across the bridge of her nose and cheeks. The little freckles shine, iridescent even in such low light.

As they should.

Someone so kind and self-sacrificing should have some outward symbol of their good nature.

Tears prick at the corners of my eyes, fighting their way free before I can blink them away. I brush a strand of hair out of Veliana's face, and she stirs. Her eyes flutter, and her lips lift into a smile as her gaze focuses on me.

Then, she sees the tears streaking down my face.

"Kivala?" she whispers. She pulls her arm from my waist and wipes the tears away with the backs of her fingers. "What's wrong?"

Shaking my head, I say, "You never see how good you truly are."

Then, I pull her closer.

Tugging her hand from my cheek, I lace our fingers together, holding her hand between us. She swallows hard, and we lie there, wide awake. Only after the Light Watchers call thirteenth sky do my eyes finally close, letting sleep come to take me away.

Chapter 30

Tyrvahn

The grey pre-dawn light that seeps from the horizon does little to chase the shadows from the corners by Soolan's bedroll. A single candle flickers in the tent, just enough light to ward off the remnants of the night, and I wonder how dark it would be away from the edge of the Sailon.

But such idle thoughts don't last long.

As Soolan hands me a bowl of silver paste, I remember Veliana's hands adorning my antlers with it, then tracing the lines over my chest. I'm to match those embellishments, enhancing my connection with the Allmother. She buzzes soothingly in my veins, offering her approval of my actions.

But my hands tremble, drawing wavering lines rather than crisp, straight ones. Vaguely, I wonder if the lines must be perfect, but more pressing concerns tug at my heart. I can still feel Veliana pressed against me, feel her tears soaking into my tunic. I can still hear the words she said before walking away.

The whole scene plays before my eyes over and again, taunting me with the knowledge that somehow she doesn't believe that I love her. Her former love must have hurt her far more dearly than I thought, because now, she thinks I offered to be Sealed to her just to purge Aia.

And what if that isn't good enough? What if she won't stand for it?

What if she runs away?

A fresh wave of hysteria threatens to overwhelm me, but I contain it. I don't have a choice. Giving in to my desperation isn't an option. So, I swallow back my fear and my dread. I make a conscious effort to still myself.

All to no avail.

I draw the last line along my collarbone, still trembling. I stand before the High Priest of Kin, hands shaking like leaves.

Yet, Soolan waits patiently.

Moving about the canvas tent, bare feet barely making an impression upon the grass, he prepares my robes for the ceremony. A soft smile plays at the corners of his lips, deepening the wrinkles of his face.

Grabbing onto that strange little quirk, desperate for a distraction, I ask, "How can you be so calm all the time?"

Turning to me, he traces his finger down the length of his nose, reminding me that I have one more line to draw.

I nod, dabbing my finger into the paste and drawing a line down my nose.

He nods approvingly and says, "I'm not calm *all the time*, Darling Prince. Dire circumstances call for an appropriate reaction. The days to come will be an example, surely. But today is a *happy* day." His smile brightens as he takes the bowl from my hands. "Today, I see my daughter Sealed. And to a worthy man, at that."

But I don't feel worthy.

I *feel* like I'm about to mess up on a far larger scale than ever before, like I won't be sufficient to purge Aia or to make Veliana happy.

As Soolan turns to retrieve my robes from atop a trunk, Veliana's rejection replays clearly in my mind. I flinch, seeing her walk away from me, yet again.

"But…" I begin, voice quiet, "does she truly want this? Or is she just doing what's best for Kin?"

Does she want me?

Soolan hands me the robes, one made of sheer white fabric and the other a dark, olive green. "Both," he answers with a knowing smile. It warms his eyes as he gazes at me.

“Now, I’ll leave you to change, Darling Prince.” He places a tender hand upon my shoulder as he passes, slowly making his way out of the tent.

And I’m left alone with my fears.

Chapter 31
Veliana

My mother leads me from my tent as the Light Watchers call first sky, sending a long hollow sound through the air, just once. I follow behind her, glancing at the border and the rising sun on the horizon.

At least I'll be able to see the sunrise as I'm Sealed.

Yet, that's little consolation. As I drag myself along in my mother's wake, my heart weeps, letting go of all hope of a Seal born of love.

Perhaps, I should've expected as much.

Maybe I shouldn't even be upset over it. My duty is to the Allmother and Kin.

My heart...

I sigh, unable to complete the thought. I can't tell myself that my heart doesn't matter, that my feelings don't matter. They do.

Just not as much as the Allmother or my people.

So, I walk onward, a lamb to the slaughter. We thread our way through the trees, making our way to the base of the oldest tree in the vicinity. My naked feet trail through the grass, each blade tickling between my toes. The birds flutter above, shifting on their perches as more come to join them at the Allmother's bidding.

My mother turns, eyes alight with warmth, and drapes a garland of Allflowers around my shoulders. The ends dangle near my wrists, and I stare down at them, unable to hold my mother's perfect blue gaze. The white flowers seem to glow with the Allmother's power, and their red centers practically pulse with it. Idly, I wrap the garland around my wrist, waiting.

But I don't have to wait long.

Footsteps approach, two sets. I put it off, holding my gaze on the flowers decorating my wrist. But I can't stay like this forever.

Taking a deep breath, I face my future.

My father leads Tyrvahn toward me, partially obscuring him from view, but as soon as he steps aside, my breath leaves me. Silver lines decorate Tyrvahn's muscular chest and collarbone, one of which plunges straight down to disappear beneath his robes.

And I remember drawing similar lines upon his skin, so many times.

My eyes dart between the silver points of his antlers, and in my mind, I see him kneeling before me to bring them into reach. Then, I'm flooded with the strangely sensual feeling of him painting the Stag's hoof onto my antlers.

I trace the silver line down the length of his nose with my gaze, wondering what it might have been like to draw that line.

My father reaches one arm behind Tyrvahn, passing one end of a garland of Allflowers behind his back to drape it over Tyrvahn's shoulders.

Tyrvahn turns to face me, and suddenly, I've nowhere left to look but into his eyes.

I swallow hard, loud, and my chest rises with a sharp breath. Silently, I hate how much I want him, how much I wish he wanted me.

I seethe, knowing that the only reason I can be with him is because we need to purge Aia, that the only reason we'll join will be to produce an heir.

My hands reach out of their own accord, aching for his touch, even as my brows furrow with the pain I'm certain will fill the rest of my days.

Maybe he'll come to love me, eventually...

The Allmother said I'd be happy.

She didn't say how or when, but... someday.

Filling my lungs with a deep, shuddering breath, I prepare myself. Tyrvahn takes the last few steps toward me, robes drifting across the ground in his wake.

And his eyes never leave mine.

Despite the sparkle of the early sun, they hold far more than just pleasant emotions. Wrinkles crease his forehead as his brows reach for each other, and his gaze seems to search mine.

When he takes my hands in his, a familiar heat radiates into me, moving through me. But my heart shrivels, wondering how long it'll take for me to get over him.

"Ready?" he whispers, voice wavering.

I take a deep breath and nod.

My parents stand on either side of the tree trunk beside us. With a nod, they branch out. As they walk, forming a large circle around us, they sprinkle Allflower seeds in their wake.

When they complete the circle and walk away, they speak soft words of congratulations, lips moving, but I can't make them out. My heart pounds behind my ears, and all I hear is the rushing of my blood as it roars through my veins.

Tyrvahn offers me a smile, eyes bright, and my stomach flutters. My breath hitches in my throat, and I close my eyes.

Together, we whisper, "Allmother, grant us the strength to plant these seeds."

At once, her power buzzes through me, soft and warm. All around us, I feel the seeds burrow their roots into the earth. The sun dims as they climb higher, and I weave them together.

Slowly, the vines join at the top, twining to enclose us within a perfect, leafy dome. Allflowers bloom, filling the air with their sweet scent. I breathe it in, hoping it will ease the tension in my shoulders.

Finally, I open my eyes and find Tyrvahn's gaze already on me. He smiles and squeezes my hands gently.

I swallow, stomach dancing with nerves. But my heart lurches, and I wonder how often he smiled at Garle like that.

I slip my hands from his and slide the garland of Allflowers from my shoulders. Their white petals sparkle delicately in the dim light, and their deep red centers fill the air with luscious sweetness.

Turning, I settle them on the ground, forming a semi-circle. Tyrvahn does the same with his, draping one end atop mine and placing the other beneath mine. Together, our garlands form a complete circle.

Nervously, I work the button of my outer robe, hands fidgeting and shaking. I haven't worn only sheer fabric around him since we met, and the prospect of doing so again makes my stomach flutter and my knees shake. Heat rushes up into my cheeks now that I know I don't hold the appeal he needs.

Swallowing back my sadness, I pull the robe from my body. I keep my eyes trained on the fabric, unable to meet his gaze, though a morbid curiosity begs me to look at him, to see what he looks like with so little between us.

I fold my robe and toss it to the ground. Then, we sit in the middle of the garlands. I cross my legs, drawing my feet up under my knees. Tyrvahn sits before me, and his knees touch mine.

I nod, signaling him, and we say in unison, "Allmother, grant us your light."

I feel the warmth of her power, though it only takes a little. We shape it, and the garlands surrounding us ignite, surrounding us with a soft ring of fire. The smoke of the Allflowers, so sweet and delicate, soothes my nerves.

A sigh lifts my chest, and I rest my hands upon my knees, palms up. Tyrvahn slides his hands into mine.

"Are you ok?" he asks. Concern creases his brows.

I nod, closing my hands over his.

This is the best path, the best way to serve the Allmother and my people.

"Yes, I'm ok," I say, but my voice comes out small.

He hesitates, mouth opening and closing. Finally, he whispers, "Veliana..."

But I can't listen to his apologies. It's bad enough that I'm about to see his heart, see all the ways he doesn't want me.

"Close your eyes," I say, closing my own as I say the words.

I don't walk him through the process of finding the Allmother's realm, trusting that he's practiced enough since I last communed with him. Soft, amber light warms my skin. I open my eyes, waiting for him, and stare up at my energy. It shines bright, gleaming a brilliant silver. Pulsing at its center, my name glows blue in the Allmother's tongue. The thick rope of the Vierna line extends into the distance, disappearing out of view.

I feel Tyrvahn arrive, feel the pull of his hand. Rising to my feet, I move toward him, weaving through the ribbons connecting the energies of Kin.

My heart flutters when I see him walking toward me, reaching his hand out for me. I keep my gaze above his shoulders, careful not to tempt myself too much. But the outlines of his body imprint themselves on my mind, regardless of my efforts. The smile on his face makes my lungs stutter, despite everything.

It almost makes me feel like things will be alright.

Almost.

He wraps his hand around mine. Somehow, the warmth from his palm supersedes that of the Allmother's realm, seeping into me.

Will it be okay?

The Allmother appears, brilliant white skin glowing, almost too radiant to look at. Her eyes dance with light as she smiles at us.

I incline my head in a gentle bow, and Tyrvahn follows my lead. Then, we sit at her feet, a perfect mirror of our posture in the mortal realm. Our knees touch, and our joined hands rest upon them.

The Allmother begins, lifting her hands. She waves them through the air, shifting the energies around us. The silky ropes tying them to each other bend and stretch, shifting through each other when necessary, as she pulls our energies toward each other.

The thick Vierna rope moves quickly, eager for another Seal. I can almost feel my ancestors' anticipation. The Allmother fills my head with their chanting, lending me the strength of their Seals.

The strangely thick rope of Tyrvahn's lineage moves almost as eagerly, and I wonder at it, yet again.

Does he hear the chanting of his forebears?

If so, I'll hear them soon enough.

But maybe they never petitioned.

The thought of only hearing my own ancestors, the same sound I've heard every time I've truly needed to call upon the Allmother, and nothing more… startles me. But I wait.

The Allmother cloaks us in a veil of amber light, and cozy warmth soaks into my bones. She tugs new ropes from our energies, silver strings bursting forth from their centers, and laces us together. Her hands dance, moving quickly as she pulls the laces tighter. Still more ribbons of silver appear, begging for her to move them.

And she obliges.

Suddenly, I see the depth of Tyrvahn's grief for his parents and his guilt over not seeing Paikon’s plans. It knocks the wind from my chest. But the love he feels for his mother and father restores my breath.

The Allmother pulls more strings loose from our hearts, weaving them together, and I see his hatred for Paikon, for Tumai. My jaw clenches, and my teeth grind together.

Another string brings me memories of his favorite foods, and another shows me the view from his window back in Jun. The entire kingdom spills out beneath him, stealing my breath.

His life flashes before my eyes, revealing who he was. I watch him overreact to a delay for a festival event, see him shout at a tailor. Briefly, the Allmother shows me the way he and Garle were together, all clipped conversations and guarded behavior. Those things contrast the man I know so sharply that I struggle to reconcile the images.

Until the Allmother shows me the change in his heart.

She shows me the smile on his face when he first saw her. He laid there, nearly dead after a poisoned bowl of soup, but it brought his energy closer to her, close enough for her to reach him. She shows me the sweet feeling of experiencing her warmth for the first time. Calm floods me as I watch him realize how much the Allmother could help Jun.

Another silver rope, and I see the forest in a blur as he ran from assassins. I feel his pounding heart, hear his desperate petition. The one that helped him punch *really* hard.

I smile, suppressing a giggle.

Then, I feel the awe that rushed through him when he first saw me, and heat rushes through me. The Allmother shows me the itch in his fingers as he ached to reach for my hand, so many times. She shows me the way his eyes lingered on me each time we met and the longing that built within him.

She shows me how quickly he pulled away from Garle and the way his heart shriveled when I turned from him, cutting his face with my antlers. My lungs collapse. A single tear rolls down my cheeks, though many more threaten to follow.

I open my eyes, and Tyrvahn smiles at me. I don't even spare a moment to wonder what parts of my life he saw. Springing onto my knees, I throw myself into his arms and kiss him with abandon. He smiles against my lips before kissing me back.

He throws his arms around my waist, and I wrap my hands in his hair, pulling him closer. My heart flutters as his hand moves up my back, skimming over my spine. He softly touches my neck, pulling back to stare into my eyes.

"I'm so sorry," I say, tracing the mostly-healed cut on his cheek.

"You were hurt…" he whispers, leaning his forehead against mine.

"But…" I swallow hard, "I hurt you."

The whole thing flashes before my eyes, but this time, I hear the agony in his voice as he says my name, see the furrow of his brows as the blood dripped down his cheek.

Tyrvahn kisses me, gentle and tender. "It's behind us, now," he says, lips moving against mine.

He rises onto his knees and pulls me into his arms. His lips press against my forehead, and I pull in a deep breath.

I shouldn't be nervous…

I know how he feels, now.

Yet, my heart skips a beat as I ease my head under his chin. His chest expands as he pulls in a deep breath. He tightens his hold on me, and my stomach flutters. I kiss the hollow at his collarbone, and he shudders against me.

Finally, he knows how I feel.

And he loves me back...

Beside us, the Allmother ties the last of our energies together, and the glowing blue symbols of our names grow brighter. Veliana pulls away, glancing up into my eyes. She glows with the ambient light of the Allmother's realm, stealing my breath away.

Chanting fills my mind, faint but there. The Allmother whispers through my mind, telling me that these are the petitions of my ancestors. My heart swells at the knowledge that, at some point, my forebears felt a strong enough connection to reach for her.

The symbols in our energies grow brighter still, though somehow, their light is soft. Veliana's eyes rake over them, but her brows furrow. "You have… three names?"

"What?"

"You have three names," she says, matter-of-fact. "I thought Jun only kept one surname."

"Well, yeah…" I say, finally realizing the oddity of it.

The Allmother smiles knowingly. "You're descended from an old line. It took some exertion, but I maintained the connection when your family did not."

I stare at her, dumbfounded.

"Your ancestors were the Naivets."

My jaw drops.

"The Naivets?" Veliana asks. "The original monarchs of Jun?"

"Yes," the Allmother says, serenely. Her hands move in the air before her. The symbols shift, rearranging amidst the glittering silver energies. "Your family weaved in and out of the monarchy, but your lineage was necessary. And it's time that the Naivet and Vierna lines merge."

She smiles at us, and some part of me wonders how much of this was planned. Veliana squeezes my hand, drawing my attention. Her eyes glow with warmth, and suddenly it doesn't matter how much was the Allmother's plan and how much was chance.

Because she's here.

"Henceforth," the Allmother says, green eyes sparkling, "You will be known as Veliana and Tyrvahn Naivier Mahrken, High Priest and High Priestess of the mortal realm. Now, reclaim Jun, so that I may heal it."

Warmth flows through me as the symbols at the heart of our energy stop shifting, burning themselves into finality. As the connection seals, the warmth around me surges, far more intense than it was just moments ago.

The chanting of Veliana's ancestors floods my mind, drumming in my ears. But their volume is comforting. I feel their ties to the Allmother, feel each and every silver strand in the long Vierna lineage. Their voices blur together, though somehow each one feels distinct. I take a deep breath, reveling in the bliss of this place and this deep connection.

This feels right. This is how I'm supposed to live, how I'm supposed to lead.

For the Allmother.

With Veliana.

A smile spreads itself over my face as a fresh wave of warmth washes through me, and I turn to Veliana. She inclines her head, and we settle onto our haunches.

"Close your eyes," she whispers, and somehow, I hear her over the chanting.

Without her direction, I imagine the soft grass beneath us and the smoke of burning Allflowers swirling around us. I concentrate on the feeling of her hands in mine and the sunlight filtering in through the woven Allflower vines above us.

The ground solidifies beneath me, and Veliana squeezes my hands. I open my eyes, and there she is.

Lovely. Dappled by sunlight.

And smiling.

Burn me alive, I've missed that smile…

The smoke of the Allflower garlands has dissipated. They've long since disintegrated with only the smallest charring on the grass they rested upon, leaving me to wonder just how long the ceremony took.

But I don't ponder it for long.

My eyes fall to Veliana's lips, and she blushes.

I've missed that, too.

Leaning forward, I reach out, placing a hand on her soft cheek. Pulling her toward me, I let my eyes roam over her, drinking in the light in her grey eyes and the pink tone hovering beneath her silver freckles. The soft outlines of her body peek up at me through the sheer fabric of her robe, tensing every muscle in my body.

Our noses touch, and her eyes close. Her lips part, so inviting, and I brush mine against hers. Her breaths come in short bursts, and though I want to draw this moment out, I can't wait any longer.

I press my lips to hers, and suddenly her hands wrap themselves in my hair, pulling me closer. Our mouths dance, and heat pools within me.

But it isn't enough.

I put an arm around her waist, needing her closer, and she obliges, climbing onto my lap. Her legs wrap around me, and my heart pounds behind my ears. I slide my hands down over her body, grasping her buttocks and pressing her to me. She moans against my lips, arching her back.

And suddenly, her hands unfasten the button of my robe and slip the fabric back over my shoulders. She kisses my neck, sending my heart racing. Her hands slide down my chest, then around to clutch my back.

Consumed by feverish desire, I unfasten her robe, pushing the fabric from her shoulders in an instant. My lips land upon her skin, hot and breathless. I kiss her neck, her shoulder.

Rising onto my knees, I lay her back on the ground, thankful for her relatively small antlers and the lack of flames around us. I cup her breasts, relishing the feel of them, and she lets out a breathy moan that drives me wild.

Desperate for her, I kiss her skin, licking her nipples as I slide my hand lower. I tease her, moving my fingers delicately over her before slipping one inside. The slick heat makes me groan against her breast.

Her nails dig into my back as I move my fingers inside her. She tips her head back, digging her antlers into the dirt and arching her back. I kiss her neck, relishing the soft feeling of her breasts pressed against me.

She releases my back, putting a hand on my neck to pull me in for a kiss. Her other hand moves downward, skimming over her body. She touches herself, but only for an instant. Her hand comes away slick, and she wraps it around me.

I bite her bottom lip, groaning as she moves her hand, up and down, picking up her pace. Then, her hand finds my hip, pulling me down into her. Waves of heat course through me, and I press deeper into her, needing her more than I need air.

Her hips move with the motion of my body, and we writhe together. My breath comes in shallow gasps. Her soft breasts press against my chest, and she grasps my buttocks, pulling me in deep, again and again.

Our eyes lock as she moans beneath me.

Clutching her hip, I pull her to me, plunging in once more. I kiss her, breathing hard. My heart pounds wildly. She drags her nails over my spine, and I shiver, eliciting a sweet gasp from her.

Releasing her hip, I dip my hand between her legs once more, working her to a fever pitch. She cries out, digging her nails into my back. So, I move faster, and she breathes out my name, convulsing as she falls to pieces beneath me, tightening around me.

And with one final, soul-shattering plunge, I find my release. The world around me becomes a bright light as my body shudders with it, and my lungs falter.

Slowly, I catch my breath. I shake, leaning all my weight on one arm.

But Veliana kisses me, lips full and breath hot. Her hands wrap in my hair, pulling me in closer. My heart swells and a smile lifts the corners of my lips. I fall to the ground beside her, rolling her to her side to face me.

Her antlers kick up little tufts of grass and flecks of dirt as she rolls, and for some reason, we can't help but laugh.

We lie there as the sun moves across the sky, reveling in the feel of each other's skin. Our fingers trace indecipherable patterns, exploring. Our minds wander, and she asks about the Sealing Ceremonies in Jun.

"They're nowhere near as grand," I tell her. "Though, people there would argue differently. An arbor replaces the bespoke latticework of Allflowers. Overly decorated gowns and suits replace the see-through robes, and everyone sticks around to watch the ceremony, even though the people being Sealed just sit there quietly, not seeing the Allmother. There's certainly no circle of fire. It's a bore, really."

She laughs, filling the air with delicate music, and though there is much to be done, my heart finds peace.

With the remnants of Fahn informed of our role in the invasion, I stand before my Rebel allies, uncertain. Kivala stands at a distance, our official ambassador to Kin.

But she turns from me as soon as I finish speaking. As she walks away, she tosses a glare at me over her shoulder. She's careful about it, obscuring her face from the Rebels who yet linger before me, unwilling to undermine me in front of them.

I contain my flinch, hoping not to give myself away.

But deep down, I'm sure they've noticed the change in our behavior, even if the look she shot at me escaped their gaze. Kivala didn't stand apart from me before. She stood right beside me, holding my hand. I can almost feel the warmth of her touch.

Almost.

My fingers curl, aching to twine with hers, but only open air greets them. An icy whisper blows through my heart as Aia reaches in to twist the knife of Kivala's rejection.

I stare after her, heart shriveling in my chest. But I know she's right to turn away from me. I expected as much when I confessed.

Yet, I had to tell her.

"They're near," the Allmother says, voice floating into my mind.

For a moment, I forget what she means, casting my gaze around. I search the border, heart thumping in my chest at the prospect of an attack. But the field beyond lies just as empty as it did when last I looked.

Then, I hear the heavy footsteps pushing through the Sailon toward us, and the Allmother whispers, "Tis only the bears, Darling Rebel."

My heart slows but doesn't quite resume its normal pace. The hairs on the back of my neck stand on end, anticipating glory and wonder.

I haven't seen one since I was a child, but they stand out in my memory. Majestic and impossibly massive, they carried our leaders with ease, traversing long distances between settlements in less than half the time it would take any of us to travel on foot.

I'm sure they only seemed so big because I was a kid...

I settle my mind, prepared to see completely normal animals. Being underwhelmed by creatures connected to my race for centuries showing up just in time to ferry us into war regardless of the danger it poses them seems ungrateful.

But my heart dares to hope, regardless.

I need this.

I need to be awed, to be inspired. I cast a glance at Kivala, then at Veliana and Tyrvahn.

All the lives I've ruined and ended, all the hearts I've broken...

I turn my gaze inward, surveying the wreckage of my own heart and mind. Aia flows within my veins, filling me with poison. The Allmother tempers him, easing the pain of his presence.

But he's there.

Breathing deeply, I close my eyes. Gritting my teeth, I hold back the waves of emotion which might otherwise overwhelm me. I can't lose control of myself here, after all. Not with all my allies watching.

The footsteps grow closer, louder, and I open my eyes.

Picking and choosing a path with branches high enough to allow them to pass, the bears lumber toward us. Luxurious black fur sparkles in the sunlight which dapples their coats. Eyes so dark as to appear black peer out at us, assessing, calculating.

My jaw drops, and the breath rushes from me.

They tower over us all, backs higher than any of our heads as they walk toward us, heads hanging low to avoid low-hanging twigs.

Vaguely, I piece my childhood home together as bits of memory spread over me like a mist. I recall these creatures moving through our villages, graceful despite their size. The trees in Fahn were so much taller, the branches so much higher. The forest seemed crafted for them, not us. And maybe it was.

One of the enormous animals flares its nostrils, searching for something, and its eyes land on me. Coming closer, it leads its fellows through the gathered Rebels, the remnants of Fahn. Other bears stop off along the way, finding the riders the Allmother tied them to.

But the first one, the leader, approaches me. A beam of sunlight dances down to light its path, and its eyes shine like honey in the light. It stares into my eyes, delicately sniffing the air, and I reach out a tentative hand.

"This is Soor," the Allmother whispers within me. "She will carry you to Jun and throughout your future. Be good to her."

My hand hangs in the air, warmed by Soor's breath. I greet her, tasting her name as it rolls from my tongue, so naturally, as if I were meant to utter it.

She takes another step forward, then sits before me. She drops her head, pressing it against my outstretched hand. My heart stutters, and my mind goes blank. The Allmother's warmth slips through my veins, quiet yet powerful.

My hand looks like that of a child, tangled in Soor's dark fur. Something in me breaks, no longer strong enough to hold back the tidal waves of agony and stress. Tears burst from my eyes, pouring out like a monsoon, dripping onto my boots. Sobs shake my body, nearly tearing me apart.

Soor presses her forehead against mine. I wrap my arms around her neck, clutching her fur. She sniffs me, letting out a soft grunt that vibrates my bones. The Allmother's warmth grows stronger, easing the weight of my burdens. My tears slow, and my breathing smoothes out.

Sniffing me again, Soor gently nudges me with her nose. I pull back, wiping my tears away with the back of my hand. She stares at me, eyes shining a smooth caramel in the light.

A soft nudge and another sniff, and she rises onto all fours. She walks past me, slow but purposeful.

Only then do I notice Kivala staring at me, watching me fall apart. She clenches her jaw, narrowing her eyes when I catch her, but she doesn't back down.

Not until Soor stands before her.

Kivala's attention centers on the massive animal before her, and her features soften. The mask of fury disappears, and she looks like the person she was before I confessed…

Sweet. Confident.

Loyal.

Three things I long to be.

Three qualities I can't possess.

She reaches out a hand, hesitant but excited. Soor settles herself to the ground, pushing her head against Kivala's palm. They share a moment, far less anguished than the one I shared with Soor just a moment ago, and Kivala's hand comes away wet with my tears.

When the bears move to the clearing near the border, luxuriating in the open air and the lack of low branches, Kivala crouches. She drags her hand across the grass, wiping my tears from her skin, staring at me all the while.

Only when she turns from me, stomping into camp, do I realize the significance of Soor approaching both of us.

We're to ride together, the whole way to Jun.

My heart constricts painfully in my chest, and I squirm before my own self-hatred. But for my allies, for the Rebels of Fahn, I lift my chin. I plaster a smile across my face despite the storm inside me, despite the embarrassment I've just made of myself and the mess I've made of my life.

Chapter 34
Veliana

I fasten the chest plate of Tyrvahn's new armor, hoping he adjusts to it quickly. The leather straps are the perfect length, and the scapulas of Tala's father fit beautifully on his chest and back, almost as if he were meant to wear this set of armor.

The Allmother's words flash through my mind. "It's time the Naivet and Vierna lines merge."

Maybe he was *meant to wear it…*

A smile lifts the corners of my lips at the Allmother's providence, and I smooth down the sleeves of his tunic, luxuriating in the feel of his strong arms.

Lifting his vambraces from the ground, he slides them on. The dark leather armguards contrast the yellowed deer femurs affixed to them. Two additional deer femurs adorn his shins, and scapulas shield his calves.

My own bone armor clings to me, lightweight and already forgotten.

Raking my eyes over Tyrvahn, I marvel at the warrior before me. His armor, though surely nothing like the armor he once wore in ceremonies in Jun, lends him the proper air of a Priest Rising.

Tracing the edge of his chest plate with one finger, I try desperately to keep my mind right here, right now. I want so badly to focus only on the man before me.

But my future awaits.

Nearby, my mother and father paint silver lines upon their skin. The same lines already adorn my flesh and shine behind Tyrvahn's armor. I stare at the vertical line that peeks out above his chest plate, swallowing back my fear.

"One more step," I whisper, voice breaking.

Taking my hands between his, he lifts them to his lips. A deep breath puffs out his chest, then leaves him on a sigh. He kisses the backs of my fingers gently, then nods.

In his eyes, I see the same hesitation, the same fear. Having lost his parents only a couple of moons ago, he understands the pain. I see it in the set of his eyes and know he'd spare me if he could.

But this is what Kin and the Allmother need.

I take another deep breath and nod back at him. We meander toward my parents, still alive and well. For the time being.

I start to speak, but my mother shakes her head. Tears glimmer in her eyes, and she whispers, "Not yet."

Choking back a sob, I acquiesce, glad to put off our goodbyes for another moment.

Kivala appears at my side, placing a tender hand on my shoulder before stepping forward to my parents. Her light brown hair hangs in a tight braid, draping down her back. She holds out a bowl of red paste, the Allflower paste we ground together.

They dip their fingers in and draw lines upon each other's faces. One line down the length of their noses and three on each cheek, extending down from their eyes.

With the bowl in hand, Kivala turns, and Tyrvahn and I draw the same lines on each other's faces. He smiles sympathetically, softly, and my eyes threaten tears. I hold them back, determined not to smudge my lines.

We take our places at the barrier, staring at Paikon's Allflower wrapped corpse and the grove of new trees beyond.

Tyrvahn grasps my hand, and warmth seeps into my palm. My mother takes my other hand, squeezing it with brittle, bony fingers as she reaches for my father. As soon as their hands join, completing the union of the High Seal and the Rising Seal, the Allmother's warmth buzzes through my veins.

Birds chirp happily overhead, and sunlight shines brightly upon my skin. A butterfly flits past.

Yet, for all this, I shiver.

The shimmering barrier before me holds back so much more than just potential attacks. Beyond it lies the responsibility of leading two nations and purging a God.

The deaths of my parents.

I take a deep breath to steady myself, but it doesn't work. My palms sweat, and my hands tremble.

Tyrvahn squeezes my hand reassuringly, and my mother whispers, "You'll do just fine, my dear."

A single tear falls, rolling silently over my cheek. I refuse to allow it's brethren to follow, gritting my teeth against the onslaught that threatens.

Together, we whisper a petition, and the barrier bursts into a shimmering mist. With the Allmother's power, we send the tiny water droplets wafting out into Jun.

My lungs shudder as I turn to face my parents. Tears well in my eyes.

It's time.

Tyrvahn releases my hand, letting me embrace them in a hug. Our antlers clack together, but I don't care. I squeeze them harder. Their frail bodies groan and pop, but they wrap their arms around me, holding me just as tightly.

Can't I just stay here?

I can't lose them.

A sob wracks my body, and my father pulls back. "Darling Daughter," he says, "it will be all right." But the waver in his voice and the tears sparkling on his eyelashes betray his words.

Another sob jerks free of my quivering lips.

"We go to the Allmother," my mother whispers. She touches my cheek, gentle and sweet. "It's time for you to lead Kin, now."

"But…" I choke back another sob, forcing myself to speak. "I can't lose you. I can’t say goodbye. And what if I'm not ready?"

"I would worry if you were certain. That you question your ability to lead tells me only that you've considered the responsibility before you and have not underestimated it. You're ready," my father says, silver eyes swimming with tears. "You've been ready for a long time. And the Allmother will guide you."

They embrace me once more, leaning their foreheads against mine in turn. My father kisses between my eyebrows, pressing the tension lines away. But they return as soon as his lips desert my skin.

"We must begin," my mother whispers. Silent tears flow over her cheeks as she kisses my forehead, and they drip onto my face.

They pull away from me, and I whisper my love for them.

"We love you, too, Darling Daughter," my father says.

Then, he turns to Tyrvahn with arms wide, beckoning him forward for a hug. My parents embrace him, whispering their goodbyes. They look so small next to him, so tiny in his embrace.

My heart stutters, and my hands tremble. I wrap my arms around myself, aching for some sort of comfort.

My father pulls away, staring earnestly into Tyrvahn's eyes. Tyrvahn nods and steps back. I reach for his hand immediately, knowing I'll need his touch to get through this.

My parents join hands at the border, standing in the moss. I want to look away, unwilling to burn the sight of their death into my mind, but I know I can't. Staring at them, I watch as they close their eyes. The Allmother's power buzzes, growing closer. It moves through their veins, and their bodies glow.

Overhead, the birds take their cue. They launch themselves into the air, following the Allmother's will. Nets laden with seeds cover the ground, spread out in every open space. Groups of four swoop down, each taking a corner of one of the many nets available.

One by one, the nets are scooped up, and the birds take to the air, flying into Jun. Wings beat the air, cacophonous and wonderful. They block out the sun, a precursor to the tree branches which will shield us from the sun in moments.

My eyes go to my parents, once more. Their grey hair glistens with the Allmother's power. Crisp blue eyes and gleaming silver ones stare out at the world beyond the border, and I shudder to think what they must have endured in their previous time there.

They no longer seem frail with age. Rather, they stand, glowing with power, and I pity any who stand against us. My chest swells with pride despite the loss clawing at my heart.

The birds lift the last net, careening into Jun with seeds filtering through the gaps. A rain of life descends upon the open fields.

Tala pads over to me, nudging my shoulder with her nose.

It's time.

A deep breath fills me, and I nod. Turning, I place a tender hand upon her neck and lean my forehead against hers. "Okay, girl," I whisper.

She kneels, and I climb atop her. Extending a hand, I help Tyrvahn up. With one last look at my parents, one last squeeze of my heart, I let Tala rise and carry me into the little clearing where Paikon's corpse waits.

Tears stream down my face, no doubt smudging the lines drawn there. Behind me, my parents' voices whisper into existence, chanting for the Allmother. She grants their petition, filling our heads with the chanting of all our forebears. The air around me reverberates with the power coursing through them, waiting to be released into the world.

Tala kneels beside Paikon's vine wrapped body, and I climb down. The grass here feels different, somehow, crunchy and brittle. It isn't the same spongy, resplendent grass of the clearings in Kin. I imagine Aia seething within every blade and almost cringe at each step.

With a whispered petition, I light a fire upon the Allflower vines. Full of life, they take a moment to catch. But when they do, the fire licks hungrily at Paikon's clothes, his hair. Smoke fills the little clearing, and my parents make their move.

Vaguely, I wonder if I'll feel the moment their energies leave this realm and our lineage centers on Tyrvahn and me.

Chapter 35

Kivala

The High Seal stands at the border, hands clasped, calling out for the Allmother's power. And she obliges. They glow with it, almost too bright to look at.

My parents approach me, and I ready myself to mount a bear named Soor. We'll ride soon, but my mother's gentle hand on my shoulder stops me.

Have I forgotten something?

I glance down, patting the sheath at my hip, then reach over my shoulder to find my quiver fully stocked. My bow is already fastened to Soor's harness, as are my provisions.

Finally, meeting her gaze, I ask her, "What is it?"

She pulls me into a hug and whispers, "Be safe, my dear."

Her voice breaks, and I wonder if she fears going to battle. My father stands beside her, eyebrows carving deep lines in his weathered forehead. He reaches out, laying a tender hand on my cheek.

His vibrant eyes shine, but not with any emotion I've seen in them in years.

But… Why should he be sad? Today, we take back what used to belong to the Allmother. Today, we bring peace to a nation in desperate need of it.

I glance at my mother and find tears brimming in her eyes.

"I'll be safe, I promise," I whisper, pulling them into my arms.

They grip me tight, putting their strength to good use. Every time they've pulled back a bowstring, every log they've cut, and every bundle of leather they've tanned seems to have been in preparation for this embrace.

My hands cup the backs of their heads, and we lean our foreheads together. Despite the calm that should envelop me, my stomach turns uneasily.

Have I underestimated this battle?

Surely not. I know it will be grueling. I know it'll be violent, but we have the Allmother on our side.

But when I look into their eyes, I can't help but think I'm missing something.

They glance at each other, coming to some sort of agreement, then my father says, "Come, now. It's time."

I pull in a deep breath, turning back to Soor. The massive animal kneels, waiting for me to climb onto her back. I turn to look for my parents, assuming that they'll ride with me. But they've already meandered to the next bear in line.

The one Garle sits upon.

They call her down and send her over to join me. She glances at me, flinching before my hardened glare. But my parents catch my eye.

A small shake of my mother's head is all it takes to chasten me.

I mouth an apology to my parents and drop my gaze, keeping the fury within me contained. I try not to watch Garle's hesitant gait, try so hard not to wish she'd trip. When she reaches my side, I force myself to lend her a hand.

She has the grace to mumble, "Sorry. I really was going to ride separately."

I don't bother replying.

Soor rises from her crouch, and I hiss beneath my breath, "Hold on. If you must."

The acid in my words leaves Garle’s touch hesitant. She grips my hips, unwilling to wrap her arms around me.

The chanting at the border intensifies. Soolan and Daerna lift their voices, louder and louder. Out beyond the new thicket of trees, the skies above Jun thicken. The clouds turn dark as the chanting builds to a crescendo, pulsing in the air around me.

Soor carries us forward, long strides propelling us past the crackling fire that used to be Paikon. The sweet smell of Allflower smoke tickles my nose. It tries so hard to soothe me, but the hands on my waist, the hands that could have killed Veliana, pull my nerves tighter than a bowstring.

We reach the new thicket of trees, and I finally lift my eyes to the procession of animals before me. Briefly, I wonder when we'll pick up speed.

But then, two familiar voices join the chanting.

I whip my head around, small antlers barely missing Garle’s. And I see them. My mother and father stand behind the

High Seal, calling out to the Allmother. My stomach plummets, and my heart lurches.

"No!" I scream, gripping Soor's fur.

But their hands land upon Soolan and Daerna's shoulders, fusing them to their communion. The Allmother's connection to this realm grows stronger, spreading to them, and their hands glow with it.

Again, I scream, but this time, no words form. Vaulting from Soor's back, I crumple to the ground. Tears pour over my cheeks, and sound rips its way free of my throat.

A single crack of lightning splits the air. Before the thunder reaches us, rain pours onto the newly scattered seeds. I sprint through the downpour, desperate to reach them, to stop them.

Behind me, Garle shouts for me to stop, and Soor skids to a halt. I hear Garle leap to the ground, slipping as she lands.

But I only run faster.

"NO!" I push myself, desperate to stop what's happening. Everything Veliana said, everything I've learned about this…

That connection will kill them.

My heart shatters as I slip, falling to my knees. My hands clutch at the grass, pushing me to my feet again.

But the glow spreads, creeping through my parents' bodies until it encloses them in light.

Garle's hands wrap around my arm, spinning me to face her. Mud stains her clothes and splatters of it coat her face.

"Don't touch me!" I jerk free of her grip, spinning to face the light that used to be my parents.

"Kivala," she begs, "it's too late."

The slick earth and the pounding rain drive me to the ground, again. I stare up at them, their forms barely discernible amongst the blinding light.

"They can't be gone," I croak, tears lost in the rain. My throat aches, squeezing itself too tightly over the words.

Garle drops to her knees beside me, whispering, "I know it hurts…" She tries to pull me into her embrace, but I shove myself free of her.

Soor approaches, pressing her muzzle to my shoulder. I turn from Garle and the shocked anguish on her face, wrapping my arms instead around Soor's neck. She buzzes with the soft warmth of the Allmother, and I weep into her fur.

Chapter 36
Tyrvahn

Tala stills beneath us, ears twitching. But thunder covers everything, drowning the sounds of the world. Rain beats down upon us, stealing still more sound from me. Veliana pats the wolf's neck affectionately, trying to calm her, but to no avail.

Turning us around, she shows us the border and the two Fahns fighting near it. Kivala shouts something, ripping herself from Garle's arms. Their bear lumbers toward them, stealing them from my view.

Veliana tenses in my arms, leaning forward to scan the people seated upon massive animals. "No…" she whispers, barely audible in the pouring rain. "Shevari… Fluros…"

The light grows brighter at the border, and realization dawns on me. It rips through me, fierce and thrashing.

"Poor Kivala…" I whisper.

But the Allmother's sweet voice sounds within my mind, urging us to carry on. "They chose wisely. It is a sad necessity. Kivala and Garle will catch up," she says. "I need you to be my eyes, and it's almost time."

Veliana answers her aloud, saying, "We'll be your eyes." But her voice breaks, and a sob shakes free of her as Tala turns us to our path once more.

Wrapping my arms around Veliana, I rest my chin atop her head. She laces her fingers through mine, wrapping her arms around herself to do so.

But I can offer her no more comfort than this.

Tala winds through the trees, avoiding low branches for our sake. The other wolves and most of the bears follow closely behind.

The rain patters angrily upon the leaves above us, amplified in this enclosed space, though very little water reaches us. Another bolt of lightning flashes in the distance, and even here, the world flickers. Thunder rolls toward us, shaking my bones, and I shiver beneath my sodden clothes.

Breaking free of the new thicket, Tala carries us into an open field. Rain pours over us once more, plastering my hair to my scalp. In the distance, the birds carry seeds throughout the land. They'll be enough to start this invasion, enough to give the Allmother a foothold in Jun.

Soor joins us, finally catching up, and I do all I can to keep from staring at Kivala. I know the wounds she's just endured all too well. My own have yet to heal. I long to offer her comfort, but I know my words will fall short.

Tala casts her gaze about the field, and I lift my eyes to the clouds above us. My eyes flinch before the onslaught of rain, blinking rapidly. I close them, truly feeling the rain in a way I've never bothered to do before. Another flash of lightning brightens the world beyond my eyelids, and thunder rumbles around us.

Then, the world falls eerily silent.

The thunder stops, far too quickly, and the rain moves further into Jun. The clouds part overhead, drenching us in sunlight. For the first time in many suns, no birds flutter or squawk overhead. No feathers rustle nearby.

The hairs stand on the back of my neck, and my skin pricks into goosebumps. The Allmother grows clearer, more present in my mind, as she reaches into our realm. Her power sprints through my veins.

I swallow a lump in my throat, thinking myself ready for what comes next even as my heart beats harder and my breathing grows shallow.

A deep rumble sounds behind us, moving closer, getting louder. The ground beneath us shakes, and the trees rattle with its approach.

But I dare not look back.

Breathing heavily, Veliana leans forward to grip Tala's fur, waiting. I tighten my hold on my Sealmate's waist. Beneath us, Tala braces herself, crouching low, bending to absorb the force, and the other animals follow suit.

The rumbling surges toward us, and the earth trembles. Leaves and branches sway violently above us. A gust of wind whips past us, sending our hair rushing forward, and the ground shudders beneath Tala. I nearly lose my hold on Veliana, clutching harder, holding tighter. My legs grasp Tala's sides, desperate not to fall.

Because I know what's to come, and I would not survive.

The deep growl moving through the earth grows louder, covering everything. I feel it in my stomach, in my bones, shaking me as it moves toward me. All around us, the trees threaten to uproot themselves, branches crashing together. Sticks and leaves fall, littering the ground.

A single jolt jerks through the ground, and a deafening crack rings out through the air. The seeds before us transform, taking root immediately. Within a single heartbeat, saplings rise, spreading out in a wave.

And Tala leads the charge, vaulting forward.

On all sides, vines sprout and trees burst from the ground. Mud sprays up around us, uprooted by the violence of the sudden growth. It splatters across us all, but Tala runs onward, surefooted.

She beelines toward the storm, sprinting ahead. My heart pounds against my eardrums, and the chanting of all my ancestors, all of Veliana's ancestors, fills my head. I cling to her, leaning my head against hers to avoid her antlers.

But I can't tear my eyes from the earthen carnage before me.

Peering up through my lashes, I watch trees erupt from the earth, and vines wrap around them. Flowers appear from nowhere, blooming and withering in a matter of a breath.

Seeds burst from plants, falling ahead of their forebears, and the Allmother takes them. Moving through the ground and our veins, seeing through our eyes, she raises them up to take shape.

And we ride into the storm, carrying her with us.

A small farming village looms ahead, gleaming in the light of the setting sun. Tala slows beneath me, and the other animals follow suit, huffing and panting.

As we slow, so too does the Allmother's reclamation. Trees burst from the ground all around us, springing free of every seed in sight. But we no longer sprint at break-neck speeds, soaring over fields and meadows.

Farmers rush out of their homes, desperate to understand the sight on the horizon and the cacophony of our arrival. Soldiers shove them aside, sprinting to meet us.

My hands clench into fists as I watch them. Their armor gleams orange in the dying light. Tala takes a step free of the new trees, carrying Tyrvahn and me forward. Bears and wolves spread out to my sides, riders lifting their bows in preparation.

The Allmother's power flows freely around us. My skin tingles with it, and I harness it. Bringing my arms forward, I cross them before myself, then lift them. A wall of stone erupts from the ground, rising just high enough to allow me to see over it.

Farmers and their partners gasp, and the approaching soldiers skid to a stop just outside town. I can almost see the colors of their eyes, but I suspect the Allmother may be helping with that. Their voices carry toward us, whispering of impossibilities.

A gentle wind blows, and seeds sprinkle free of the trees around us. They land just beyond the wall, and I smile. The Allmother lets them take root, slowly raising them up. Those closest to the wall reach its height, but the rest wait patiently.

A villager faints, black antlers digging into the dirt where he lands.

"For those who do not know me," I begin, and the Allmother amplifies my voice, carrying it to all in town. "I am Veliana Naivier Mahrken," I say, testing my new name, "High Priestess of Kin."

My heart twists painfully as I say my new title, but I control my voice.

Gesturing to Tyrvahn, I say, "And I believe you know the High Priest, Tyrvahn Naivier Mahrken. He is not dead, as Paikon and Tumai would have had you believe. But my parents and your King and Queen are. And as of a few suns ago, so is Paikon."

The soldiers still, but smiles slip hesitantly onto the faces of a few villagers.

There might be hope…

"You need not shed blood here, today. You don't have to follow them to their graves. But Tumai will, as will anyone who stands in our way."

The villagers glance nervously amongst themselves and at the soldiers before them. My heart quickens as hope floods me.

Do they feel the Allmother's warmth yet?

"For too long, Aia has twisted your land, contorting hearts with greed and vengeance. Famine, poverty, and injustice have wrecked Jun. Beyond the Allmother's reach, your leaders fell prey to him."

Tyrvahn tightens his arms around my waist. For the first time in two moons, he addresses his people. But today, he offers them hope.

"The legends we learned as children are true," he says. "The Allmother is far more real than I ever imagined her to be. And so is Aia. I have felt his influence, felt the cold oppression of his presence. But the Allmother is light. She is warmth."

A deep breath puffs out his chest. "And she is here, now."

Gesturing to the trees around us and the saplings beyond the wall, I say, "We have brought her with us to heal the pain in your land and your hearts. Can you feel her reaching for you?"

Because I can...

She strains at the boundary of the new growth, aching to ease their suffering. She whispers to me, begging me to convince them that she can help them.

"Please," she croons. "Please, let them see me."

Vines of Allflowers reach over the wall, snaking through the saplings toward the village. Bushes spring up in the mud left in the storm's wake, and sweet berries ripen on their limbs. Clovers and moss coat the ground, spreading to fill the gaps. Tiny white flowers sprinkle across them.

"All who accept her warmth will find ease and a peaceful life in harmony with the Allmother and her land, the life we were meant to have. No more starving while your leaders feast every night." I glance out at the faces staring up at me. They gaze at me with wonder and fear in their eyes. "But those who stand against us, those who deny the Allmother… will meet her."

A shudder rolls through the crowd at my words, and the soldiers grip their swords tighter.

But the Allmother continues forward. Berry bushes huddle close to buildings, and flowers bloom all around.

A small child with dirt smudged on her arms delights in the beauty of it all, reaching for a sweet rehlberry. Plucking it free, she considers its plump purple skin carefully, then pops it into her mouth. As she bites down, she smiles, and I can almost see the Allmother's warmth soothing her.

"Mommy, try one," she says, offering a berry to her mother. The woman takes it tentatively, analyzing it far more thoroughly than did her child.

Her head jerks up, alarmed. "Who said that?" she asks, concerned.

"She heard me!" the Allmother whispers, voice breaking in my mind.

"The Allmother speaks to you," I say, smiling from ear to ear.

"Are these… Are they really safe?"

I nod to her daughter, feasting upon berry after berry. Each time she pulls one free, another springs up to take its place.

"They're better than safe," I tell her. "Rehlberries are my favorite."

She hesitates but eventually eats it. A smile washes over her face, and the Allmother brightens in my mind. Her eyes crinkle with a smile, filling with tears.

"They hear me," she croons. "They feel me."

She reaches further into the town, sending plants spiraling toward seed. They spread throughout the village, and her energy pulses through every leaf, every branch, every flower. Each fruit glows with her power, and the villagers reach for them.

Only then do I see how thin they are. Their clothes hang from their light frames, baggy and limp.

But…

“Shouldn’t the farmers be healthier?” I whisper to Tyrvahn. “They can grow their own food.”

“They don’t make enough coin off it to eat much of it,” he admits with shame burning in his words.

The Allmother pulls trees up closer to their homes, and fresh fruits swell on their branches, ready for consumption. And a soldier drops his sword to reach for one.

Vines reach for the weapon, tangling over the blade.

Sitting in the opening of my tent, I watch the people of Railen celebrate. They sing and dance, delighting in the Allmother's warmth. A few drink. Many talk.

Several thank me, stopping by my tent on their rounds through our camp. I smile at them, assuring them that it's merely the right thing to do, that I stand to gain as much from this as they do.

Aia seethes in my veins. He itches to move my hand to my dagger or send me through the village tempting hearts and wrecking homes. He aches for chaos, for power.

Yet, his vicious heart and his greedy thoughts serve only to remind me just how much I stand to lose. The Allmother keeps him weak, shriveled in a corner of my mind. She spares me his wrath and the pain of standing against him.

But she can't spare me the pain of my broken heart.

As my eyes scan the crowd in the middle of Railen, I search for one face. It doesn't take long to find her.

Holding a lute, Kivala plays along with the people of the village, smiling wide. She takes a break, but only to chug the mug of ale they offer her. Veliana and Tyrvahn dance to her music, their steps quick and lively, eyes sparkling brighter than the stars.

Despite everything, despite all their recent losses, they've all found happiness here, if only for tonight. Yet, here I sit, festering in my own unworthiness and weakness.

My eyes drift once more to Kivala, to the smile on her face and the strands of hair hanging loose from her braid. A pang of grief strikes my heart, tugging at the corners of my lips.

How many hearts have I torn apart?

How many times have I fallen to Aia's control?

"You're far too hard on yourself, Darling Rebel," the Allmother whispers to me. Her warmth flows through me, thawing my frigid heart. "Aia is not weak. You underestimate him, just as you underestimate yourself."

She warms the skin of my cheek, as if she reached out to cup my face. "Give yourself a break."

I can't...

I hurt them. Kivala will never forgive me.

And she shouldn't.

"She is more reasonable than all that, Dear Child. She hurts, just as you do. She fears another loss," the Allmother says.

I stare down at my knees, drawn up to my chest. Picking at my nails, I ask, "Is there anything I can do to show her..." I choke back a sob. Unable to say the words, I let my mind continue.

How can I show her I didn't want *to kill Veliana?*

The Allmother draws closer, filling my heart with her warmth. In my mind, I see her soft smile, her luminous green eyes. "You may have to show her Aia's power," she finally says.

I recoil from her words, knowing I'll have to expose myself to his cold heart to do so.

What might he make me do?

"As long as you stay close to me, he won't be able to make you do anything. You'll feel him. You'll hear him. But so long as you're close, he won't be able to force your hand."

But… I can't do it. I can't force her to feel him, to endure his violence.

"I wish you didn't have to, Darling Rebel," the Allmother sighs. "But she fights an enemy she doesn't know. Veliana felt the chill of him on the coast, but her lineage protected her from feeling more than that. Tyrvahn has felt his presence since birth, though he only recently saw it for what it was."

In my mind, I watch the Allmother shake her head, luscious red hair sliding gracefully over her bare breasts. "Kivala will follow you and the Rebels into the castle after Tumai, and she cannot go into this fight unprepared," she says. "But if you show her, she'll understand."

I nod, knowing the Allmother speaks the truth. Yet, my heart runs cold at the thought of willingly seeking Aia, at the thought of being the one to chill Kivala's heart with his presence.

Another stone around my neck.

I swallow back my fears. This is what the Allmother needs from me, so this I will do.

"Just don't stray too far from me, Darling Rebel."

I lift my gaze to Kivala once more.

A woman from the village approaches her, hips swaying as she carries over yet another mug of ale. Deeply tanned skin peeks out from her neckline, and locks of ink-black hair tumble down between her breasts. She stands just a little closer to Kivala than I like. After Kivala takes the mug, the villager reaches for her, smoothing back a lock of light brown hair.

My palms sweat, and heat rises within me. Aia surges forth to twist the knife, stoking my jealousy to a raging inferno. But I clench my fists, willing him back into his little corner.

Kivala's eyes dart upward, landing on me, and my breath catches. But anger draws her brows together, and the woman before her easily pulls her attention away. My poor heart shrivels in my chest as Kivala smiles at the villager, reaching out to touch her arm.

Footsteps approach, and I quickly wipe away an errant tear. Flahren sits beside me, face split open with a smile. He sits close enough for his bushy hair to tickle my ear, and for a moment, I find myself thankful for the shield it offers. I compose my face into something reminiscent of a smile before daring to meet his gaze.

"You don't have to pretend, you know," he says.

"What do you mean?"

"You know *exactly* what I mean," he says, tipping his head and eyeing me without patience. "I mean *her*. I don't know what happened, but you don't have to act like it doesn't hurt. Not with me."

And I break. Sobbing, I curl into myself, face falling onto my knees.

"Come, now," Flahren says, pulling me against him.

I lean my head on his shoulder, ever careful of my antlers. Tears blur my vision, but they quickly fall away, letting me see her.

She smiles at the villager, but her eyes find me, again. Her jaw drops as she surveys Flahren, apparently misreading his comforting embrace as something more. A scowl darkens her face, and she excuses herself from the tiny woman before her. Chugging the rest of her ale as she walks, Kivala slams the mug on a table and storms off to her tent.

Sickly waves of relief wash over me as my jealousy abates. Flahren tightens his hold on me. He nods, shaking me with the motion. “Maybe there’s still hope,” he whispers.

Maybe…

I just have to darken her heart.

Cowering at the thought of hurting her yet again, I vow to let her sleep, tonight.

I can break her again, tomorrow.

We ride through the fields, and the Allmother sees the wreckage Aia made of our realm. She weeps over the pain he filled these people with, over the barren land.

But with every step we take, she reaches just a little farther, heals the land just a little more, warms the hearts of just a few more people.

Yet, my throat constricts.

The Allmother's power warms my veins and buzzes on the air around me, more tangible than ever. But only through sacrifice. Back at the border, my parents yet stand, forever linked with Shevari and Fluros. With so much of the Allmother pouring through them, the lines between our realm and the Allmother's realm blur.

When we return, *if* we return, I'll find their energies gone, pulled into the Allmother's realm at the moment of connection. Their bodies, turned to crystal, will remain.

A single tear slips free of my control, but I don't wipe it away for fear of drawing attention to it. We have more pressing matters to concern ourselves with. But our slow progress, necessary for the moment to allow the wolves and bears some rest, lets my mind wander all too much.

Before us, another sapling bursts free of the dirt, perfectly placed by the Allmother's hand. Not a single one of us must change course to avoid its growth.

They would've loved to see this.

My heart twists, and another tear falls.

"They do see it, Darling Daughter," the Allmother whispers within my mind. Her voice is clearer than I've ever heard it, sweet and delicate. "They watch my Rising, even now."

A lump forms in my throat, and tears prick at the corners of my eyes. I nod once, knowing this is right.

***

Another small farming village welcomes her, soldiers and all, and my heart glows. Songs ring out from the village as we ride away from them after lunch. A smile tugs at my lips. Taking a deep breath, I rejoice in the scent of fresh Sarflowers, sweet as honey. Vaguely, I wonder if the villagers we leave behind have ever used their petals for tea.

Tyrvahn plants a kiss on the top of my head, and warmth floods through me. Tala picks up speed, rising to a trot, and I lean forward, gripping the straps of her harness. Tyrvahn clutches my waist, arms wrapped tight around me.

Soor carries Kivala and Garle forward, peeking into my periphery as she plays with Tala. They run faster, teasing each other with sudden bursts of speed. The Allmother keeps pace, pulling trees and bushes and vines from the earth with ease. The air around us crackles with her power. The cacophony of an entire forest rising from the ground at once surrounds us.

Soor pulls ahead, and I catch a glimpse of Kivala and Garle on her back. Kivala bows over Soor's neck, as she should so as not to gouge Garle's eyes out.

Just days ago, the two were inseparable, but now, something holds them apart. Garle clenches the harness on Soor's back, reaching over Kivala's legs to do so rather than clinging to Kivala. She sits, rigid and guarded.

Whatever happened between them needs to be sorted.

She can't ride like that the whole way to Ivlan. She needs to hold onto Kivala or switch to another bear. She's going to strain something or fall off.

Tala surges forward, overtaking Soor and stealing the Fahn Rebel from my sight as we pass them. A sigh puffs out my chest. I decided not to intervene a few days ago, but I can't have her falling off a bear and getting trampled because they had a fight.

I'll talk to them tonight.

The Allmother curls the forest out around a field, and we set up camp beneath a window of open sky. Trees wrap around us, filling our hearts with the Allmother's warmth. I stake out my tent quickly, then my eyes seek Kivala.

The tent Tyrvahn slept in before being Sealed to Veliana lies at her feet, and she takes her time assembling it. I tap my toes impatiently, waiting for her to finish. Nervously, I nibble at dried venison, sitting in the mouth of my tent.

Finally, she finishes, and I rush up to her before I lose my nerve. My heart beats unevenly, but my feet are steady, carrying me onward.

"Kivala?" I say, voice small and fragile.

She stills, and her shoulders rise in a slow breath before she turns. She doesn't speak, only arches a brow, daring me to say something, anything.

"Will you…" I clear my throat, picking at my nails, then try again. "Will you come with me? Please. I need to talk to you, and… The Allmother said I should."

Tipping her head back, she stares up at the sky and pulls in another long breath. Her lips purse, and she shakes her head, braid whipping back and forth against her shoulders.

My palms sweat, and I wipe them on my trousers. Dread fills me, and Aia whispers savagely in my head.

"Even at the Allmother's bidding, she won't listen to you. She's going to walk away from you and never look back. Because she knows what you are." He laughs at me and calls me a savage.

His voice is faint and distant, flickering through the trees. Yet, I flinch, and suddenly, I'm thankful Kivala won't meet my gaze. It means she didn't see me wince.

But at long last, her gaze finds mine. Her once-luscious blue eyes are hard, staring into my soul. "Fine," she says. "But only because the Allmother told me to."

She asked? She didn't believe me?

A lance of pain shoots through me, but I understand.

Why would she trust me to tell her the truth? After what I almost did...

But I have my chance to prove to her that I didn't want to, and I can't let that slip away. I grab Kivala's hand. I don't have time to wait around for her to follow at her own pace. I can only hope she sees what I mean quickly. I shudder to think what Aia may inflict upon me outside the forest.

"You'll understand, soon," I whisper, over and over, hoping it's true.

She has to understand.

I don't want to hurt Veliana. I never wanted to.

I didn't want to hurt Kivala, either, but I've already done that.

As if I needed reminding, she pulls her hand from mine as soon as we leave the trees behind. A sharp stab of pain racks my body at the loss of contact because I know how angry she is.

And I can't fault her for it.

Yet, she follows, willing to hear me out. Despite the Allmother having to convince her to go with me, my heart tries to tell me she wants to believe I'm not so vicious.

But my hope dries up quickly.

As we move further and further beyond the Allmother's reach, Aia awakens within my heart. He slithers through me, twisting like a corkscrew as he winds his way through my veins.

I hear his sinister laugh, and I flinch.

Cold settles into my heart, then spreads out, following in his wake. It shakes the sweet, lingering warmth of the Allmother from my bones, wrings me dry of it.

He laughs again, cruel and mocking, and I grit my teeth. My feet trod a steady path, but I keep my head down. Kivala keeps pace beside me, and I feel her gaze on my face. Her eyes bore holes in my flesh, but I can't meet her gaze. I can't look at her, can't bear her fury.

Desperate for a distraction from the monster inside me, I ask, "Have you ever felt Aia?" My voice is weak, a hollow mockery of its usual cadence.

"No," Kivala spits. "I ran *into* the forest after the absorption. Not *away* from it."

Her words hit me like a landslide, nearly taking my feet out from under me.

But I couldn't run deeper into the Sailon... Tumai chased my parents and me. He forced us out.

Aia flashes the scene before my eyes, shows me the dark trees blurring past as we ran from Tumai, shows me the fire chasing after us. He shows me the root I didn't see that night, the one that tripped me. He shows me Tumai, dark hair falling free of its oils to shutter his eyes as he stood over me with his blade raised and shining in the flickering fire light.

I couldn't fight Tumai, then. How could I fight him, now?

He took everything from me once. Why wouldn't he do it, again?

"Kivala knows how weak you are," Aia says within my mind. His voice rumbles through me, shaking my bones as he grows stronger. "She's seen just how broken you are. She'll never want you, now. Why would she?"

My chest rises and falls quickly, and tears prick at the corners of my eyes as he tells me everything I've feared for so long.

I'll be alone... Again.

"Of course, you will," he answers. "Because you were stupid enough to tell her just how much of a savage you really are."

But I'm not. You're the savage. You made me do all of that.

I try to fight him, arguing with a God, but it's no use. He slithers into my heart once more, having made his rounds through my veins, chasing the Allmother's warmth from every fiber of my being.

I didn't want to hurt Veliana. I didn't want to kill the loggers.

Just the soldiers.

Just Tumai.

"Quit lying to yourself. You're a savage, and you know it. You enjoyed hurting them." He laughs, and I tremble as he throws their broken bodies into my mind, again.

I've seen them so often since that night that I know exactly how they fell, know the expressions on their faces as they breathed their last breaths. I know their eyes, know the way their hair splayed out in the grass beneath them.

I know the shadows that flickered over their lifeless bodies, tricking my eyes and making me think it took longer for them to die than it did.

Darkness clouds my heart, and only one path emerges before me. A single light shines in the distance. I grasp my wrist, sparing it a surreptitious glance. Just long enough to find a vein. I dig my nail in, squeezing as hard as I can.

And Aia helps.

He surges through my veins, strengthening my nail and tensing my hand until my nail breaks skin.

"Does Kivala know you could have saved Tyrvahn's parents? Had you only had the nerve to say something, to be honest for once in your pitiful life?" he whispers.

And we dig my nail deeper.

Kivala latches onto my wrist, jerking me around to face her. My nail comes away from my wrist, and a droplet of blood hangs on my broken skin.

So close…

But rage contorts her features, curling her lips into a snarl. I reel from the sight of her fury, and my shattered heart beats a little faster.

Two more drops of blood trickle from my wrist, and she squeezes my unopened wrist harder.

Another path out of the darkness opens before me, and though I never wanted to die by her hand, I nod, accepting my fate.

Aia laughs within me, knowing she's felt his will, now.

Knowing she'll be my end.

Garle tugs at my hand, insisting that I'll understand soon enough. But I don't want her to touch me. As soon as I step out of the forest, I pull my hand from hers. She winces as if I've slapped her, but carries on, leading me into the open field.

As we move away from the Sailon, my mouth runs dry. The Allmother's presence fades with each step until I can no longer see her in my mind, no matter how hard I try. Her warmth vanishes from my veins, quickly replaced by a deep, unsettling chill. I shiver with it, staring hard at Garle.

Why would she want to subject me to this?

"Have you ever felt Aia?" Garle asks, meekly.

But anger surges through me.

"No," I say. Acid drips from the word. "I ran *into* the forest after the absorption. Not *away* from it."

I realize my words after they fall from my lips and wonder only then if I blame her for the little influence Aia supposedly has over her.

She could have run into the Sailon. Just like she could've refused to consider killing Veliana.

Aia is weak. He can't actually control her. Even the Allmother can't do that.

"I *don't* do that," the Allmother corrects me, voice faint and barely intelligible.

Still, I glare at Garle, but she won't meet my gaze. Her eyes glue themselves to the ground, and her shoulders slump forward. She crosses one arm in front of herself, grabbing her wrist. She digs a nail in desperately, pushing far too hard. Her knuckles go white with the effort.

Stepping forward quickly, I wrench her hand off her wrist, only to find a drop of blood hanging from the indentation she's made in her other arm.

Something dark seethes in my belly, twisting and expanding. It snakes through me, and a cold voice whispers in my mind, "Kill her. You hate her, don't you?"

My grip tightens on her arm of its own accord as rage floods my body, far stronger than any I've felt before. It boils my veins, bares my teeth. My lungs work faster, huffing angrily.

"You saw her wrist. She was going to kill herself. But someone like her, a *murderer* like her, doesn't deserve such a quick death," the voice hisses within me, savoring the violence it speaks. "She would have killed Veliana without a second thought."

Garle stares at me with a mixture of horror and acceptance twisting her features.

A pang of shock rattles me, and I release her wrist. I stare down at my hand, disgusted with the cruelty writhing within my gut.

Aia is far stronger than I thought.

Fear washes over me in cold waves. Swallowing, I lace my fingers into hers and run, pulling her toward the Sailon. "We need to get out of here."

Before Aia pushes us into some other horrific act.

The drop of blood on her wrist flashes through my mind, and I know it was him. He pushed her to do that, just like he pushed me to grab her wrist, to squeeze so tight.

Did I hurt her?

My insides clench, and I hear him laughing at me. He calls me weak, tells me that I'm leading a murderer back to my people, to my best friend.

So, I run faster, pushing myself harder. My feet pound the earth, and my blood rushes in my ears, drowning out the sound of my ragged breathing. Garle sprints at my side, every bit as desperate to feel the Allmother's warmth as I am.

Aia's laughter grows faint as we run, fading into the distance. I feel the Allmother reaching for me, begging me to return to her embrace. Her warmth seeps out of the forest, so close. Her voice whispers to me, indecipherable, but I hear her.

Another burst of speed, and I see her smiling in my mind, feel a tinge of warmth in my heart. Garle pushes faster, passing me, dragging me by the hand, and I strain to keep up with her.

"Darling Children," the Allmother whispers as we burst through the undergrowth. Her warmth floods my body, and the light of her realm slowly chases Aia from my heart.

But I keep running.

Panic drives me further and further into the forest, one step after another. Vibrant shades of green pass by in a blur. Sunlight, then shadow, then sunlight, then shadow… I run from one dappled patch of grass to another, desperate to be away from Aia.

I run until the Allmother forces the last of him from my heart, and Garle slows, tugging at my hand. Spinning to face her,

I gasp. My ragged breathing burns my lungs, and my side aches from the sudden burst of exertion. Pulling Garle to me, I throw my arms around her with abandon, leaning my forehead against hers.

That was just one moment, just one step into the open.

She felt that for fourteen renewals?

The Allmother answers me, though I hadn't expected her to. "It was worse today than usual. He knows how close we are to purging him. He's desperate."

But it's been close to that before? He's that strong?

"He is a God. I never said he was weak, Darling Child. He is merely weak in my presence."

Garle wraps her arms around my waist, burying her head in my shoulder and crying openly. Her shoulders shake with rough breaths and terrible sobs.

I close my eyes, trying desperately to control my breathing. I slide my hand around to Garle's neck and tip her head back to gaze into her eyes.

"I'm sorry," I whisper.

She shakes her head and mumbles, "You didn't know."

"That doesn't matter," I say.

I press my lips to hers, and a fresh wave of tears falls down her cheeks. It soaks our kiss, coating it in salt, and pulls tears from my eyes.

"You didn't know," she repeats, whispering against my lips.

"But I should've believed you."

I close my eyes, ashamed of myself. In my mind, I watch her unravel before me as she confessed what she might have done, what she might have been *forced* to do.

Again, I see her trembling hands and hear her words, choked by sobs.

And I knew she'd felt Aia's touch. I knew.

But I underestimated a God...

How arrogant can I be? How stupid *can I be? To think a God incapable of such things. I even underestimated the Allmother, mistaking her restraint for the inability to control us.*

A tear slides down my cheek, and I whisper, "I should've believed you."

Because I've seen her heart. She's bared herself to me, so many times. And now, it's my turn.

I kiss her lips, hard and desperate. Her hands tangle in my hair, pulling me closer. My heart stutters at her touch, and the Allmother's warmth floods me. And for a moment, I forget the monstrous God we must purge and the savage man we must fight.

Clutching Garle's hips, I press myself against her, deepening our kiss. Sliding my hands around, I grasp her buttocks, squeezing lightly. She moans against my lips, and heat pools within me.

Her arms wrap around me. I kiss her lips, her neck, her collarbone. Lightly, I nip at the sensitive flesh where her neck meets her shoulder, and she tips her head back.

I come up for another kiss, and our mouths move together. Molten rock shifts within me, burning me up, and I push her back against a tree. She gasps and meets my gaze, breathing hard. Her lids hang heavy over smoldering dark eyes.

But I want to be closer.

I claim her mouth once more and slide my hand beneath her shirt, slowly caressing the soft skin of her waist. She slides her hand down my back, grasping my buttock.

Slowly, my hand moves up to cup her full breast, and she squirms against me. I bite her neck, aching for her.

But this is for her.

Tearing her shirt over her head, catching it on her small antlers, I let my mouth taste her exposed flesh, teasing her nipple with my tongue. She whispers my name, voice breaking over the sound.

Her long black hair drapes over her shoulders, tumbling around her breasts and teasing my nose with a sweet floral scent.

I drop a gentle kiss between her breasts, then tease the other with my tongue. Garle's hand wraps in my hair, desperate for more, and I oblige. I unfasten her pants, and slide them down, caressing her powerful thighs and letting my fingers drift softly over the backs of her knees.

My lips find her bare stomach, dropping soft kisses all the way down. Kneeling before her, I kiss her thighs, teasing her. She arches her back, antlers scraping the bark of the tree as she tips her head back.

"Please," she whispers, and I nearly fall apart.

Pulling her down to her knees, I kiss her soft, full lips. My hand slides down between her legs. I move one finger over her, teasing, stoking the fire. Her breath comes in shallow gasps.

But so does mine.

Slowly, I dip my fingers inside her, aching at the warmth of her, and she cries out for more. She hangs onto me, thighs shaking as I move my fingers within her. My thumb moves in slow circles, pushing her closer and closer to release.

Her hand finds my breast, teasing sensitive flesh through the fabric of my shirt, and I gasp. She pulls me in for another kiss, and I work her faster, desperate to give her the release she needs. And finally, her legs tremble as she shatters, hanging onto me for support.

My name rings out from her lips, broken and stuttered, and I move faster, bringing her to yet another peak.

And slowly, she slides her hand down my stomach and into my pants, touching me tentatively. Her fingers move at an agonizingly slow pace. My entire body tenses, begging her for release.

And it doesn't take her long to bring me crashing down alongside her.

We collapse to the ground, falling into each other's arms.

A single tear breaks free of my control, for I know she's forgiven me. She never would have touched me, otherwise.

Placing a gentle hand on her face, I kiss her, breathing hard. I marvel at her, gazing at long lashes fanned out over dark grey freckles.

She wraps an arm around my waist, mumbling, "You're not naked enough…"

"Well, that's easy to fix," I whisper, sitting up. I rip my shirt off, barely taking the time to unbutton it, and unfasten my trousers quickly. Laying back down, I lift my hips and slide them down. I kick them away and roll back to face her. "Better?"

She kisses me softly, trailing her fingertips up my bare thigh. "Much better."

I shudder at her touch, smiling all the while. Gazing into her eyes, I nod. Pulling her against me, I tuck her head beneath my chin, staring at the sharp points of her antlers.

My heart stops, waiting.

But she doesn't pull away, and her antlers never tip forward.

Soft lips find the hollow at the base of my neck, and she slips her arm around my waist.

I pull in a deep breath, relieved and full of warmth.

Chapter 42

Tyrvahn

Veliana leans against me, staring up at the stars. The nearly-full moon shines overhead with only a portion of it missing from our sight. With our stilled progress, the Allmother's storm has dissipated, letting us enjoy the twinkling of the night.

Gentle giggling wafts toward us on a familiar voice, and I turn to find Kivala tugging Garle along into camp. I smile, nudging Veliana to draw her notice.

She follows my gaze just in time to watch the two collide. Their lips melt together hungrily, and Garle nudges Kivala toward her tent, right next to ours.

Veliana breathes a sigh of relief. "That saves me an uncomfortable conversation," she says, chuckling.

I laugh. "Could the Allmother deafen us to the noise they're about to make?"

Veliana giggles then turns to me with mischief in her eyes. "We could make our own noise and drown them out."

Swallowing hard, I nod. "I like your plan much better."

She giggles, again, and a perfect blush creeps over her skin. Crawling past me into the tent, she casts a glance back over her shoulder. "Are you coming?" she asks, expectantly.

I've never been so eager to crawl into a tent before.

***

I glance around, marveling at the change the Allmother has made in Jun. Every village we've left behind us so far has gracefully accepted her love, relishing the freedom and abundance she offers them. My heart glows with warmth at the mere memory of their smiles.

In just a few short suns, we've traveled more than half the distance to Ivlan. I lean forward, reaching over Veliana's thigh to pet Tala's neck appreciatively. This journey would have been grueling without her, without the other wolves and the bears.

And it would have taken far too long.

We would have reached Ivlan days after Paikon would have been expected back, and an army would have awaited us. But the Allmother provided a way to reach them while maintaining the element of surprise.

How could I not have known about her before?

How could we have turned from her all those years ago?

My mind boggles at the thought of abandoning the only God that ever truly cared for us. And yet, she forgives. She welcomes us back with open arms, with branches and bushes heavily laden with sustenance.

A deep breath lifts my chest as I marvel at her divinity, and a smile lifts the corners of my lips. I plant a delicate kiss on the back of Veliana's head.

She reaches back, caressing my thigh with a gentle hand, then whispers, "Hold on."

Leaning forward, she grips Tala's harness. I take the hint, leaning over her and reaching under her arms to grasp the harness, as well. My head rests at the base of her neck. Her backside presses against me, sending a delicate trill of pleasure through me.

But Tala gathers speed beneath us, ready for the first sprint of the day. On all sides, the other wolves and bears lope alongside us.

And the Allmother reaches farther into Jun, transforming the landscape from barren and sallow to lush and vibrant. The land I once knew morphs before my eyes as the Sailon Forest spreads further, shaking the earth. The air rumbles with the rapid growth and the Allmother's power.

A smile lifts my lips, sparkling in my eyes.

***

Vrali waits in the distance, homes and market stalls sprawling over the landscape as the town stares at us. The Light Watchers call seventh sky, and the Allmother's power buzzes, aching to move further. But roughly one hundred soldiers stand in our way, assembled in the open field before us.

I knew it would come to a fight, at some point. It had to.

But some small part of me held out hope that the people of Jun, even the soldiers, would come around once purged of Aia's influence. And thus far, my hopes were fulfilled.

But the people staring back from the field snarl within their helmets. The buckles fastening them around their antlers shine in the light of the sun, making me wish for a helmet of my own. If it comes to hand to hand combat, I can only hope the blessed bone armor I wear holds up.

The Allmother sends a wave of trees bursting from the ground, wrapping around us and the soldiers. They flinch, but quickly regain their composure, not realizing the advantage she's just given us.

A single man steps forward from the front line, shouting, "Turn back, now. We have no need of savages, here."

The Allmother's anger surges through me, and I see them flinch before it.

Does she call to them as she called to the villagers before?

"Yes, Darling Prince," the Allmother whispers to me. Then, as if through gritted teeth, she spits, "But they turn their ears from my voice."

Fury boils in my veins, and I don't know how much is mine and how much is the Allmother's. My hands clench into tight fists upon my knees.

And then I remember. This is where Tumai was born, where he grew up. Paikon met his wife here. Of course, they have allies here. Of course, they turn the Allmother away, fear and loyalty holding them against her.

If she moves in, they stand to lose their nobility, their riches. All the things they've built on the backs of others will crumble.

Veliana lifts one arm, and a platform of rock rises beside Tala. The great wolf doesn't flinch, trusting her and the Allmother implicitly. But the soldiers startle.

Sliding from Tala's back, Veliana reaches a hand to me, yet her eyes never leave the soldiers. I take her hand, sliding onto the platform. Her skin glows with the Allmother's power, and I recall wondering when I first met her if she was the Allmother. Now, I can't help but wonder if these soldiers think so, too.

What is your plan, dearest?

Sealed to me by the Allmother, she hears my question and responds, "They get one more chance." Her lips never move, yet I hear her answer clearly in my head.

I barely keep from flinching, still adjusting to this new path for conversation.

Lifting my hand, I raise a walkway from the earth. As we move to its end, I marvel at my progress in controlling the power the Allmother affords me. The archers opposing us raise their bows at our approach. I smile but wait.

"We are the High Seal of Kin," Veliana says aloud. Her voice carries down to the soldiers, filling the little meadow the Allmother created for us. "Tyrvahn and I bring you the Allmother."

Gesturing to the earth before us, I call out, "For those who accept her and shun Aia, we bring gifts of her abundance."

Right on cue, berry bushes and fruit-bearing trees spring from the ground at the base of our walkway.

Dropping my voice lower, knowing they'll hear me, I say, "For those who turn from her, for those who seek to oppress others to lift themselves, we bring wrath."

I watch them flinch as her anger burns their veins.

"The choice is yours," I say. "Aia has worked misery upon this land. He has twisted the hearts of Jun. But we will see him gone, soon."

Driving the point home, Veliana says, “Paikon is dead. Tumai will soon follow him, with Aia close behind. Choose wisely.”

Kivala and Garle dismount from Soor’s back, standing on the rocky plinth behind us. Below us, the soldiers glance nervously amongst themselves. A few swords lower, wavering on the edge of surrender.

The Allmother hangs in my mind, waiting for their decision as moments drag out into eternity. My heart pounds, unsteady beneath the tension.

But the Allmother’s face twists in my mind, eyes filling with sorrow and disappointment even as she bares her teeth in a snarl.

I know the choice they’ve made before they lift their swords to charge.

The archers loose their arrows, sending a hail of death toward us. But I wave a hand through the air, and every arrow turns to a sapling. Branches sprout from the wooden shafts, and leaves unfurl.

And the saplings grow larger, heavier.

They fall from the sky long before they reach us, and a thicket of nearly mature trees falls upon the soldiers.

Those few who escape charge at us, but Tala and Soor burst forward. The massive animals clamp their jaws around two and three soldiers at a time. They chomp down, driving teeth and shards of broken metal armor into flesh. Screams erupt into the air.

And in a few heartbeats, the soldiers lie broken upon the earth.

The Allmother pulls blankets of moss over their bodies, tucking them in to nourish the earth. She wraps the roots of the arrow trees into the ground, pulling them slowly upright.

And where once stood a field of enemies twisted by Aia's influence, laboring beneath the rule of Tumai and Paikon, the Sailon Forest now sways in the breeze.

The noises of Vrali waft into the tent, wrapping themselves around me. With Tumai's forces out of the way and the Allmother's warmth running through their veins and sprouting edible plants all around, the townspeople welcomed us.

Now, they wake to the Allmother's bounty. Joy fills their words as they mill about, trying to accept that it wasn't a dream.

And even though their sweet praise and bewilderment warm my heart, here in my tent, I shudder beneath the weight of my burdens.

Garle sits behind me, legs spread around me. I draw my knees up, bracing my arms atop them. She trails a comb through my hair, pulling the knots loose. When she finishes, I turn my head to make her work easier.

She ties most of my hair off to the side, holding it out of her way. But on the left, my head will hold two braids. One for my mother. One for my father.

Her hands go to work. Starting the first braid just above my temple, she runs it along the side of my head, just below my antler. Her fingers tickle my scalp, brushing it delicately.

But my mind wanders.

Still reeling from everything that's happened, I struggle to process their loss and the true scale of our enemy. Tumai and his army are formidable enough, but they're mortals. Flesh and blood, I understand how to kill them.

But Aia...

He's a different beast altogether. I've never felt myself bend so completely to the will of another before. For the first time in many renewals, fear wraps itself around me, pulling me into icy waters.

Garle ties a small ribbon around the braid just behind my ear, then starts on the second one. Meanwhile, the Allmother reaches for me. She sees the black depths I sink toward and grasps my hand. Her warmth radiates into me, but my doubts remain.

After all, if I was so blind as to miss the severity of our situation, what else have I missed?

My mind casts about, looking for answers and drumming up only the worst possible ones. A million times over, I watch my friends die from blows I could have prevented. I see Veliana, the only family I have left, twist beneath Aia's influence, driving a blade into Tyrvahn's heart. I see Garle wither beneath Aia's cold words, as she nearly did in the field.

In my darkest imaginings, I see Tumai somehow manage to purge the Allmother. I shudder, and tears fall over my cheeks.

How long has death hung over me?

How long have I refused to look at it simply because I didn't have to?

I don't have to search my heart long to know. Since losing my brothers in the Absorption, I've thought of death as little as possible. I thought my serene life in the Sailon immune to such violence.

But this is war, and war, by its very nature, demands death and sacrifice.

Visions of my parents' bodies, glowing as the connection took them, flash before my eyes. They reach for the High Seal with linked hands, smiling as the warm light of the Allmother's realm consumed them.

Another pit opens within me, trying so hard to swallow me up. My chest falls in on itself, and a lump forms in my throat. Slamming my eyes shut, I grit my teeth, trying to force the image from my mind. But to no avail. Their deaths are part of me now, just as my brothers' deaths became part of me.

"They are at peace, Darling Child," the Allmother says softly. Her voice whispers through me, a warm caress easing the cold hands of anguish from around my heart. "They smile upon you, even now."

Choking back a sob, I let her words sink in. And though the agony of facing the rest of my life without them is still there, gnawing at my insides, the knowledge of their happiness eases my suffering, just a little.

Garle ties a ribbon around the second braid behind my ear, then frees the rest of my light brown hair from its tie. The strands beyond the end of the braids weave into the rest of my hair as their deaths will weave into the rest of my life.

It doesn't feel like it's been long enough, doesn't feel like I've had time to mourn them. And I haven't. But my life is moving faster with every rising sun, and so many changes lie ahead.

Swallowing back a lump in my throat, I take a deep breath and wipe my tears away. I nod, accepting the solitary path that waits before me.

"You misunderstand your braids, my Darling." I still at the Allmother's words, wondering what else I've been wrong about.

But she shows herself to me, and her eyes soften. Her warmth centers on my cheek in a tender caress. "Accepting your braids does not mean you have to move on or forget your loss. It merely means that you acknowledge the impact it will have on you, while also accepting that it should not stop you from moving forward when you are ready."

Breathing deeply, I struggle to contain a fresh burst of sobs. Garle moves one hand in comforting circles on my back.

As I move to stand, Garle sniffles quietly. I turn to face her, only to find a tear track glistening on her velvet skin. Her blue eyes swim with them, full to the brim.

My heart breaks open, and tears scramble over my cheeks as I remember that I'm not alone in my pain. I settle back down, and pat the ground before me.

"Come," I say. "Switch with me. It's about time you got your braids."

***

As we pack up camp and prepare for the day's travel, my mind drifts over the battles to come. Very little was required of me in battle last night, but I know I can't stand aside and let Veliana and Tyrvahn do everything.

Not when we reach Ivlan.

Our roles have already been assigned, and I know I'll have to act. I'll have to fight.

The Absorption flashes through my mind, as vivid as it was that night.

Bathed in the light of too many fires, I watch my brothers push a soldier away from my parents and me, screaming all the while for us to run. I watch them die at the hands of another Jun soldier.

I remember the rage that filled me. And suddenly, I'm back there.

A deep need for justice courses through my blood as I charge the man who killed them. He stares at their bodies, wiping blood from his busted lip with the back of his wrist. His dagger hangs at his waist, and I take it, so easy. His blood pours over my hands as the blade plunges into his neck.

I let him fall, and my parents grab my arms, pulling me away. Tears pour from their eyes, and we run to the river. In our haste, I trip over roots I know I never would have stumbled over otherwise.

Cold water rushes over my skin as we plunge into the river, swimming across. Running for our shadows, we leave the fires to consume my brothers.

Blinking rapidly, I call myself back to the present. My hands shake freely, and tears fall for my brothers, for my parents.

But it's time to face my enemy.

And this time, I won't run.

***

The sun shines brightly overhead, beating down upon us as we ride at the forefront of the Allmother's reclamation. Wind batters my face with strands of Garle's hair as Soor propels us forward.

I lift my head above the whips of her hair, gazing into the distance. Ivlan looms on the horizon, cowering behind thick walls.

Leaning my head forward, I drop a kiss between Garle's shoulder blades. The Allmother whispers within my mind, telling me to prepare myself. Something in her tone makes me look forward again, just in time to see a flood of soldiers pour out through the walls of Ivlan. They crowd in front of the openings, waiting for us.

But… We'll never get in, now.

My heart drops, but Soor never flinches. Rather, she runs faster, pushing us closer and closer to the oncoming army. The bears follow suit, weaving through the dire wolves and pushing the Rebels ahead.

My heart hammers in my chest, and my blood drowns out all other sounds.

Behind us, the wolves slow, and Rangers draw their bows.

Soldiers flood through the walls, and I grit my teeth. This isn’t quite how we planned it, but this is war, after all. Plans change.

The Allmother urges the wolves to slow beneath us. They oblige, and her voice floats through my head.

“Dismount,” she says.

So, I do.

Veliana and I slide from Tala’s back before she stops moving, and she takes off again, sprinting headlong for the soldiers. Veliana watches, eyes tight with worry.

I squeeze her hand. Her lips purse, but she nods. We raise our hands before us, palms up, shaping the earth, forming a column beneath our feet. It lifts us up above the battle.

All around the base of our pedestal, Rangers ready their bows. Bears carry Rebels into battle, and wolves charge after them. The unearthly cacophony of so many massive, snarling animals stampeding across the field rattles the soldiers. Their swords tremble in their hands, and their gazes dart back and forth from one to another.

Pausing our ascension just above the tree line, Veliana and I spread our arms wide, then drop to our knees. The walls of Ivlan crumble, sending plumes of dust into the air. Chunks of stone fall outward, rolling into the ranks of soldiers. Their screams barely reach us. The Allmother spares the city, holding the rubble out and sparing civilians.

And all around, everywhere our eyes land, she spreads her roots. The landscape of an entire country shifts, becoming lush and fertile once more.

As Veliana and I rise to our feet, the soldiers charge toward the stampede, pushed by idiotic loyalty to a vicious king. The bears slow, discharging their cargo as the wolves catch up.

But Veliana and I raise our hands, palms up. The pedestal beneath our feet rises, carrying us up and up and up. The battle beneath us becomes small, and the Allmother reaches further, wrapping leafy tendrils around the very edges of the horizon.

My head spins as I look down, staring at a lethal fall. Something cold slithers through my veins, and I know Aia is here.

"It's such a long way down from here…" he sneers.

My stomach drops as I imagine the fall.

"Oh, yes… I hadn't even meant that." He chuckles in my mind, and I can almost see the mischievous arch of a dark eyebrow. "What will you do when your people find out you couldn't save them? Because I'm not going anywhere. You fool yourself if you think yourself strong enough to purge me."

My eyes flutter as his cold hands grip my heart.

"Do you think your people would forgive such a weak leader? Would they forgive a man who led them to war, *to slaughter*… for nothing?"

His voice drops to a sinister whisper as he says, "Could you forgive yourself?"

My palms sweat, and doubt clouds my mind.

"You could jump, spare yourself the pain of disappointing them."

Veliana turns from the ledge, putting her hands up.

She's waiting for me.

But Aia twists another blade into my heart.

"Could she forgive you for failing her? For failing them?"

Chapter 45

Garle

Behind us, the earth groans, shaking violently. Soor stumbles but quickly regains her footing. The soldiers before us aren't so lucky. Several trip. A few lose their footing altogether.

Dipping my head to keep from scraping Kivala's face, I turn to see what could have made such noise. My jaw drops as I take in the massive podium of stone, towering above the Sailon Forest. Tyrvahn and Veliana stand atop it, gesturing smoothly as it rises.

When it stops, I turn to face the foes ahead, just in time to watch the walls of Ivlan collapse before us, crumbling and exploding outward. Reflex jerks my head down to avoid debris, but the Allmother pours the stones upon the soldiers, thinning their ranks. Screams ring out, rising above the noise of the collapsing stone. The remnants of Tumai's army charges, closing the gap. But Soor slows, as do all the other bears.

"Dismount," the Allmother tells me, and I oblige. Kivala and I slip to the ground, landing just as the wolves catch up to us.

Behind us, another rumbling groan crashes into the air, shaking the ground beneath us, and I can only assume that Tyrvahn and Veliana rise higher on their stone platform. The soldiers still charge, but nervous glances pull their eyes from us to each other.

"Brace yourselves," the Allmother whispers.

For what?

I don't wait for her answer, though. Spreading my feet wide, I crouch, ready for whatever may come for us. My stomach ties itself into knots, waiting for mayhem, waiting for the soldiers to fall upon us. On all sides, wolves and bears lower themselves, bending as if to absorb a blow.

A deafening crack shatters the air, and my ears ring. All other sound fades in and out. Then, a shockwave hits us, pushing us forward. I take a step to keep from falling, as do the other Rebels.

Soldiers fall to their backs, defenseless.

And I use their moment of weakness to cast a glance over my shoulder.

With a gasp, I survey the stone columns spiraled around the pedestal. Twisted tight like vines, nothing of the platform inside is visible. A few reach outward, reaching into the air like tree branches.

Turning back around, I stare at the soldiers before me, clamoring to their feet.

Hushed whispers reverberate through them, and undertones of awe and fear play in their words. A few clamor to their feet, running for the safety of the city. But most who yet live stare openly. At us. At the massive animals standing at our sides.

At the Allmother Rising.

Kivala takes my hand, and we step forward. Soor shifts to stand behind us, staring down at them.

And their attention falls to us.

"We will fight, if necessary," I begin, hands trembling at my side. Queasy with so many eyes upon me, I try to swallow back a lump of fear. But it doesn't move. "Aia must be purged and Tumai must die today. Stand with them, and you will die, as well."

But this doesn't feel right.

Threatening and posturing… that's what Aia has always forced me to do, and I hate it.

I've always hated it.

I drop my gaze, clearing my throat as I reconsider my words. All around us, grass takes root in barren soil. Clover spreads, sprinkled with tiny white flowers. They crawl toward the soldiers, and saplings follow in their wake, rising slowly and unfurling their leaves.

Lifting my chin, I try, again.

"We bring you the Allmother, and she brings life. Can you feel her?"

I reach out to a ranner sapling nearby, watching it climb. It reaches my height, and bright orange flowers blossom on its branches. The soldiers watch in amazement as the flowers fall away, and dark blue fruits take their places.

Plucking one from the tree, I take a bite, reveling in its sweetness. Tossing it to the nearest soldier, I say, "She is warmth and light. She whispers to us, smiling and comforting us through hard times."

"Can you feel her chasing Aia and his cold heart from your veins? I lived with his will in Jun for 14 renewals, and he nearly crushed me. He twists mortals, tainting their hearts. But he is weak when the Allmother is near."

Civilians peek out through windows, glance out through cracked doors. They stare, openly curious. Children with dirty faces catch sight of the new foliage, and their faces light up. Giggling, they beg their parents to let them go play.

The soldier nearest me unbuckles his helmet, and it falls away with a clank. He takes a bite of the ranner I threw him and smiles as the juice drips down his chin.

Whispers float through the crowd before me, all still firmly planted on their backsides. The Allmother whispers delightedly in my mind, and excitement bubbles in her words.

"They hear me," she says. "Oh, Darling Children… I've waited so long for you to come home."

But a cacophony rattles through the city proper.

Nervous eyes turn to face the oncoming parade of steel and hooves. The soldiers rise to their feet, turning to face the ranks of cavalry approaching us. More armed men and women pour out through a gap in the shattered walls, and their horses charge.

Closing the distance quickly, they face Jun blades and armor, turned for the Allmother. The man with ranner juice drying on his chin raises his sword against an approaching officer, taking him by surprise.

And chaos erupts.

Turning toward Tyrvahn, I put my hands out. He hesitates, sweating beneath Aia's cruelty. And I feel him, too.

The god of greed, power, and violence berates me. He belittles my parents' sacrifice and our trek here. He calls the Allmother weak. He calls me weak, calls me a sorry excuse for a leader, echoing my fears. My heart sags beneath the weight of his words.

We need to do this quickly.

"Tyrvahn," I whisper.

Slowly, he turns to me with desperation in his eyes. With trembling hands, I say, "We have to move."

He nods, pressing his palms against mine. We shove our hands upward, and spikes of stone shoot out of the earth, spiraling around our pedestal with a deafening crash. In a mere heartbeat, they rise above us, twining together overhead and plunging us into darkness as the stone closes over us.

Lowering our hands, we close our eyes. We've had so little practice, but the Allmother guides us through the motions, helping us to shape her power. Hands out to our sides, palms up, we slowly pull Allflower vines from the earth. They twist and twine, climbing stone spirals.

Silence weighs upon us, thick and heavy.

Shouldn't there be some sort of noise outside?

"You would think so, wouldn't you?" Aia says, nonchalant and crystal clear. "I wonder what that means for your friends."

His implications aren't lost on me, but he throws bloody images of Kivala into my mind, for good measure. I shiver, trying to block it out, but he surrounds me with it, dropping my mind right into the middle of a field of bodies.

No... That's not real.

Gathering all my will, I resume my work, pulling more strands of Allflower vines from the ground. They twist up the stone columns, climbing ever higher. A few reach the top of our tower, sending little tendrils in through cracks between spiraled spikes. They hang around us, reaching for my hair.

Taking a deep breath, I whisper, "Now."

Opening our eyes, Tyrvahn and I sit, cross-legged and facing each other in the darkness. Our knees touch, and I take comfort from that small contact.

The cold stone beneath me leeches heat from my skin, just as Aia draws the warmth from my heart. But not for long.

"One, Two," Tyrvahn counts. "Three."

We snap our fingers, and the vines of Allflower ignite. They burn brighter than any plant should, filling our little chamber with light, and for a moment, I wish I could see the spectacle we've made from outside.

Tyrvahn's chest rises and falls quickly. Only then do I realize how fast my own breath rattles my chest. My fingers tremble on my knees, so I wrap my hands around Tyrvahn's, squeezing tight to settle myself.

The sweet smoke of the Allflowers eases the tension Aia builds within me, but he hovers, far too close. My mind fills with a thousand images of Kin falling, of the Sailon burning. And every scenario is my fault.

"You're too weak for such a burden, too weak to lead. You'll crack beneath the pressure," he says, so convincing.

Because isn't that exactly what I've feared my whole life? That I'm not good enough? That I'm not strong enough?

"But you are, Darling Daughter," the Allmother whispers. "And I am here. Just bring me closer to the mortal realm, so I can help you."

Nodding to Tyrvahn, I say, "Ready?"

He swallows. "Ready."

And though I'm not sure either of us is truly prepared, we begin. Our eyes close, and we focus on the Allmother's voice, her image. I imagine her realm, all amber light and blissful warmth. Our little room, this bespoke temple resembles it in those two most important aspects.

And as our minds reflect upon her realm, the lines between here and there blur.

Chanting in the language of our symbols, *her* language, we petition her, not for her power, but for her presence. Turning our hands over, we rest them palm upon our knees. My right hand lies atop his left, and his right lies atop my left.

We raise our voices, filling the air with our petition.

And the air grows warmer. Impossibly, the Allflower vines burn brighter.

But Aia squeezes my heart.

"That isn't the Allflower burning," he hisses. "That's the Sailon. Tumai held true to Paikon's threats. You sit here in this tower, above it all, but your people are suffering. Already, you fail them, and you've only been their leader for a few suns."

My heart withers from his words, but my lips never stop chanting. The Allmother reaches for me, so close. I feel Aia's icy touch moving through Tyrvahn, but his voice never falters, blending with mine.

Crystals of ice form on my fingers, locking my hands onto Tyrvahn's. The Allmother reaches into my veins, warming my hands, but the ice keeps coming, crawling up my wrists in agonizing branches.

"He would have done it," Aia whispers, malevolently. "He would have jumped. Had you not turned his face from that ledge exactly when you did, he would have left you behind. Because he never wanted you. Just like Materva."

An old wound rips open, and ancient insecurities seep through me. The ice climbs higher, moving over my forearms. Still, I chant, but my voice grows quieter, choked by tears.

"You worry so much over your body, but it's far deeper. Such a timid little thing like you could never truly hold a man's attention. But you already know that, don't you?"

I almost argue, almost acknowledge him.

But a surge of warmth from the Allmother stops me.

Don't give in. Don't argue with him.

Don't give him that power.

Breathing deeply, I scrunch my eyes to force the tears out. They freeze upon my cheeks in an instant, despite the Allflowers burning brightly all around us.

And the Allmother's language never stops flowing from my lips.

The Allmother's storm gathers over Ivlan, and dark clouds swirl over the city. Lightning flashes, silhouetting armored forms. Metal clashes with metal, and shouts of fury fill the air. Mounted soldiers slash unapologetically at foot soldiers, spilling blood without question.

The Allmother weeps in my mind, and I hear her begging them to accept her. But they refuse.

Soor, Tala, and all the other bears and wolves rush forward, leaping over our newest allies. They tear into the ranks which oppose us, clearing a path into the city with ease. The snap of bowstrings sounds behind us as the Rangers let loose a hail of arrows, and the Allmother guides them, sparing those who accept her.

Arrows sink into those who stand with Aia, knocking several from their mounts.

An explosion of light casts our shadows over the soldiers. I spare a glance for the tower behind me, and my jaw drops. Vines of fire coat the mass of spiraled stone, reaching up into the clouds. They cling to curled offshoots of rock, defying gravity. The sweet scent of Allflower smoke wafts toward us, drifting on a gentle breeze.

The fire burns hotter, and the stone itself glows a dull red.

But the sounds of clashing swords draw my attention.

"Move!" I shout, raising my hand. Still linked with fingers laced together, Kivala's hand rises with mine.

And the Rebels join the fray.

Surging forward, we slash with daggers of bone. Whispered petitions pull the Allmother's power into our bodies. Moving our hands with precise coordination, we turn hair into vines, wrapping green tendrils around necks. Snapping our fingers, we light undergarments on fire, baking and burning the enemy beneath their armor.

One by one, the cavalry falls away, and we gain entrance to the city.

Taking the lead, I sprint for the castle. The Allmother reaches into the city with a flash of lightning and a crack of thunder. Rain pours from the sky, and she shapes the world to her will. Trees burst from the earth, and gardens grow abundant in patches of light. The ground shakes with the transformation, and people stumble from their homes, stunned.

A woman in a tattered dress falls to her knees, hair plastered to her skull. She weeps openly, tears mingling with the rain which drenches Ivlan. A child no older than three renewals totters out of her house, splashing in puddles as I pass.

My heart warms, glowing with the Allmother's power and the effect she has on the people around me. Memories of Ivlan clash wickedly with the quiet hope that fills the streets now, pushing me further, faster.

The castle looms over me, a dark cloud, a stronghold of greed and power. Heavy and foreboding, the stone fortress stares down at its citizens with contempt.

But it's time we take it back.

People trickle from every door, stumbling into the rain as their city transforms before their eyes. Yet, so close to this place, my head fills with one thing.

Tumai.

As I lead the party of Rebels and liberated soldiers through one hall after another, I see that bastard chasing my parents and me from our home. My mind drifts back to that night, and all I see is him. Through backward glances, I watch him pull a dagger from his belt.

As my feet slam into the marble floors of the castle, all I hear is the crackle of fire and the sick sound of a dagger whirring through the air to sink into my father's back. Climbing the stairs, I hear my father fall with a thud.

Kivala runs at my side now, following me through the castle's maze of halls and stairs. But I fell that night. Rolling my father onto his side, I stared into his dead eyes. My mother tugged at my arms, trying to pull me along.

And Tumai caught us.

Now, my heart hammers in my chest, far too fast and far too loud. My lungs scream with ragged breaths, and my throat dries out. A stab of pain bursts across my side with the exertion of sprinting for so long.

But I'm so close.

The Allmother shows me where he is, but I would've guessed it.

Guards charge us from a side hall, splitting our group. Half of our party stays behind, fighting them off and shouting for us to carry on. Rounding another corner, we barrel through a small cluster of soldiers.

Almost there…

Dashing up a flight of stairs, I come up against two guards on either side of the door. A whispered petition pulls some of the Allmother's power into me. Pushing my hands down, I collapse the stone beneath their feet, dropping them to the floor below. I never could have managed such a thing all those renewals ago, but I've been practicing.

Muffled shouting fills the room beyond the door, and I recognize the voice. Just a touch higher than seems appropriate for his frame, Tumai's voice is unmistakable.

With a silent thank you to the Allmother and a wave of my hand, I send the door of Tyrvahn's old bedroom splintering inward. Shards of wood shower the room, and Tumai screams. A few strands of oily hair fall over his face as he jumps.

Rushing forward with the remnants of my group on my heels, I take the room. Slamming into Tumai, I push him against the wall. Ripping his dagger from the sheath at his waist, I press it against his neck. Tan skin beads with sweat as I press the blade just a bit closer.

He swallows, neck bobbing against the cool steel.

Behind me, the room is a mass of chaos. Blades clash and metal slams into blessed bone armor. Shouts and grunts reverberate through the air.

But all I see is fear, shining in the cruel eyes that widened with pleasure as he drove his sword into my mother's stomach. All I hear is ragged breathing wincing through lips that laughed when he kicked me to the ground.

"Do you even remember me?" I hiss.

"Garle," he chokes out. The word pushes his neck against the blade, and a drop of blood leaks out.

"No, I mean do you remember me from before? Do you remember my parents, dying by your blade in the Absorption? Do you remember the woman that grabbed your ankle, even with a sword in her stomach, and tripped you when you kicked her daughter?"

"Do you truly remember me?" My jaw clenches, and I spit my next words through gritted teeth. "Because I remember you."

Recognition flickers in his eyes, and I smile.

"Look," he begs, "You don't understand. Let me just explain."

"No," I hiss, recalling perfectly every time he and his uncle gloated about their conquest at dinner parties. "*You* don't understand. I'm not here for excuses."

His eyes go wide with fear, and he tries to shove me away.

But I'm faster than him. The dagger slices through his neck, and blood gushes over his chest. He falls to his knees, clutching his neck. Tumai crumples into a heap before me, and his blood wicks across the cold, stone floor, wrapping around my feet.

My lungs scream in agony, but I laugh. Finally free of him, of the need for revenge, I fall to the ground.

The room around me falls silent. Bodies litter the floor. Some ours, some his.

Kivala rushes forward, crashing to her knees beside me. She grabs my shoulders and turns me to face her. "Are you okay?" she asks.

And the only words I can force past the lump in my throat are, "He's gone… He's finally gone."

Tears trickle down my cheeks, and Kivala wraps me in her arms.

I finally did it…

I'm sorry it took me so long, Mom, Dad.

The stone grows hot beneath me, but still, I chant. I stumble over the words, so unfamiliar and fluid. But I never stop.

Because I know that if I do, Aia will find a way to kill me.

“Oh, silly boy,” he says. “Why would I dispose of you? There are so many ways to use you.” He laughs, and a chill creeps down my spine.

In my mind, I see myself setting fire to the Sailon, using the Allmother’s power to feed the flames and spread the blaze. I watch my hands wrap around Veliana’s throat, watch the life drain from her as she batters my arms.

But my lips never stop moving, whispering the soft, gentle words of the Allmother’s language.

Veliana’s cold hands rest with mine upon our knees. She isn’t hitting me, because I’m not hurting her, not choking her.

The warmth seeps from my hands, and my skin prickles with pain. Little solid chunks of ice form on my fingers, on Veliana’s fingers. The frost spreads to my palms, to the back of my hands. Pain lances through me as it moves further and further.

I focus on the words, the strange sounds I'm making. I don't understand the language, don't truly know what I'm saying to the Allmother.

But she tells me what to say, and I feel her getting closer. She surges through me, pushing back the frozen tide that slowly consumes my arms, thawing my skin. Pins and needles prick my forearms as Aia surges forward, claiming more of my body.

Crystals of ice hang from my eyelashes, growing heavy. Every joint in my body aches with the cold, and my teeth chatter, chopping my words into bits. Yet, I speak, breathing the Allmother into this world with every exhalation, pulling her closer.

The world beyond my eyelids glows red, and the stone I sit upon grows warmer and warmer. Veliana and I chant louder. Our voices join forces with the crack of the flames around us, trying so hard to drown out Aia's voice.

"Open your eyes," the Allmother whispers to me. "Show me the world."

So, I do.

Veliana's eyes meet mine, shining grey in the light. But her skin glows with the Allmother's power.

Dropping my gaze to our hands, I find myself aglow, as well, shining through an agonizing sheen of frost on my forearms and hands. My fingers refuse to move, too frigid to obey my commands. My wrists refuse to bend. Strands of hair fall into view, stiff and tinged with frost.

But every strand shines, regardless.

A small laugh of shock erupts from me, but I recover quickly.

The stone around and beneath us burns, glowing a fierce orange. Yet, somehow, that doesn't hurt us.

Thank you, Allmother.

She flows through my veins easily. A sudden burst of her warmth shatters the ice encasing my fingers and wrists. It all falls away in chunks, melting on the glowing stone beneath us.

"Rise, and show me the wounds Aia has inflicted upon the mortal realm."

We oblige. Rising to our feet, Veliana and I stand back to back, taking in the entirety of our stone temple.

"Show me," the Allmother whispers.

Our voices still, and only the crackle of the fire remains. Even Aia pauses, and I can almost feel him trembling. Ice pricks at my feet, at my knees.

But the Allmother is too close, now.

Veliana and I drop to our knees, slamming our aching hands on the near-molten stone, turning it translucent. Branching out from our fingertips, from our palms, the stone crystallizes. It creaks and groans, deafening compared to the stillness that preceded it, as the Allmother forces Aia out of this realm, cleansing the stone.

She moves through the tower, through swirls of stone which reach into the air. In her wake, she leaves only perfect prisms and refracted light.

Within a heartbeat, the entire tower sparkles in the sunlight, but she doesn't stop there. At the base of the tower, clearly visible through the pure crystal beneath us, a burst of lightning spreads through the ground, moving in every direction.

It streaks through the earth, leaving twisting veins of perfect crystal in its wake. The Sailon springs up around the veins, spreading to encompass all of Jun.

Staring out at the once-barren, now-lush landscape, I shake with relief. And only the Allmother's warmth whispers through my veins.

The cold cruelty of Aia… is gone.

Sitting back on my haunches, I gape at what we've done.

Spinning to face me, Veliana throws her arms around me, leaning her head against the back of my shoulder. Falling onto my backside, I turn and reach for her. Our lips meet, and I touch her face, just below her braids.

Tears glisten in her eyes, as she says, "We did it…"

I nod, and we laugh merrily, clutching at each other in disbelief. Our skin still glows with the power of the Allmother's realm, yet none of this seems real. At any moment, I expect to wake in the forest, on the run from assassins.

But the crystal beneath me buzzes with warmth, and Veliana's lips find mine once more. She smiles, moving them softly against mine.

Beside us, the crystal splinters, splitting and transforming. A spiral staircase opens up beneath us at the Allmother's bidding, ready to take us down to the battlefield below.

I look at Ivlan, but find no battle outside its crumpled walls.

"It is done, Darling Children," the Allmother says, voice reverberating through the crystal. "I cannot thank you enough for bringing me peace."

Her warmth flows through me, easing the tension of the day.

Voice a whisper, she adds, "You are needed below."

***

As we near the base of the crystal tower, we watch the Rebels stream out of Ivlan. Carried on the backs of every surviving wolf and bear, they barrel toward us. Tala leads them, hurtling through thick foliage. Trees shake before the force of such a stampede, showing us their progress, and I smile.

By the time we step through a finely wrought opening in the crystal, they wait before us. Bloodied and battered with armor scratched and chipped, they stand proud.

Yet, Garle drops to her knee before us. And Kivala falls, as well.

For a moment, I think them exhausted.

But Garle speaks. "None of our lineages are strong enough to lead. We can't commune with the Allmother well enough to truly know her will, to guide Fahn accordingly. Our only hope is to join Kin."

Shocked at her humility, knowing how deeply this must grieve her, my chest collapses. After all this time, all this effort…

"In her infinite wisdom," Veliana says, "the Allmother reshaped Fahn territory during her Rising." Her voice breaks, and I feel her grief over her parents' deaths. The reclamation flashes before my eyes, showing me her parents' sacrifice, once more.

"Your new home awaits," I say. "Even now, she fortifies your lineages. The two of you must take in a child, and they will inherit your lines, adding to those they already possess. Fahn will breathe, again."

Tears prick at the corners of my eyes. Garle and Kivala's eyes pour rivers over their cheeks. Refracted light plays across the faces of everyone before us, painting every face a different shade.

"In the meantime, commune with the Allmother every day," Veliana says. Taking a deep, steadying breath, she adds, "It's a great responsibility, but I believe you're equal to the task."

About the Author

Elexis Bell is a quiet nerd with too many hobbies, including everything from gaming to shower-singing and even archery, weather permitting. She specializes in sarcasm and writing stories that make people feel. She's made a home for herself with her husband and a small army of cats.

She writes dark, gritty stories, sprinkling gut-wrenching emotions over high fantasy romance, thrillers, post-apocalyptic romance, and science fiction.

For further information, follow her on Instagram, Twitter, or Facebook, or check out her blog on her website. There, you can sign up for her newsletter to stay up to date on all future book releases, giveaways, and on-going projects.

www.elexisbell.com

Other Books by this Author

Soul Bearer

The return of dragons? Slow burn romance? A part-Orc, underdog of a heroine? Yes, please.

The Gem of Meruna

Oppression and a magical gem that can defeat a dictator? Slow burn romance? Yes, please.

Annabelle

Vigilante justice thriller set in a western? Weaponized parasol? Yes, please.

World for the Broken

Slow burn romance in a dark, post-apocalyptic world? No holds barred, no punches pulled? Yes, please.

A Heart of Salt & Silver

Blood and broken hearts? Immortals, magic, and inner demons? Yes, please.

All of these books can be found right here:

http://author.to/ElexisBell

www.ingramcontent.com/pod-product-compliance
Lightning Source LLC
Chambersburg PA
CBHW020339310726
48979CB00015B/2425/J

* 9 7 8 1 9 5 1 3 3 5 1 4 4 *